I0606492

MARI

WHY I NEEDED TO RETURN FROM THE FUTURE

DR WINFRIED SEDHOFF

Copyright © 2019 Dr Winfried Sedhoff

Cover Design by Jeff Brown Graphics

978-0-9946091-5-1 (paperback)
978-0-9946091-2-0 (ebook)

This book is a work of fiction. The characters, incidents, and dialogues are products of the author's imagination and are not to be construed as real. Any resemblance to actual events or persons, living or dead, is entirely coincidental.

All rights reserved. No part of this publication may be reproduced, stored in a retrieval system or transmitted in any form or by any means, electronic, mechanical, photocopying, recording or otherwise, without the prior permission of the copyright holder.

With joy and love raised skyward, I meekly bear witness to the fulfill-ment of thy divine womanly presence … Thy very being, its grace and honesty, unlocks the celestial spirit of bliss, setting the gods in rages of jealously for the gifts thy heart and very being have bestowed upon me. No matter the roughness of road or the height of jagged cliff, know my arms are ever ready for comfort's embrace, my trusted hand to clasp thee from trouble's wrath. In a life all too brief, let time hold no barrier that I may fully honor thee.

Thy dearest friend, eternal.

Extract from letter dated 2023. Author unknown.

1

Cold emptiness of despair filled my chest as I watched Mari's confused and scared face search around in the darkness for me. Police flashlights blinded her. She fell to her knees, her hands behind her head. They soon threw her face down into the paddock's dry grass, then tied and bound her. I could see it all, helpless, from above, through images on a screen of the stealth craft from another time I was now trapped in. I had been abducted, away from the one whose heart enticed me beyond my imagining, captured to go back to a future where I needed to answer for serious crimes. On the forward monitor, the coordinates were set:

Year: 2183 AD
Month: May
Day: 22
Time: 13:00
Location: Earth, 27.48° S, 153.04° E
Altitude: 5,000 meters

West End, Brisbane, Queensland, Australia, late twenty-second century—the place I had recently left. The screen blurred for a moment as we traveled to our destination, quietly—without a bump. My eyes closed with dread—would I ever see my beloved Mari again?

Had you told me barely a month ago I'd be marched like some criminal into an interrogation room, I'd have thought you insane. Preposterous! Rarely, if ever, has a respected arbitrator, let alone of ambassador standing, been indicted on any serious matter for over ninety-five years—it was a most trusted position in our advanced, peace-loving time. Yet here I was. But I desperately needed to get back. Mari was being arrested because of me; I had to help her. More than that, I had to be with her!

I won't lie, I thought about stealing a TC—a disklike time travel–capable ship we call a travel craft, like the one I had just been snatched in. I would go back in time, illegally—just wait for the opportunity. But what would be the point? They could travel through time and pick me up whenever they wanted. Convincing those I answered to, I knew, was my only desperate hope of not only returning to Mari but building a life with her. It wouldn't be easy: what I proposed potentially threatened the lives and destiny of billions.

Two tall temporal justice officers in smart light-blue uniforms escorted me down mostly bland gray corridors into Interrogation Room 12. Still in period clothes of the year 2020—dusty jeans, checked shirt, jacket, and riding boots—I was gently thrust into a formless white space about three meters square. The light was soft, white, and appeared to emanate from everywhere, making it hard to distinguish the walls from the floor or the ceiling. Taylor Van Hoyden, an arbitrator of the same order as myself, though of lesser rank, entered past me, found the white couches, and invited me to sit opposite.

I'd met Taylor once before, a few years back at a conference. He was still the tall gentleman I remembered—light-chocolate skin contrasting light-blue eyes, his big hands still as gentle. Although we were both in our midforties, I was paler, shorter, and slimmer of frame than the more athletic Taylor, and I had more hair, even if it did have flecks of gray.

Taylor maintained the expected persona of an arbitrator— amicable and nonthreatening, at peace within himself. As I made myself comfortable, I found it hard to take my eyes off his bright almost-navy-blue arbitrator uniform jacket, especially the gold insignia of the Institute on his left lapel. The contrast to the blandness of the room demanded my attention—as the interrogation room, or "debriefing office," was designed to do.

"Before we begin," Taylor said firmly, "it is my duty, Mr. Ambassador, to inform you of your rights and let you know this conversation is being recorded. According to article sixteen of—"

"I understand the formalities, Mr. Van Hoyden," I interrupted. "Consider me informed." I then leaned forward. "May I make a request?" I asked humbly. Taylor looked suspicious. "May I ask you to call me Ben? Mr. Ambassador is way too formal. With your permission, may I call you Taylor?"

"Very well." Taylor nodded.

I leaned forward and put out my hand. "Good afternoon, Taylor."

"Good afternoon, Mr. … Ben." Cautiously Taylor took my hand. I shook it with affection. It was a tactic I had previously taught interrogators from our department. It quickly built rapport and made the other person more receptive to one's concerns. Clearly, Taylor had missed the memo.

"Great. How can I help you, Taylor?" I offered calmly.

"Beginning at time zero, in your own words and for the record, what is the first, most outstanding memory of the event of your arrival?"

"Hmm. After the crash?"

"Yes."

I hesitated a moment as I recalled the events. "Ah, yes, being sick as a dog!"

Taylor's eyebrows rose. "A dog?"

"You know, four legs, goes bow-wow."

"I know what a dog is." I knew he hadn't heard of the analogy: it was from the past.

"Of course you do. I like dogs—trustworthy, always aim to please.

Do you like dogs, Taylor?"

He didn't answer.

"What have you got against dogs?"

"Nothing. Let us get back to topic, shall we? You said you were sick. Care to elaborate? Were you injured?"

"You should consider a pug—small, short snout, not particularly bright though."

"Were you ill?"

"A poodle? No?"

Taylor glared at me silently.

"Was I injured? No. It was the phase-shift variance from the escape pod. Threw up for several minutes, dry retching mostly."

"Ah, yes, the escape pod, from the destroyed craft. What was that like? I hear they are very different from ours."

"Like being locked in an oversize coffin … surrounded by hell," I said with conviction.

"Sounds terrifying," Taylor empathized, a genuinely caring expression on his face.

Suddenly the memory flooded back. Chaos! Alarms blaring, flashing lights, being shoved within seconds into a small, enclosed space. There was a flash of fire outside. Suddenly the ship and bloodied crew disappeared. Next thing I knew, I was being pushed from the opened pod into darkness, through a shimmering—like the shimmering surface of a large pond. Then the world was going around and around; the nausea was overwhelming. I fell to my knees onto a hard, dark, cold, flat surface I'd never known before and couldn't stop vomiting. Behind me the pod just disappeared.

I regathered my thoughts, then continued. "More disturbing," I said, "was almost being run over."

"Run over?"

"I landed on a road."

"A real road, with cars?"

"Yes. Hate them, horrible contraptions. One swerved around me with an alarm sounding. Then yelling I couldn't make out. Missed me by centimeters."

"But you arrived safely?" Taylor asked, his face one of concern.

"I thought so. Then a completely new set of lights came after me."

"A vehicle pursued you?"

"You know, it would have been better if they had just introduced themselves instead of trying to run me down. They'll have to work on that," I added.

"They?" Taylor sat forward, awaiting my every word.

"The HRU."

"Ah, the History Rescue Unit, of course. They were there to collect and protect you. What a relief it must have been to know you were in their experienced and trusted hands." Taylor breathed a sigh of relief and sat back.

"I think I struck one of them."

"You did what?"

"Self-defense. Wasn't seeing the world very clearly. I think I left a scar."

"You left one bleeding?"

Taylor seemed totally shocked. I expected him to be. He knew arbitrators, above all things, value peace. We are taught self-defense, but most of us can go decades before we have to use it, if at all. We are also skilled in self-control; we should never need restraining. To hear I had actually caused physical harm to someone would have appalled him. For a high-ranking arbitrator to act so uncontrollably … unimaginable.

"Could have been worse. Later I was almost shot."

"By a gun?"

"Yes. They have those in that time too."

"The HRU almost shot you?"

"An old lady, actually, before we had to run from the cops."

"Cops?"

"Local law enforcement."

"Their authorities. You broke their laws as well?"

"It wasn't like that," I tried to correct him.

"What was it like?" Taylor now looked at me with intensity and suspicion. "Was it like deciding to violate at least nine temporal directives, and disregarding your oath?" Taylor peered at me earnestly. "Help me understand, Ben, Mr. Ambassador, why a high initiate of the Institute of Mind, touted to someday be one of the High Council of Five, would break his solemn oath to humanity, to himself, and in the past, no less?"

"That's a great question, Taylor." I stood up and started pacing. "It seems puzzling, doesn't it?" I took a few steps, stopped, and looked at him. "First, let me ask you, how deep, how intimate, would you say your deepest relationship with another human being has ever reached?"

Taylor squirmed slightly in his seat. "On the Progressive Connection Scale?"

"Yes, if you like."

"I can't say."

"Can't? Really? All right, let me ask another question. How many of the Council of Five are in deep, fulfilling relationships?"

"Three of them are in couplets."

"Yes, but how many are really close?"

"That is not for public disclosure," Taylor replied, uncomfortably.

"I sense you are not in a close relationship with anyone at present either, are you?" I asked.

Taylor sat motionless, his eyes looking away, sheepishly.

"It's OK. Neither are most of the rest of us. Often our training precludes it, makes it next to impossible. When did you last hold a lover in your arms whose level of connection touched the depths of your soul? Transformed you?"

Taylor's eyes continued to avoid me.

"I didn't think so."

Taylor then looked at me directly. "I don't see the relevance—"

"You don't see the relevance?" I interrupted.

Taylor continued. "Surely our individual feelings must come secondary to risking the very lives we have vowed to honor and improve?"

"And that, kind Mr. Van Hoyden, is why this debriefing should stop right here. I might as well be talking to a blind man about rainbows."

I walked to the wall, knowing someone was watching behind it. "We've played the game," I said to the blank white in front of me. "You know he will never get what you want. Are you ready to really talk, or would you prefer I begin to play with him? You know I have the skill."

Suddenly the lights dimmed and the door opened to my left. The silhouette of a small figure was engulfed by a brighter light. It stood motionless for a moment, then stepped in slowly, with a limp.

"Madam Li, an honor," I said, bowing slightly, my relaxed, cupped hands open before me as if to receive, as was custom. She responded in kind, her ancient hands wasted and knobbly.

"Thank you, Mr. Taylor. I'll take it from here," Madam Li, one of the High Council of Five, announced softly.

Already standing, Taylor bowed his head to us, then slowly left as if strolling on a summer's day.

"Walk with me," she insisted.

We turned left down the corridor. It was smooth and gray, difficult to distinguish floors from ceilings and walls, like the room. Soon broad windows opened to our right. I walked to her left and slightly behind in reverence and respect.

"You were hard on poor Taylor, don't you think?" Madam Li asked as she shuffled along slowly, her ankle-length, embroidered red silk dress hanging loosely over an almost emaciated form, barely covering her white sneakers.

Someone had asked her once why she always wore running shoes—she was too old to run. "Even a walking foot enjoys the dream of running someday," she'd replied. Later she'd admitted she just liked that they were so comfortable for her well-worn feet. She didn't care how they looked.

"I thought I was very measured," I replied. "Needs to brush up on technique—too easily distracted and particularly poor friendship-building skills. Why him?"

"Staff shortage."

"At least the Ministry knows we have completed the formalities." A debriefing could now be marked as recorded for the appropriate departments.

Madam Li nodded.

We walked a few more steps in silence before Madam Li added, "You will be happy to know the new Noretian ambassador from Earth—your replacement—has arrived and has been accepted graciously. Their ambassador wished to convey their deepest apologies to you and hope you are well."

"I received the message in 2020. I was saddened to hear they lost three lives."

"Mmm, so were they. It allowed us a commonality of social bonding, however—better for us than for them." That meant it helped us diplomatically to build greater trust: the Noretians felt they now owed us. "So, tell me, young Benjamin, what troubles your heart?"

"I must get back," I stated, without thinking and almost desperately.

"Must you now."

"I mean, I seek to return to the time of my departure in the year 2020 as soon as permission allows," I said, more calmly.

"What if permission does not allow? I sense you will try to return anyway."

"I know I have broken several laws …"

"Yes, several."

"If I could only explain."

As we walked, I peered through the window into the sky. It was just as bright blue and vivid in this time as over a century ago—timeless. The landscape looked totally different though—gone were the skyscrapers, and there were far more trees now. So too no roads and traffic. It seemed more serene, more natural, but also more incomplete. There was an emptiness to it this time that I'd never experienced before.

In the distance, at the end of the corridor, stood a sole female figure wearing standard arbitrator uniform, appearing to wait for us.

"You will have your chance, young Benjamin. Then the Council will decide."

"The Council?"

"You didn't just land in any time. As you are fully aware, this was the era of the birth of great hope and change, before the upheaval and the great transformation," Madam Li explained. "If you go back, you could threaten us all, trigger a catastrophic divergence. The future of all humanity is not worthy of sufficient consideration and attention?"

"I could help them through the transition," I offered. Then it occurred to me, with delight: "Perhaps I already have."

"I'm listening."

"What if I am a major reason the Institute exists? With my knowledge I could guide them in the past to look into their hearts, teach them to understand the desires that define us, that start us on the road to lasting …"

Madam Li started to laugh, then cough. "So quick to think of being a savior. I thought I taught you better than that. What if the present is as it is because we never sent you back?"

She was right. Two main outcomes may have already been decided: I could have gone back and ensured the future as we know it, perhaps because I didn't interfere, or because I managed to help someway in their development. Or I might have been made to stay here, never see Mari again, and the future is as it is now because of it. The latter thought almost stopped my heart in my chest.

"You don't understand," I said under my breath, the desperate pain of possibly never seeing Mari again burning cold within.

"So sure, you are. Come, I'd like you to meet someone."

The woman at the end of the corridor had a plain but pleasant face, slightly tanned, perhaps Spanish, black hair tied up neatly. She looked to be in her late twenties or early thirties, trim. Except for the uniform, I would have thought she was one of our bodyguards.

"Benjamin, Fiorella. Fiorella, Benjamin," Madam Li announced.

We shook hands gently. Hers were very soft—definitely not those of a bodyguard.

"This exceptional young woman," Madam Li explained earnestly, "is one of our most promising recent graduates. Her wisdom and perceptions exceed her years, much like yours once did." Was that sarcasm in Madam Li's voice? "You will sit together over the next three days, and she will take your story and present it only to me. What is said will then never be spoken again. You don't have to convince me, you have to convince her. What she says to me will determine my recommendation to the Council. I have been given full authority in this matter."

Fiorella looked shocked. So was I. I was expecting a board of peers from the Institute or a meeting with the Ministry of Time to make my case. I never considered I would have to convince a young woman, let alone one who was also such an inexperienced arbitrator—as a recent graduate, she wouldn't have even had a posting. It would be worse than trying to convince Taylor—how could she possibly understand my feelings and motivations in the matter?

"But, you can't possibly—" I began to protest.

"It is decided," Madam Li announced boldly as she stepped into the elevator.

"There must be some other way," I pleaded.

"Perhaps you prefer a more permanent solution. Coconuts and turtles?"

"You wouldn't."

"I don't think you understand the risk you pose."

Images flooded my mind of the dreaded possibility: permanent relocation to an isolated island over forty thousand years ago, never to be seen or heard from again—to live among coconuts, fish, and turtles. So far back no human contact would be possible. The world a permanent jail cell.

"Be grateful I do not shut you down here and now."

She was right; I should be grateful. At least there was still some hope of returning to Mari, however slim.

"All travel craft rights rescinded—you understand." The door started to close. Madam Li's voice projected loudly with her no longer in view. "Three days! No more, no less!"

The closing doors had a finality to them.

"Three days it is, then," I whispered to myself.

Fiorella stood there for a moment, still and seemingly emotionless.

As I walked to the window to stare outside, forlorn and lost, Fiorella walked over and stood beside me. "Shall we go for a walk?" she suggested. "I know a quiet café. Their apple Danish is exceptional."

"Sure."

2

I didn't notice the elevator ride or the walk by the river. It wasn't until we'd walked halfway across the new walking bridge to the other side that I even noticed where I was. I couldn't get Mari's face from my mind, smiling, laughing, snuggled up to my shoulder. Then her despair as she searched for me. An intense weight gripped my chest. I stopped. Peering down, I noticed the clear blue water flowing beneath me. It was as if my heart had been thrown into its coldest, darkest depths, never to know the warmth of light ever again.

Fiorella handed me a wipe. I hadn't realized I had tears flowing down my cheeks. "It's not over," she remarked, her hand resting gently on my shoulder. "We still have seventy-two hours. I have no idea what you are supposed to convince me of, but I'm willing to listen. If I can, I'd like to help."

"She hasn't told you?"

"Told me? Madam Li? No. She just pulled me from a tutorial I was giving at the Melbourne Centre, and next thing I know, I'm here."

"That cunning old ..." Madam Li had done it again, surprised me as few people could. Before me was a blank slate, a woman who knew nothing about me or my suspected crimes. A student that, just perhaps, I could guide to see past what she wanted or was reluctant to see, to accept the merits of my case.

"You want to update me?" she asked.

Memories flooded back of standing on a similar bridge over the same river, only then it was like brown, churning soup, a flowing collection of mud and water in a growing city in an almost tropical part of the old world. What was once murky was now becoming clear.

"Apple Danish, you said?"

"You won't be disappointed."

As we walked, many an old acquaintance recognized me by name and wanted to stop and chat. After introducing my guest, I had to politely decline several of them and move on. Some, surprisingly, knew Fiorella, and she introduced them to me. The café was old and quaint, with a Germanic feel. The aroma of sweet coffee and chocolate spread onto the wide and open street. We sat outside. Only a few tables were taken; it was 2 p.m., after lunch and an hour before closing.

"Fee!" A bright young blond woman, who couldn't have been more than twenty, head half-shaved—the new trend, apparently—shouted out warmly for all to hear. Dressed in black-and-red jeans, pink boots, black tank top, and apron, she emitted the odor of the local brew. I noticed it as she hugged my companion.

"This is Benjamin," Fiorella said.

"Tippy." The young lady thrust her hand out to shake, then just gave me a hug too. "Hi, Benjamin."

"Hi, Tippy. I hear the apple Danish is the go."

"The go? I like it. Yep, I'll have to see what we can do. It might be all gone." She then whispered, "Don't worry, I usually keep some stashed aside for special people." She winked. "To drink?"

"The usual for me," Fiorella replied.

"Me? A large hot chocolate, please."

"No probs, see you in a sniff." Tippy hurried back inside.

The village was alive. Store owners were talking to each other, laughing, greeting customers like old friends, and many of them were.

Families walked past, and I could see some playing in the park less than fifty meters away, grandparents included. Everyone greeted everyone else; most knew each other by name.

"You seem popular around here. I'm surprised you don't know this place," Fiorella commented.

"I used to be the arbitrator for the inner west region, around twenty kilometers from here. That was over five years ago."

"That explains it. This place has only been open a couple of years. Lovely people, the Hahndorfs. I used to attend the Institute at the old university a few corners away, down near the garden. I'd indulge here at least a few times a week."

"I know that garden—river walks, great big old and wise trees to contemplate under."

"Exactly. That's what I said, but my friends told me I was being too romantic; they couldn't see it."

"They didn't attend the Institute?"

"Some, but I like to experience beyond the teachings."

That was a good sign. It meant Fiorella was taking the time to personally and privately know her feelings, to look beyond what she was taught, and was probably able to keep an open mind.

"Sounds like you live nearby. A couple of my old friends we bumped into, Trish and Tom, knew you," I commented.

"Nice people. I studied with their daughter, Phoebe. I live twenty minutes' walk that way." Fiorella pointed east.

"The Valley?"

"No. Just before the old Valley. It's a new honeycomb suburb just in from the river. There used to be old offices there, I believe."

"And you teach in Melbourne?"

"I tutor in Melbourne, but prefer living here, close to friends. My community tribe and dreaming is here now."

"Melbourne, that's, what, ten minutes away?"

"Closer to fifteen. I enjoy a slower walk."

"What a crazy world. Ten minutes to travel over thirteen hundred kilometers." I had memories of longer trips with Mari, and we'd still hardly traveled any distance at all.

"Not as crazy as arriving before you leave, but temporal directives and laws, being what they are, won't allow that—not yet, anyway."

"Speaking of temporal directives …"

Suddenly Tippy appeared with our order. There was only one large piece of Danish. Apple sauce was dripping from the lightly icing-sugar-sprinkled crusted pastry.

"Last piece," Tippy said with a smile. "All warmed up. I hope you don't mind having to share." I noticed her wink to Fiorella. In return she received an awkward smile.

"Hope you don't mind sharing," Fiorella apologized.

"Not at all." I ate some of the frothy chocolate on top of my drink with the small spoon provided, then took a sip as Fiorella smiled with delight at her first mouthful of the crispy, apple-centered treat.

"You were saying?" Fiorella spoke with mouth half-full.

"What do you know about the temporal directives?" I asked.

"You really should try this before I eat it all," she said as she pointed her fork to the large morsel in front of her. Swallowing, she replied, "Not much. Set up within five years of the invention of temporal drive, part of the UN charter, policed by a combined federal force internationally. Prevents me from getting to work as early as I'd like. Why? Planning on breaking any?"

I sat motionless, staring at her.

"You're not."

I smiled.

Fiorella stopped chewing. "Forward or back?" she asked.

"Back."

"How far?"

"Well, Fiorella—"

"It's Fee, by the way."

"Hi, Fee, Ben. About a hundred and fifty years."

"To the time before …?"

"Yes."

Fee thought about it a moment, then quickly stood up, agitated. "What the hell? I need to make a call." She opened a small wallet the size of a credit card and took out her phone, expanded it to hand-comfortable size, then made a call. "Madam Li, please. No, I'll wait."

Fee paced back and forth. Other people stopped to stare, then looked at me. I smiled back, making it all look OK. Then they moved on.

"Madam, sorry to bother you …" Fee stopped speaking a while. "But …" Fee stood still for what seemed like minutes; then she glanced at me and put away the phone.

"Let me guess. You wanted to tell her this was too important for someone of your experience. This could affect countless lives. She knew you would say that and said she chose you personally, had faith in you. And no, you had no choice, and should consider this an honor."

"How did you—?"

"She was my mentor for over a decade. Besides, we are trained to know people."

"She said you needed to convince me. Convince me of what? How bad an idea it is to mess with time, to threaten millions of lives?"

"Billions."

"Pardon me?"

"Potentially billions of lives are at stake."

Fee sat down slowly in disbelief.

"Then why would you travel back and threaten …?" She stopped midsentence, stared into my eyes. "What's her name?" she then asked, with a look mixed between compassion and confusion.

"You do your training proud," I commented with genuine praise.

"When did you first meet?" Fee asked. She wasn't touching the Danish, or her drink.

"Perhaps I should start from the beginning," I suggested.

Fee nodded as she sat back, a look of concern and deep concentration on her face, her legs crossed, her hands clasped on her lap.

"Whenever you're ready," she replied.

"You have to understand," I preempted, "this isn't what I wanted or expected at all."

"Of course."

I changed position in my seat to get more comfortable. "Best I offer as complete a picture as I can so as to give the best view of the circumstances."

Fee nodded.

I took another sip of the hot chocolate. I didn't taste it at all.

3

The air was warm and fresh, the sky the deep, bright blue I was familiar with and accustomed to. I guessed it was around twenty-four degrees on the Celsius scale—autumn in Brisbane was always the best time of year.

A shadow slowly began to cover us. Looking up, I saw a dull gray, disk-shaped travel craft hovering slowly, approximately three hundred meters above us. This was a large one, over a hundred and fifty meters in diameter, completely smooth, with a thicker center that tapered outward—the more traditional shape. I knew it was off course: the visual-pollution laws restricted craft flights to designated corridors. They certainly weren't supposed to fly over this village. As I watched it silently and effortlessly head toward the West End landing facility, it brought back clear images of my fateful trip. The Noretian craft was a similar design, only larger in the middle. It, too, had been off course, much like I would be, in more ways than I imagined. Gazing into Fee's interested eyes, I realized now was the time for some sharing, and convincing. *Here I go.*

With my mug of hot chocolate in hand, I began by explaining about my ambassadorial mission to the Noretian home world, about having completed my advanced arbitrator training just months before, and how this had been my first interworld assignment. I had been excited but, I clarified, not for the reasons most people might have thought. I didn't care for the new technology, space, skies, or landscape. I was interested in the evolution of the minds of their people, a humanoid species not unlike us, only half a meter taller on average. It would have been two centuries—their time—after their development of interstellar temporal travel that they had decided to connect with other worlds. Another century before, they had agreed to connect with us. What interested me was what led to their awakening, what world and social traumas had occurred, and how this was still reflected in their culture, in their minds. When did they, too, abandon cities and reconnect with their land? When did their minds stop fighting themselves and the natural world and return to being part of it? The mission had been to try to recognize as many social similarities as possible between our two peoples so we could use them to develop an increasing bond of friendship, but also help us learn about ourselves. If I could have learned the same information from here on Earth, I'd have jumped at it—travel was not my thing.

"You still haven't told me her name," Fee insisted.

I was coming to that, hoping to edge myself back into that time slowly.

I explained the crash, and the events of my rescue. Fee agreed that being thrown unexpectedly into another time was always going to be traumatic. Only a well-trained historian thoroughly prepared for the conditions, she rightly reminded me, could thrive in such a scenario, and I certainly wasn't one of those.

"Mariana," I finally revealed, and my heart both lifted and sank at the same time.

"Lovely name," Fee responded politely. "How did you meet?"

"By chance."

"And you believe in chance, even after our training?"

"Perhaps."

As I spoke, the images of being back in the early twenty-first century flooded my mind as if I was there once again.

✻ ✻ ✻

It was approximately 2 p.m., three days after the crash. I was in deep contemplation, reworking the recent traumas, emotionally accessing them, rewriting them, preventing them leaving deep fears—emotional scars—in the future. The chair beside the double bed of the hotel room I had been confined to was acceptable for such a purpose.

Suddenly the door burst open. Martino, the leader of the HRU, overweight and bald as a nut, cap and glasses in hand, stormed in with two of his crew, Tina and Bob, both in their mid to late twenties by the look of them. The two rolled in a couple of travel cases—"suit-cases" they were called here, I later found out.

"This really annoys me." Martino's Italian accent was more obvious today. "You should be gone!" he said as he pointed his assistants to the closet. As Martino took a call, Tina and Bob unpacked all manner of clothes. Bob supplied the bathroom.

I went over to ask Tina—she seemed the more approachable type. "Is there a problem?" I asked.

Tina sneaked a look at her boss, then whispered, "You have passed the forty-eight-hour rule. No one has contacted us. We have no idea how long you'll stay. This is highly irregular."

Martino swore, in Italian by the sound of it, grasped his bald head, rubbed it furiously, then threw his arms down as he paced the room.

"Trouble?"

"What? Yes, trouble—supplies, staff, plumbing." Then he poked me in my chest. "You, you, big trouble!"

"Anything I can do?"

Martino clicked his fingers, and Tina brought him an open blue bag that seemed to be made of hard paper with some cloth cord as handles.

"Now pay attention," he said sternly, pulling items from the bag. "To stay, you need this. This is your license. It has a photo of you." He pulled out a card with a picture of me on one side. "It allows you to drive a car," he explained. "You cannot drive a car. You will crash. Do not drive a car, but this license says you can. Your name is here." He pointed it out: BENJAMIN MICHAEL DUBOIS, DOB 02.12.1979. The address was Wilston. I knew Wilston, a small suburb not far away. "Remember, do not drive. Clear?"

"Clear."

Then he handed me a smooth metal-and-glass device.

"This is your phone. This is how you turn it on." He pressed two buttons, one either side, then slid a colored circle on the screen. "Your password is 'asses1.'"

"Nice."

"You listening? I don't have time to repeat."

"Yes, listening."

"You make calls like this. You access net like this." His hands darted across the changing screen.

"Net?"

"Radio waves to worldwide database. You take special care of this. Don't drop it, get it wet; don't give it to someone else. OK?" I nodded. "It has GPS, so we always find you."

I was confused.

Tina spoke up. "Global Positioning System. Satellites can locate this phone anywhere in the world."

Satellites, how quaint, I thought. They'd been cleaned up over a century ago in our time.

"You lose this," Martino said abruptly, "we lose you. I lose you, I'm in big dog poo. Understand?"

"I understand. Dog poo."

Then he handed me a small folding leather pouch.

"This is your wallet." He grabbed my license and slid it in a pocket. Then he took out a gold plastic card from another pocket of the wallet, about the same size. "This is a credit card. It is how you buy. Don't share it or give it to anyone else—ever! You swipe this over control unit when asked by staff to pay. If you need, you type in 'ass1' to pay.

This is password. No one must know this word. You have sufficient credit. Don't waste it."

Ass1, asses1, nice—I was getting the hint I was quite an annoyance. I noticed the card had my name on it too—my alias. He put it into another pocket in the wallet, then took out a green-colored card, then a darker blue card. What was swiping? I wondered. The green card read "Medicare." It had my alias and numbers on it, including my new date of birth.

"Medicare?"

"If you are ill, call us. If you are injured, call us. The number is in the contact list on your phone. Call me now." Martino handed me the phone.

I fumbled as he guided me to call him.

"If you ill and not able to contact Martino, you go to hospital or doctor and show them Medicare card and private health card." He pulled out the blue card and waved it around. "You may need credit card. First you try call us. Always call us. Clear?"

"Sure."

"Remember, you Benjamin Michael Dubois. You work with computers, IT. You are a consultant and project manager. It is sufficiently boring job no one ask any more." He handed me the wallet, then told me not to lose it either, or I'd have to answer to him, personally.

Then he handed me a plain gray plastic card. "This will get you in and out of your accommodation. Keep the door closed at all times."

Martino's phone rang. He answered it, and swore again, for quite some time. He finished and thrust it into his pocket.

"I have to go. Any questions?" He didn't give me time to answer. "Keep quiet, keep ordinary, keep safe. We contact you again in three days."

"What about going home?" I asked.

Martino swore again and threw his hands into the air as he left. Bob followed him. Tina stayed back a moment. "Don't worry, he's just a bit stressed. Business to run that is struggling, now you show up. They are supposed to have arranged pickup by now."

"They?"

"The Temporal Directorate." The Ministry of Time. "Protocol states all unplanned incursions are to be returned within forty-eight hours to help preserve the time thread. They are supposed to have given an indication of when you will leave. They haven't."

"Maybe they haven't got around to it."

"You're kidding, right? It could take them ten years to assess your case, and they could still send someone to get you a minute after you arrive. No. Something else is going on and we aren't being kept in the loop. The Ministry of History is making a formal complaint. Just remember, it is our duty as visitors to be ordinary, unseen, be like all the other sheep."

"So I'm free to walk around?"

"Of course. We can't keep you here indefinitely: we aren't barbarians. My advice, keep it local and don't interact any more than you have to."

"Keep a low profile."

"Yep. Oh, and whatever you do, don't tell anyone who you really are. Next thing you know, they'll lock you up!"

"Really?"

"Good luck, Mr. Dubois. See you in three days," Tina said as she closed the door behind her.

For a time, I was in shock. They had no idea when I'd be going home? It wasn't what I wanted to hear. I also wondered what had happened to the Noretian ship. Were there any other survivors? I asked Martino on each of the occasions of his daily visits, but he was just in and out with food and off again, his usual cheery and carefree self—like he was just then. Every day, I would gaze out the window, but all I saw was a glimpse of sky, and the windowless building wall beside this one. I felt like I had been caged in a box—but, aha! Now I had the key. With a touch of excited trepidation, I decided to go for a short walk—test out my new-found freedom. It was 4 p.m. on a Thursday.

They called it the Brisbane Mall. It was wide, open, and busy; there were plenty of people around. Yet stepping into the Brisbane Mall was like stumbling into sorrow: everyone looked so miserable. No one smiled. No one looked at each other. Everyone seemed like they were in a hurry. Almost no one made eye contact. I couldn't count how many had these devices in their ears with their heads bowed down, looking at their phones as they sat or walked around. Almost no one was talking, only occasionally a few small groups. It was heartbreaking; I felt lonely just walking among them. Then there was the noise and traffic.

It took some time to get used to the corner colored lights and to only walking when the green figure appeared. I was almost hit by cars a few times crossing the street. Ah, cars, and buses. What smelly, noisy contraptions. They looked terribly unsafe. And I had a license to drive one. Not on your life!

Everything was new and unfamiliar: the tall buildings, the streets made of asphalt—they are nothing like what we have in the future— and the clothes some people wore looked so bulky. I was amazed the first time I saw an aircraft. With such flimsy-looking wings and bulky engines, I wondered how on earth they stayed in the air. They were kind of graceful though, like a slow, giant bird. Not that you would ever get me in one. Did you know these people let themselves be confined in them for up to twenty hours at a time? Amazing!

By the afternoon of my first day of freedom—as I called it—I began to feel hungry. It wasn't hard to find places selling food. I ordered some Asian cuisine from what they called a food court. It was the first time I used my credit card. I felt proud it worked, once I was shown what "swiping" meant. It was heartening to know I had at least some of the survival skills necessary to make it in this hostile, unfriendly place.

Next day I felt bolder. I started to explore. I walked across the river over an old stone bridge shared with cars and buses—very bulky compared to the one we know now. I found the library and had a quick look. I was pleased it was quiet. Then I met her.

It was lunchtime. I looked around carefully and found a small-to-medium café in the city. It was very busy. *Must be a good place to eat to have so many people*, I thought. I ordered a coffee and a sandwich, then searched my pockets for my wallet. It wasn't there! I apologized profusely as I kept searching. "I can't pay you," I said as I stepped back and others let themselves through.

Just then a young woman stepped up from her seat and came over and paid for me. I hadn't seen anyone do that since I'd been here. It seemed people were very careful not to share: their credit was precious.

"Let me," she said. She then handed me my meal.

I thanked her graciously. I looked around; there were no tables free to sit at.

"You look lost," she commented.

"Pardon?"

"You're not from around here, are you?"

I smiled.

"Here, take a seat." She cleared her bags from the one beside her. "Lunchtime rush."

I noticed a pleasant sense about her, almost content, the only person I'd met with such an aura. I hadn't noticed her age much, early thirties perhaps, neatly dressed, blond hair in a single braid down to her shoulders. Then the words of Martino started echoing in my mind: *Stay ordinary, and don't lose it*—referring to my wallet. I dreaded having to tell him I'd misplaced it after only one day. I especially dreaded not looking ordinary, affecting the time thread. I stood there a moment, contemplating my choices.

"It's OK. I don't bite. My name's Mariana. My friends call me Mari." She stood up to shake my hand. I put my coffee down and answered the greeting.

"My name is Ben. Thank you, Mariana."

"No." She smiled. "Just Mari will be fine."

"OK, Mari." I gingerly sat down. On the small table, beside her almost finished bread roll, I noticed a book. I could just make out the word "Mind." *A book this old, how rare*, I thought. She must have noticed me staring.

"Do you read?" she asked.

"I can read."

She smiled. "That's good, not quite what I meant. Do you read much?"

"Oh, sometimes. I prefer contemplation. You?" I began eating.

"Contemplation? You're a thinker?"

I'd forgotten. It wasn't as well thought of in this time: the search for knowledge—information—was more important here than personal insight. I nodded and decided on a new tactic: I'd try to keep my mouth full. That way I wouldn't have to speak as much.

"You're a bit of an odd one, Ben."

"Hmm, how is that?" I mumbled with a full mouth.

"Well, I don't know. Perfectly pressed trousers, new tennis shoes, brand-new T-shirt, and not a penny to your name. Yeah, some might think that odd."

I nodded.

"You aren't a spy, are you?" she asked.

Food caught in my throat and I started coughing. A few people started looking. Mari offered me my drink, and it helped.

"You OK?"

"I think so." I drank some more. "So, tell me about you. Do you like to read?"

"Yeah. I sometimes inhale books." Her face filled with whimsy.

"Sounds painful. I didn't think that was possible."

"No. I just start a book, and before I know it, I'm ready for the next one."

"What does that do for you?" I asked.

"For me? Sometimes it helps me see the world through different eyes. Other times it sends me off to wondrous lands. Some help me settle, find a sense of peace."

"And this one?" I motioned to the book on the table.

Her hands turned it over as she handed it to me. *Comfort of Mind*, by an author I can't recall. I began to read the back cover.

"This helps me connect with my self."

I stopped chewing. I never thought I'd hear these words in this time—*connect with self*. I took a sip of coffee. "Really?"

"I think it's good to know yourself. Don't you?" Her gaze seemed intent on creating a reaction. I noticed my heart skip a beat.

"What do you mean?"

"They say the truth of heart is discovered inside. So many people go looking for it elsewhere when it is right there in front of them the whole time."

I stopped. I couldn't believe what I was hearing.

"Well, that's what this book claims. What do you think?"

"About searching inside our hearts for the truth?"

"You know you're the first guy I've spoken to who got it? I've shared this with twelve other guys, and not one of them picked it: they had no idea that's what it meant."

"Perhaps they weren't ready to look."

Musical chimes began to emanate from her loose-weave cotton bag. She rummaged around, looked at her phone, and began packing up.

"Sorry, Ben. Lovely to meet you. I have to rush."

"Lovely to meet you too." I stood up as she readied herself.

"It's been a pleasure."

"Thank you again, for this." I indicated the meal.

"Oh, it was nothing. Cheers." We shook hands, her eyes gazing deeply into mine for an all-penetrating split second. "Maybe we'll meet again," she said.

"Maybe."

Then, she was gone.

To be honest, the rest of the afternoon was a blur. The conversation with Mari played over and over in my mind. Somehow I meandered over to the gardens by the river. Large Moreton Bay fig trees were spread sparsely among manicured lawns, and some formed a grove with a walking and cycling path—I saw people using the path for both. I found the wisest tree I could and sat, trying to connect with it, as I had done with trees since my troubled teens. I was failing miserably.

Eventually I made my way back to my room. There was my wallet on the nightstand. I remembered leaving it there last night. I'd just forgotten to take it with me: it wasn't part of my routine yet. *How fortuitous*, I thought. If I hadn't forgotten it, I'd have never met that remarkable young lady. She offered me hope for our future, a reflection of seeds planted tens of decades ago that blossomed into the amazing world we call home.

My phone sprang to life. Tina said she had news she didn't want to share over the phone. I was to meet them at Martino's store. She explained the directions; it was barely a block away.

* * *

On the second story of a shopping complex was a small coffee establishment. Martino was behind the machine. Tina was serving. Only one other young man was helping. Sweat poured from Martino's bald dome, and he wiped it regularly with a small dark towel. He waved me over. We talked as he crushed coffee beans, compressed them, and locked them into the machine.

"Two have the flu." He had two coffees ready in a moment. Tina served them; then it was on to the next order. "I have a message."

"From home?"

"From our friends. Three died; two made it safely."

"That's terrible. What happened?"

"No word. Also spoke with our ministry." The next order was

ready. He tried to smile at the customers, but he wasn't very convincing. "You are a bomb, Mr. Dubois."

"What does that mean?"

"You either sleep and all is good, or you explode, and history falls to pieces. You should not be here."

"Great, tell them to pick me up, anytime."

There was a short break between orders. Martino looked me in the eyes. "Someone is playing with us. This is not our job. We only have the resources to keep well-trained staff." I knew he meant well-trained historians, like himself, Tina, and Bob, trained to blend in. He shook his head. "You make trouble, they check your cover, you be caught."

"Caught by who?"

"You know why I come here, Mr. Dubois?" He tried smiling again at customers as they paid and left. "It is troubled time. Great fear, paranoia, hurtfulness. I'm here to detail how it fall apart."

"But we know how."

"We see it; we not live it. You see that young boy?" He pointed to his other staff member. "Troy is a good boy, will be a great father and community leader, I checked. Yet every day, he come here to pay for his car. A car! He is nineteen, lives at home, and he just spend time working for a primo car. He dream of it, he tell me. Why? Why not people? Why he not work to help his parents, and his sick uncle? Why his sister live overseas, alone with two bambini, than come here to stay? This, we must record this, so we know how to stay and make better."

"I hear what you say. All of us are important. All of us play a part in our world; we cannot forget who we are and who we are doing this for."

"Then why you here to blow it up? I see the simulations. What is wrong with you people? History doesn't lie!"

He continued filling another order.

"I don't know. I just don't know. Trust me, if I thought I would cause more suffering than these people are about to go through, I'd end it in a second. It isn't just you they are keeping out of the loop. This is all well beyond me."

I'm not sure Martino believed me.

"You been a good boy today?" he suddenly asked. I felt like I was answering to an overbearing father.

"I been a good boy, Mr. Alfonsi. I been a good boy." I didn't have the heart to tell him about my wallet—luckily, it was never missing after all. Informing him about the interesting young lady seemed over the top, too inclusive and irrelevant. Besides, he had enough to worry about.

He was right though. If I was such a risk to the future, they should have pulled me out ages ago. What game were they playing, and why me? I had much to contemplate.

Then I met her, again.

4

All the other outside tables and chairs had been packed inside. Tippy had left. Johan, the assistant manager, kindly let us talk a bit longer, until he needed to go home. The Danish was enjoyed by Fee a few more times until its final demise. Long shadows were casting themselves over the row of stores onto the communal village walkway. Johan leaned in the doorway and seemed bored—we had extended our welcome beyond being respectful. We thanked him and headed for the garden by the river, the one where I'd sat under a tree just weeks ago, or so it seemed. As we walked, the conversation changed focus.

"Me?" Fee asked. "Not much to say, nothing special." I sensed her modesty was genuine. However, it wasn't true. To be accepted into the Institute was an honor few attained. For her to be given Madam Li's praise meant she was special indeed. "Grew up in Wagga."

"A country girl, then?" Wagga was a large collection of villages—once a city. A rural community, it was surrounded by farmers mostly, part of inland New South Wales, one of the larger states of the East Coast.

Fee nodded, walking at a leisurely stroll. "Eldest of three," she continued. "A younger brother and sister. Father was a former mechanical engineer, Mother a nurse. Later they owned a fresh produce store."

"Fresh produce, sounds satisfying."

"My parents thought so. It was part of the local co-op. We were fortunate: we felt connected to a greater productive tribe and dreaming."

"May I ask what triggered your awakening?"

"You mean, what emotional pains or discomforts?"

"Third law of self-awareness: it is only triggered among the discontent. Do you mind?"

"No. You can look it up in my Institute dossier—I know you have access. Short version: I suffered a new and poorly understood type of severe fatigue in my mid to early teens. Left me almost bedridden for years. It meant I spent most of high school at home."

"Away from friends?"

"All except Mary-Anne. We were almost inseparable since we were five," Fee said as if in fond remembrance. Her face seemed sad as she continued. "Then one Wednesday afternoon—it was our regular time and had been for months—I sat waiting on our veranda. I waited. And waited. Then my mother came and told me Mary-Anne wouldn't be coming anymore. I cried for days. I kept to myself after that."

"I'm so sorry."

"Actually, it was a positive: it meant more time reading." Fee tried to smile. "Then one day I came across a text about how to explore within, from a graduate of the Institute."

"As a teenager?"

"Yes."

"You learnt to connect with your intuition so young? Very impressive."

"Very necessary. It helped give me hope and soothe the pains."

"The pains of loneliness?"

"Among others, yes."

"So now you were both intuitive and comfortable in your own company."

"Over time, yes."

"It must have been hard, being social again, I mean, when you were better."

"In some ways."

"How so?"

"Let's just say I made a few relationship choices I'd rather forget."

"Regrets?"

"If you mean, would I do things differently if I had the time over again? Never. It made me who I am. I cherish this." She touched her heart with both hands, then her forehead.

Fee then turned it around. "What about you? Would you change your past? Perhaps more relevant, would you really go back into the past and change it for everyone no matter the cost?"

"It's not that simple."

"Maybe you can explain. You met her again, you said?"

"Yes, the next day."

* * *

I was up early and more careful about how I dressed—I had a keener eye on men's dress habits from wandering around the hotel. Dark blue shirt with collar and sleeves, smart black trousers, and black laced shoes—I sacrificed comfort to look "ordinary." I made sure not to forget my wallet, phone, and the card to get into my room.

Skipping breakfast, I took the clear glass elevator to the first floor. The mall was already starting to get busy. People were running in shorts, sneakers, small sleeveless tops, and with devices coming out of their ears as before. It was sad: they'd just run right past you as if you weren't even there. I tried waving once; the fellow looked at me like I was a strange annoyance, then ran past. Once again, almost everyone was alone, or part of a group of three or less. No one smiled; no one laughed; no one wanted to know you. Looking back, it was probably a good thing—fewer questions and less having to remember the lies about me I sometimes struggled to recall. This day, I decided, I would be more adventurous, see just what kind of place I'd landed in.

The mall led up a slight hill. Across the road at the top to the left was a large, majestic sandstone building with columns framing its entrance. It was a casino, a place for gambling. Yes, such a place existed. It confirmed the high levels of emotional pain these people must have been feeling—as we know, contentment fuels no motivations to give our power and efforts away to the uncertainties of chance. There was a strange and open place opposite it, with large metal sculptures of geometric shapes. I would find more artwork on the other side of the river.

The bridge was as before. I followed some people and kept left. Halfway along I stopped to look around. Behind me were great towers of buildings of mostly block shapes, varying in height, black or gray mostly, and features reaching to a mostly clear blue sky. Up the river, the buildings were smaller. Down the river, on the opposite bank, was a massive wheel with what looked like many pods for people—I definitely wouldn't get in that. The river had boats moving back and forth, but it was the brown murkiness of the water that captured my attention. It reminded me of miso soup, the Japanese soup with many fine particles you can stir up and notice churning, hot areas rising, creating mini currents in a small open bowl. To me, it was another depressing sight: it seemed so dirty compared to the beautiful, clean river we know.

As I continued, to my right I noticed people standing under a narrow shelter, waiting for buses—large rectangular boxes with wheels front and back, carrying up to thirty people. Here they would drop them off or pick them up. On the other side of the shelter was an interesting metal insect sculpture with wings like those of a dragonfly, folded back—it was nice.

To my left was a music conservatory or theater of some kind. Large, colorful banners of people dancing and smiling enticed the eye. It was the first smile I'd seen so far in my day. The street, I learned from the signs, was called Melbourne Street. It was wide, with some trees here and there. It didn't remind me at all of the Melbourne I knew—too dull, sterile, and unlively. Coming off the bridge, I turned left, deciding to walk along the river.

Now there were even more runners. I was starting to feel I wasn't properly dressed. The big wheel was to my right. It wasn't moving and seemed empty. Further up I came across a comforting and familiar sight. They called this area South Bank, and in the 1980s they held a world expo here. Hidden behind some trees before me was an immaculately carved small wooden hut imported from Nepal for the occasion. Perhaps you know it? It was strange to touch the wood: I was used to seeing it encased in a clear, weatherproof box. The reddish material was cool, smooth, and had a lovely sweet smell, and covered almost the whole building up to the square, sloping roof. The whole place had a serenity to it I missed. I took off my shoes, sat in a corner on the cold concrete, and meditated for what must have been an hour—a cleansing meditation, to give my mind much-needed rejuvenation and rest. No one seemed to notice: it was as if the place didn't exist, except to me. It was the tonic I needed.

Brushing myself off, shoes tied up, I continued my stroll until I found a beach. Yes, a small beach, with real sand, in the middle of a city! It was part of a small human-made lagoon. Some people were swimming; others were undressing into bathing suits and lying in the sand. There were some enticing female figures. I didn't stay long: I didn't want to stare and show disrespect.

I remember walking past many food establishments, past many houses—wooden most of them, rectangular windows, metal roofs, some on stilts. Then I reached West End. It was nothing like I remembered.

The busy transport hub we know was nowhere to be seen. Replacing it was a narrower street full of many stores. No tall buildings here. It was closer to the villages we're familiar with, except for the cars.

I noticed a scruffy-looking man in an alleyway, dirty, with thin bags full of who knows what around him. He looked like he needed help. I asked how he was, and he barely moved, sitting as if in a stupor. The smell was terrible, a mix of urine and alcohol of some type. I returned to the street and asked for assistance. People kept walking. I tried the store next door; it sold women's shoes. The lady seemed friendly enough.

"Oh, Bill? He's fine. It's where he lives."

"He lives outside in an alleyway?"

"He prefers it."

"He looks like he needs medical attention," I insisted.

The lady, in her fifties, I'd guess, walked around the corner. "Hey, Bill! You OK?" she shouted. The fellow raised his hand, then lay down. "He's fine." We walked back inside.

"What about his family?" I asked.

"Only family wants to know him is Jim Beam."

"Where's he? I think we should let him know."

The woman laughed. "I think Jim is part of the problem."

"Why? Is he a person of disrepute?"

"Some think so." The woman shook her hand as if holding a glass and pouring it out. "Jim Beam, whiskey?"

I'd completely forgotten: this was a time of homelessness, alcoholism, and broken families. I thanked the lady but still wanted to help. I introduced myself to Bill and asked whether I could assist him. He put out his hand as if wanting something.

"I'm sorry, I don't have anything to give you," I said. Without a word he waved me away, then told me to "piss off." Reluctantly, I left him to his troubles.

Just as I returned to the street, an emaciated lady with loose clothes, rough hair, and pictures up her arms asked me for a light. What was a light? I wondered. It was sunny. Why would she need light now?

"A ciggy? Got a light and a ciggy?"

What the heck was a ciggy?

She asked a young fellow walking by. He stopped, lit her a cigarette, and went on his way. "Thanks, love," she said, as she moved on.

And it was a time of smoking. I'd forgotten that too. How different this West End was from the one I knew.

It was further down the street that I noticed a small, cozy bookstore. The window was emblazoned with copies and images of some boy wizard, Harry somebody, saying "He's Back." Had he been missing? I didn't care. I was curious about what books I'd find inside. Yeah, I know, real books!

I walked between cramped aisles, some book covers facing me, some just showing their spine. It was the self-help and nearby spirituality sections that caught my eye. I was looking for any books by … well, an author well known in our time who made a start in this era. I found a few on friendship, but none from the author I was looking for. You know the one, pivotal to the world's amazing transformation. I pulled out a few books here and there. Then a familiar voice piped up.

"Are you stalking me?"

"What?" I turned quickly and took a step back, startled.

"Fancy that. It must be fate. Ben, isn't it? The guy who gets it. Unless, of course, you don't, in which case you *are* just stalking me."

I must have looked confused or scared. I had no idea what she was talking about. She touched me reassuringly on my arm. "It's OK. I'm kidding. Really, you can chill. I'm not going to post you on Facebook and write nasty blogs about you or anything."

"Mari," I blurted out without realizing it. I had absolutely no idea what she'd just said.

"You remember. I'm touched. I like the duds," she remarked, taking a step back to look me over. "What, no tennis this afternoon?"

"No, no tennis."

"Work, by the looks of it. You work nearby?"

"No. Just on a stroll."

"And just happened to stroll into a bookshop. So, you aren't totally against books after all?"

"Um, no."

"See anything you like?" She searched the section in front of us.

"The friendship books look interesting," I commented.

"Hmm. Haven't read many of them. Perhaps I should. Any recommendations?"

"None here I can see."

Then she seemed slightly nervous. "Do you have a few minutes? Could I buy you a coffee?"

"Coffee? Sure, but I think this time I should pay, if that's OK."

"OK."

A couple of stores down was another café. It was like they were everywhere around here. This one was more open, with dark decor, a slight Greek feel about it. I ordered us drinks; then the young guy at the counter asked whether I had any cash. The electronic bank connection had been down all morning; it couldn't accept my credit card. Cash, I never even knew what it looked like. Mari noticed and paid for us both. I was terribly embarrassed.

"Now you owe me two coffees," she said with a smile as she was sitting down. "I'll hold you to that."

"OK, two, definitely, next time." If there was a next time.

"Tell me, Ben, what do you like to think about?" she asked, sipping her hot beverage from a large black mug.

"Think about?"

"I remember, you said you liked to think more than read. You weren't talking crap, were you?"

"No, no crap."

"Great, tell me more. What thoughts grab you?"

I didn't know what to say. *Keep it ordinary*, I reminded myself, but I also wanted to be honest. "About matters of the heart," I said.

"Such as?"

"Feelings, mostly."

That brought a skeptical look. "You're screwing with me. This isn't some macho get-a-girl-in-bed trick, is it? Step three, talk about feelings—women dig that stuff. If it is—"

"No screwing. I don't do that, promise."

She sat forward, looked me straight in the eye. I could tell she didn't believe me. I sat calmly. Was this really what the men did in this part of the century, emotional manipulation for sex?

"Very well," I said, "I'd like you to try something. Take a few deep breaths. Focus on the cup on the table. Let all the noises disappear, all the thoughts drift away, and tell me what you feel. What does your heart tell you about what I said?"

She seemed reluctant at first, but eventually tried it.

"Take your time," I said softly. "What do you notice, inside, beyond the clutter and racing thoughts, in the feelings deeper and deeper inside you?"

Several seconds passed until slowly she looked up into my eyes and a tear fell onto her left cheek. Embarrassed, she quickly snatched a paper napkin, turned away, and blotted under her eyes, trying not to disturb her eyeliner.

"What did you say you did again?" she asked.

"Oh, I work in it. As a consultant," I said definitively.

"In what?"

"Computers, specialist consultant. Very boring."

"Oh, IT, information technology."

"Yes, IT. Very ordinary."

"OK," she said slowly with a strong air of skepticism.

"You don't believe me?"

"It's just that most people I know in IT have ASD and wouldn't know a feeling if it bit them on the bum."

"ASD?"

"Autistic spectrum disorder? Autism, you know, poor communication skills, great with computers, bad with people."

"Oh, yes, ASD. No, I don't think I have that."

"So where do you consult?"

I was struggling to come up with an option.

"It's OK," she interrupted. "If it's confidential, I don't want you to break any rules on my account."

I smiled, in half agreement and half relief. "What about you?"

"Me? Where do I start?"

"You seem very intuitive."

"Uh …" She seemed reluctant to share. "I work in counseling. I'm studying a master's on the side."

A healer of hearts and minds. That explained the aura I sensed when we met. I think I smiled.

"I'm impressed," she said. "You're not nervous or making an excuse to leave. Most guys get a bit scared by it. They get uncomfortable, worried what secrets I might discover, what mind tricks I might be up to."

"Mind tricks?"

"It's just, not many people understand what counseling is and think we have some kind of hidden knowledge that allows us to manipulate people. It can scare some."

"Do you have a hidden knowledge and manipulate people?"

"What do you think?" Honest curiosity in her eyes.

"Me? I think if you know yourself, you don't need to worry about secret knowledge, manipulation, or any tricks. Hard to help people change, though, if they aren't prepared to touch this, wouldn't you say?" I rested my hand over my heart.

"Uh, yes, very difficult," she replied. "IT, huh?" The look of skepticism and bewilderment returned.

I nodded. "What made you become a counselor?" I deflected.

"Oh, did admin for a while, beauty therapy on the side. Found I enjoyed talking and listening to people more. So I decided to take the next logical step. Thought it would be better to understand what I was doing. Didn't want to make people worse."

"How could talking to them make them worse?"

"It's not everyone, usually those who have suffered severe traumas. You know, like being severely abused, involved in a serious accident, or experienced near death and the like. Explore too deeply, and they can experience the trauma all over again—trigger them—and it can make them worse. It can get very serious."

"I see. So counseling allows you to help people carefully, then?"

"Yes, exactly, yes!"

"Helping others is a noble cause. If only more people thought the same as you," I commented genuinely.

"Thank you, Ben. Yes, I sometimes wonder what the world would be like if there was more caring than making a buck."

"A buck."

"Cash, moola?"

"Oh, yes, I wonder." But I already knew, my mind returning to a time I was beginning to miss.

Suddenly my phone started making a ringing sound. I ignored it. It rang again. I ignored it again. Then it chimed. It kept chiming.

"It's OK," Mari said. "I don't mind. Sounds like someone really wants your attention."

I fumbled with it, not knowing what to do. It rang again. I pressed the green button on the screen to answer—that much I worked out.

"Yes?" Martino informed me there was a new arrival, no specifics. "That's nice," I said. And that I would be on my own for at least another three days as they sorted it out. "Anything I can do?" I asked. He laughed. That went on for quite a while. Then he asked the expected question. "Yes, I am being good," I replied. He hung up.

I smiled at Mari as if it was nothing. She seemed curious.

We spoke about a range of topics. She shared about growing up around Melbourne, then working in Sydney, then eventually moving to Brisbane. She was very open. I learned her young single mother had abandoned her to an older uncle and aunt on her mother's side— Mari's mother had been struggling with mental illness and couldn't cope, and her father had been nowhere to be seen.

"It wasn't that bad," she said. "I still felt very loved. Even managed to catch up with bio-Mum a few years back. The artist type and a bit of a greenie."

"Greenie?"

"Into social causes. You know, into saving the forests, making the world a better place." She smiled. I must have looked lost, as she continued. "Stopping wars, tackling global warming? Mum had quite a crazy dream." Mari stared into the distance.

"Are these issues important to you?" I asked.

"Definitely. Babies before guns, trees ahead of profit, I say. Wouldn't that be something?"

"Yes, it would," I said with a smile. "Yes, it would indeed." This young woman's kind heart was beginning to intrigue me.

Hours passed. We smiled, we joked, we shared a light lunch. She paid, again. It was getting embarrassing, but she didn't seem to mind, so I made no further mention of it.

Later, as lunch turned to afternoon, she turned to me slightly nervously. "So, if you don't mind me asking, have you any plans for tomorrow?"

"Tomorrow? Not that I can think of."

"Great. I was planning on a trip up the coast. Would you be interested in joining me?"

OK, wasn't expecting that.

"Just a bit of time on the beach. Do you like the beach?" she asked.

"It can be nice, sure."

"Great. I'll pick you up at seven. Where's the best place?"

I didn't think I'd said yes, had I?

We agreed out the back of the hotel was optimal.

As we said our farewells, she turned back to me. "Don't forget your bathers, and a towel."

"Sure. Great." After she left, I muttered, "Where the heck will I find a beach towel and bathers?" I'd only ever worn a bathing suit twice.

After I asked around the stores at West End for bathing suits, I was recommended to go to the city. I was told I'd better hurry, as they closed in forty minutes. I started walking briskly, then started to jog. I felt a sense of panic I hadn't known since childhood.

Soon I ran, gasping, down Melbourne Street, across the bridge, down the mall. Sweat was pouring off me like I'd just stepped out of a steam bath. I finally made it into a surf-and-swimwear store. I ran up to the counter to a young lady, trying to catch my breath, desperate, blurting out, "I need bathers!"

Thankfully, Anna, the staff attendant, had a calm disposition. Over the next who knows how long, I tried on shirts, bathing shorts, rubber sandals called thongs, a hat, and some reflective sunglasses. I said I wanted to look like a local, to fit in.

I just completed my purchase before closing time—thank goodness the credit card worked. Uncomfortably I had to type in "ass1," as I was told it was over the card's swipe limit—whatever that meant. Bags in hand I made it back to my room and flopped on the bed.

As drowsiness started to consume me, all I could hear in my head was Martino's voice: *Be ordinary, be good, be ordinary, be good.* Well, ordinary people of Brisbane went to the beach, so the lady at the store said. All I was doing was what Martino had suggested.

As I drifted off, I noticed that the anticipation of tomorrow felt nice. The trick, I knew, was to stay out of trouble. Surely I could manage that.

5

Lights began to appear across the river as the sun set behind us. Interestingly, I noticed the big steel bridge—the Story Bridge—and its arches of lights were missing—it was prominent in the other time, back in 2020. There wasn't any water traffic now. This felt more normal: it felt more open, peaceful, closer to being home. Fee was sitting with legs crossed. I was lying back, playing with the grass between my fingers. "You're telling me," she began, "a fully trained arbitrator, trained in self-control, able to step back and see the greater perspective of any situation, felt fear and ran to find a pair of swimmers?"

"Yeah. Perplexing, isn't it?"

"How do you account for it?" Fee asked, with genuine curiosity.

"On contemplation, I'd say it was a mixture of instinct, having so much to deal with in a foreign environment, and not wanting to make any drastic mistakes—upset the future."

"Nothing to do with your personal past, then?"

"True, a lack of experience played a role."

"Lack of experience with women?" Fee asked.

I had to think about that.

"Hadn't you been in a relationship before?" Fee continued.

"What? Yes, of course."

"And you do know untrained personnel from our time cannot

remain in the past. It is the law."

"Yes, but she was a counselor. I was interested in her own level of insight, what level of wisdom existed in this time—it is my field of expertise."

"But you were exceeding your mandate; your level of engagement with her was clearly becoming unacceptable."

"Did I know that to continue to engage with her held risks? Yes. But, as you said, we are trained to remain detached. I would be careful what I revealed; the risks would be minimal."

"So you intentionally ignored her feelings in the matter."

"What do you mean?"

"She was clearly developing an emotional interest in you. Didn't you notice it?"

"Yes … no. It wasn't foremost on my mind. We were just being friendly, nothing more. Was I looking at having a relationship with her? Of course not. I could be called back at any time."

"And yet you went on a date."

"That wasn't how I saw it."

"So I see."

We decided to continue our discussion over dinner. Nearby was an Italian establishment. I felt like pizza, some bruschetta, and a nice salad. This pizza was exceptional, with a thin and slightly sweet crust, divine spiced tomato sauce, melted buffalo mozzarella, a sprinkle of spices and fresh basil. We shared; I talked. There was much to cover before Fee had to report her recommendations in less than another two and a half days.

"The beach was enjoyable?" Fee asked.

"Part of it, yes. Being in the intensive care section of a hospital wasn't ideal."

"You needed medical attention?"

"You have no idea how difficult it can be, trying to be 'ordinary.'"

* * *

My eyes opened to the dark. Thankfully, I hadn't overslept. My phone indicated 3:34 a.m. Then I noticed the symbol for the battery, signaling that it was low. *Wonderful. How do I replace it?*

After searching through the bags the HRU had left, I found the box for the phone and, of all things, a charger. We are so used to constant electricity being freely available to all devices that it took me a moment to get my mind around having to plug in a device just so it would function. It seemed to work … but was very slow.

I performed my routine morning stretches and muscle work as I waited, then went looking for something to eat. The buffet didn't open for a few hours, so I strolled around the mall and found an all-night store. I bought some fruit and sliced potatoes in a packet—they called them "chips"—then headed back upstairs. I felt like something healthy; fruit and vegetables would do nicely. Waiting, I decided to read the instructions to my bulky communication device.

I was amazed. It had so many "apps"—applications—too many to properly investigate. It did have one app that had immediate practical application though: a map. I played with it, learning where I was and where we would be going. The phone's added camera was a crude but effective toy. I learned from the weather app that today would be twenty-six degrees Celsius, with a ten percent chance of rain, not much different from the typical weather this time of year in our time. Then I meditated.

Relaxed and dressed for the day, I headed down early. I used one of the strong paperlike rectangular bags with cloth handles to carry what I needed: my rolled-up towel, wallet, and phone. I was careful to observe how people entered and exited cars. It wasn't at all like our travel pods, where entering and exiting all happens almost automatically—doors open, seats rotate, and we sit in. Here they were low and fixed, facing forward. The cars seemed fairly functional, and they had a compartment in the back for storage. I was a bit apprehensive: it would be my first time in a car. I reassured myself I'd be fine; all I had to do was just act like everyone else. Surely I could do that.

Mari arrived right on time. The car window on my side opened, and she waved me over. I opened the door successfully and was about to be seated.

"Throw that in the back," she said with a smile. I tried but there wasn't much room between the seats. "You could have used the back door, but that's OK. Chanel, impressive." It was written on the bag. I had no idea what it meant. "Get in."

I sat down in the small fabric-covered seat. It was very cramped. She looked me over and said, "*OK, then*," as though making a comment I didn't understand. "I hope you brought sunscreen. You'll burn," she commented as I finally found the handle to pull the door shut.

"A sun screen? No. Should I buy one?"

"Nah." She smiled. "I've got a bit. It'll probably do."

We had started to move when Mari told me to buckle up. I looked at her, perplexed. "If the cops catch us, I'm the one who has to pay the fine. Do you mind?" She indicated with her hand the strap covering her chest, over the lovely white-and-blue sarong coming up under her arms.

Oh, great, I thought, *a vehicle that needs a restraint!* I fumbled a few times but eventually clicked it in and adjusted it to comfort, to look the same as hers. The car was moving back and forth and side to side. I gripped on tightly to the seat. A few hundred meters later, she pulled the car over.

"Are you sure you don't want to drive?"

"Me?" I was horrified.

"You seem nervous with my driving. Some guys prefer to drive. I don't mind. I'm sure Nancy won't either."

"Nancy?"

Mari tapped the control panel behind the front glass window. "She's my new baby. I trust you." She started to unbuckle her restraint and open her door.

"No! No!" I insisted. "You drive. That will be fine." I heard Martino's words echoing inside my head: *You cannot drive a car. You will crash. Do not drive.* Absolutely do not drive—the prospect already gave me nervous shakes.

"OK, then. This is going to be great!"

I closed my eyes and took some deep breaths. When I opened them, I found myself watching all the traffic. It was all around us—some going in front, some behind. I closed my eyes again, took more breaths, and practiced mental focus. It helped. Then I noticed other passengers in other cars we passed or who passed us were just looking ahead, so I decided to do the same. I put my hands on my lap and just looked to the car in front. They had red warning lights that came on for stopping—like those at intersections for people walking. We slowed down quickly at times. There was swearing involved; Mari seemed a bit stressed. Soon we were on a longer road with only four lanes—two each way—with signs indicating the Sunshine Coast, no more stopping or turning. I finally started to relax.

"What a glorious day," Mari then said, with just one hand on the wheel, looking at me, not at what was in front of her. I found myself looking to the front instead of her for cars about to turn or stop.

"Uh-huh," I agreed, nervously.

"Any particular choice of beach?"

"Oh, no. You can choose."

"Great, I know just the one. Thanks for yesterday, by the way," she said. "I enjoyed our chat. Fancy running into each other like that again? The universe must be speaking."

"Yes, I enjoyed it too. Thank you for the lunch and coffee."

"No problem. So, Ben, tell me, where are you from, if you don't mind me asking?"

I was expecting that one—it had to come at some time.

"Oh, no, it's OK. I'm from the co-op of …" I had to stop myself. "Australia."

"No kidding. I think your accent gave it away."

"Really? I guess it would."

"What, another secret, like your job? You can't tell me where—"

"Yackandandah. I grew up in a village community called Yackandandah, in Victoria." Which was true, for a short time, until I moved to the reclaimed land of central Queensland.

Her face beamed. "No kidding! I know that place. We used to stop by on our trips to Melbourne growing up. Loved the ice cream. A great feel to it—very homely and quaint. What was that like?"

"Good. Lots of creeks and paddocks to go for long walks, lots of trees."

"Trees? I love trees. You know that's one reason I'd never travel to Mars. You know, like this billionaire guy Elon Musk, trying to set up a colony there. I could never do it. I'd miss the grass, the beaches, and the trees."

Mars, I thought, *what a barren place*. Why go there when there were so many beautiful, lush planets around, with grass and trees, and the occasional creature that would bite but you could avoid? There were thousands upon thousands to choose from.

"And I'd probably get lonely," Mari added.

"Lonely? Wouldn't there be others too?"

"Yeah, but I'd be in a foreign place, strange people. I'd miss my friends."

"I know what you mean." I felt a mild melancholy come over me, remembering the people and supportive community I'd left behind. Similar to the feeling I'd had when I stepped onto the Noretian TC not that long ago, my time.

"You do?"

"Yeah. Friendship and community are important."

"Yackandandah has a close community, doesn't it?"

"Yes. The whole town has been a co-op for dec … years."

"Really? How's that?"

It seemed unusual she would ask such a question. In my time everyone intimately knew of cooperatives: they dominated most of our towns and cities. I had to remind myself it wasn't very common here. I tried to explain the basics. "Everyone owns part of the local businesses and properties through a community cooperative to share and support one another. No outside businesses allowed. Lots of small group meetings, talking, stage productions, dancing—"

"You dance?" She seemed excited.

"Not really. I was a bit shy for that."

"Kept to yourself?"

"Pretty much. I was a scared kid growing up, I'm afraid. Liked being on my own."

"And on a computer?"

"What? Yes, of course." I forgot I was supposed to have an affinity with computers—PDs, or processing devices, as we know them. For a time I actually did get on well with the digital devices. "Or outside," I added. "My mother used to get very disturbed when she didn't know where I was. Often I'd just be gone all day, without a word."

"Sometimes we just need our space."

"Yes, sometimes we do."

As we drove, I noticed the Glass House Mountains to our left. Large dormant volcanic towers formed through erosion and named by Captain Cook as he sailed up the coast in the late eighteenth century. They had reminded him of giant glass furnaces in England. They looked bigger than I remembered. In our time I've flown over them occasionally; I've never driven past them.

The mood was solemn in the car by now, until Mari sparked up.

"And sometimes we need music!"

As she touched the center console screen, loud music started blaring. I almost covered my ears. Then Mari started singing, or was it shouting? It was hard to tell. "You are the dancing queen, young and free, only seventeen!" Apparently, the tune was by a group called ABBA, whoever they were. Then, "We built this city, we built this city on rock and roll! Built this city!" Her head was bouncing up and down. "Join in anytime," she offered as she chose another track when it finished. The next she said was a classic, a tune called "Bohemian

Rhapsody." Sounded like a sad tale about a criminal. Lots more head bobbing this time. I must admit I smiled a few times at her enthusiasm.

"You choose one," she insisted.

I scrolled through the names on the screen, and none struck a chord—all very old classics, well before my time. Then I found an interesting title, kind of familiar.

"Ground control to Major Tom. Ground control to Major Tom. Take your protein pills and put your helmet on."

"David Bowie!" Mari was delighted and sang along. "This is ground control to Major Tom. You've really made the grade."

Sounded prophetic. I was moving slightly to the beat.

"Another!"

"Life is a highway. I wanna ride it all night long." I actually started singing that one—softly. Now I also knew what a highway was, in real life—I was experiencing it.

Suddenly I wasn't well.

"I think I'm going to throw up," I blurted out as I felt I was about to let breakfast go.

"No, wait! Not in the car!" Mari quickly pulled over. Just as I opened the door, up it all came. Mari kindly came around my side and helped clean me. Some had landed on my shorts. She told me I looked "as sick as a dog" and offered to turn back.

"Thanks. No. I'll be fine."

"Not good with car trips, huh? Was like that for a while when I was five. Maybe less bouncing around."

Mari kept the songs a bit less hectic after that. I remembered a few. I checked them when I arrived back at the hotel: "Piano Man," "Stairway to Heaven," then "Rocket Man" by a guy called Elton John. I gazed wistfully at her fine, pale, handsome features as she mouthed the words, wondering—if she only knew it, she was with a real rocket man, of sorts. Only this man was from a space vehicle far more advanced than a rocket.

We arrived in Mooloolaba, a seaside resort city with high-rise apartments facing the beach. We found a park for her vehicle. It was busy—I was told this was because it was a Sunday, lots of people from Brisbane. Mari insisted we go to a chemist, a place that dispensed medicines, and bought me motion sickness tablets. "Just in case," she said. Then we took another road, another "car park," and headed toward the sand. She recommended I leave my wallet and phone locked in the car "glove box." Strange, I saw no one wearing gloves. I was reluctant. Martino had made it clear I should keep them close at all times. But I trusted Mari; they were locked away.

With towels in hand, fully reflective sunglasses on, hats in place, we headed for the beach. An elderly couple seemed to be struggling with some chairs and beach-related paraphernalia. Mari asked whether she could help. Alice seemed very grateful, Ernest less so. Mari and I both shared the extra load and helped them settle. Alice whispered to us that Ernest insisted they could carry it all at one time; she was particularly grateful for the extra hands.

The sand was soft yellow-white, very fine, and made scrunching sounds with each step. Once we had helped Ernest and Alice set up, we headed toward yellow-and-red flags. There was a small wooden tower on a metal frame with a few people in yellow-and-red caps looking out over the ocean from behind glass. More were seated or standing nearby. Some sort of safety patrol, I assumed. The sign by the water said to swim between the flags. Who was I to argue? We dumped our gear and Mari took a tube from her bag.

"Take it off," she said.

Really? I didn't see anyone else naked.

"Your T-shirt. You're white as a sheet. You need this more than me. I'll do your back."

The cream was cold; I flinched.

"Sissy. Keep still."

Her hands felt soothing, like a soft massage.

"You do the rest. My turn."

She dropped the sarong to reveal a tight black one-piece bathing suit covering an immaculate hourglass figure. My heart skipped a beat. It skipped more than a few more when she dropped her shoulder straps, held her hair to the side, and told me to rub the cream into her almost fully exposed back.

"Give it a good rub in, and don't miss any, or I'll pay for it tomorrow."

I struggled: my hands were starting to shake. I started some controlled breathing to gather my composure and distance.

Next, we both finished applying the cream to ourselves. I must admit my eyes peeked in Mari's direction a couple of times.

"Up for a dip? Come on!" She raced to the water.

I stood, petrified: I could barely swim. She raced back and took me by the hand and dragged me toward the water. It was surprisingly warm but with a mild chill.

"Come on!" Her head ducked under a wave.

I gingerly followed, checking behind me to see whether the patrol was watching. Then, just as I was jumping to avoid the cool water on my stomach, Mari started splashing me. "Just get under. It's wonderful."

I ducked under the next wave, the loud washing water and tinny sound lasting but a moment, the chill all over in an instant.

"See!"

It did start to feel warmer, and I had to admit it did feel good. Until I was hit by a wave.

"First time, huh?"

I nodded as another wave almost washed me off my feet.

"Just keep watching the waves and duck under them."

Some were almost a meter high. I started to walk back.

She grabbed my hand. "Please don't. I'd like to share this with you."

Reluctantly I turned to her. We were both hit by a wave, it pushing her into my arms unexpectedly. I held her up. We were less than an arm's length apart.

"Thank you. Come out a bit further, before the break."

I was nervous: I hadn't swum since I was a child. We were chest deep.

When the waves seemed to stop breaking over us, Mari came closer. "Nice, huh?" she said, peering into my eyes.

I nodded nervously.

Another wave brought us even closer together. Soon her body was against mine. I felt her warm, sweet breath on my face. Time stood still, the moment lasting an eternity.

"Who are you, Ben Dubois?" she asked.

For an instant I began to move closer still, as if magnetized. There was almost no water between us. Then I stepped back.

Suddenly a wave crashed into us, sending me tumbling underwater. I scrambled to my feet only to have another wave hit me as I gasped for breath. I inhaled water, coughing terribly. Again I rose. Again I inhaled water. I couldn't breathe! Struggling to gain a footing, I pushed myself toward the beach, waves hitting me over and over as I went. Mari soon helped me, and a member of the patrol checked I was OK. I waved him away reassuringly, coughing on all fours in the shallows.

I finally stood up, and Mari sat by my side.

Then, "Mars? It is you!"

"Kells. What a surprise to run into you here." Mari's tone wasn't very convincing.

"He OK?"

I was stumbling.

"Kelly, this is Ben. Ben, this is Kelly, a friend from work."

I sat down, waved briefly, and smiled. "Pleasure." I coughed a few more times.

"You might want to see a doctor," Kelly recommended.

"No! Um, no, thank you. Just give me a minute. I'll be fine."

"So, this is … him?" Kelly tried to whisper to Mari. I noticed Mari nod. "What a wonderful coincidence!" Kelly said louder, all bubbly.

"Mark and the munchkins are just over there. You're welcome to join us."

Mari looked at me with an awkward smile.

"Sure, be delighted." Spitting the foul, salty taste onto the sand.

"Be right over," Mari replied.

"Great. Emma's going to be thrilled." Kelly bounced off.

"Sorry," Mari whispered. "I think I mentioned you, and that we were coming to the beach. You don't have to—"

"No, really, it's OK. I'd be honored to meet your friends."

Mari's comforting hand rested on my shoulder a moment as if to say thank you.

Next thing, a five-year-old girl grabbed Mari around the hips with a big hug.

"Emma, my sweet, what a pleasant surprise!" Mari said with an exaggerated smile. Mari then crouched to her level. "Emma, I'd like you to meet a friend of mine, Ben. Emma, this is Ben."

"Emma, is it? Don't you look pretty today? I love your bathers." Pink, one-piece, had a glitter unicorn on the front.

"It's Toppo. She's my favorite." She pointed.

"She looks very nice. Does she have friends?" I asked. She started listing the names, very serious and adultlike. "Emma, I think they are very lucky to have a friend like you." She smiled. Mari gave her a warm hug. Emma grabbed my hand.

"You must come. Daddy and I are building Toppo a castle. It has a moat and everything!"

"Wow, sounds impressive. I'd love to see!"

Emma led us to her father crouching on the ground, patting wet sand down in a small bucket. Kelly held a baby boy in her arms, must have been barely eight months old. Mari took the baby, gave him a cuddle, and started making funny faces. He smiled. Kelly and Mari started to talk, looking in my direction occasionally. Emma began to explain about the castle and where Toppo lived.

The tanned, somewhat unfit-looking guy in his midthirties wiped his hands on his shorts, then held one out. "Mark."

I shook his hand confidently. He had a strong grip. "Ben."

"OK, Ems, I wonder whether Toppo and the herd could do with another room over here. Do you think you could help me make it for them? You're doing such a good job. They're going to have a wonderful home." He tipped the full bucket upside down next to some mounds. Emma gently pulled the bucket away, and it held its shape. "Shall we make it bigger still?" Mark said, enthusiastically. He handed Emma a small shovel and the bucket. "That looks like just the right sand there. What do you think?" Emma agreed and started filling the small plastic piece. Mark helped.

"Hear you work in IT? All hush-hush," he asked as he grabbed wet sand.

I was shocked.

"It's OK. Software engineer myself, project management. Brother in the air force. I get secrecy. Can't be too careful these days, not with the Chinese."

I didn't say a word.

Between building the sandcastle and giving Emma attention, Mark started asking questions about computer programming language, whether I'd had similar problems, and whether I had any ideas. It seemed he was testing me. I think he was surprised when I offered a few different approaches. What I didn't tell him was that I had done my thesis on intertemporal digital transfer processing—how to communicate with processors we run in a different time field so they can run hundreds of thousands of times faster than if they were in our time. The problem was how to get an ultraquick computer to talk with one much slower—to account for the interface. We sorted it out in the end. The solution had to do with information packet size and buffering. Compared to those issues, the software problems he was talking about were like simple ancient history.

"What do you think about the new Tesla Roadster? Thinking of getting one. Zero to a hundred in under two seconds. Insane!"

"Yeah, insane." I had no idea what he was talking about.

"Have a new Beemer, M8. Kells hated I bought it behind her back. She didn't mind the badge though. It's a dream to drive. Women just don't get cars."

Cars? Those sick-inducing death traps? I nodded my head in agreement, trying to build rapport.

Emma looked bored and ran over to Mari. She gave both the children her attention—caring, kind. For a moment, warm feelings of endearment embraced my soul.

"Let's go for a walk. I need to get out of here," Mark said as he brushed the sand off.

As we walked, he spoke about interest rates, about how big his mortgage was—"up to the hilt" I think was the term he used. They'd moved up here for the better pay—Kelly and Mark's families lived in Adelaide, and so did their friends. It sounded like he enjoyed getting drunk on weekends, or whenever he could get away with it. Then we spoke about politics.

"It's gonna get bad," he said. "The Chinese have us by the balls." Whatever that meant, it didn't sound good. "Fingers in every pie, military growing by the day; the Chinks are trouncing the US, controlling the markets. I think someone needs to just stand up to the bastards."

"Put them in their place?"

"Exactly!"

"You think we should fight them?"

"What? No. Too big. That's the US's job."

"You don't think it could end badly?"

"Someone walks over you, that ain't the time to look all weak. You show strength."

"And if there is a war?"

"We join in, do our bit. I don't want my kids growing up under a bloody red flag."

"What do your friends—sorry, *mates*—think?"

"All behind it. You should meet 'em. Good blokes. We should go out on the town. What d'ya say?" He put his arm around my neck affectionately.

"If I'm here, sounds good."

As we walked back, his grip around my neck tightened. "You know, you're all right, Ben. You're all right."

As the anguish inside me built during our discussion, I couldn't help wondering, how the hell did friendship ever take off? How did the world ever change so much? That was right: the bombs played a big role, and some amazing, courageous people.

On our return it was decided we'd all go for some ice cream. Emma was particularly eager. As we walked up the broad metal-and-wooden stairs toward the stores, I noticed a flash in the corner my eye. I looked up. For a second I swore I saw a TC, but that was impossible. They were never to be seen in this time period: it was strictly forbidden. As I turned, I saw a small drone flying overhead. It distracted me. Not looking where I was going, I tripped, fell, and felt a searing pain in the back of my head. Then everything went black.

6

The dessert menu was tempting, but we abstained. The place was almost our own: only one other couple remained. Light dim, the sweet aroma of coffee wafting our way, I ordered a short black. Fee ordered the same. For a moment there was silence as Fee stared, blankly, at the table, her face hard to read. She was sitting back, hands across her lap, her head tilted slightly to her left as if curious, as her eyes searched mine.

"In the water, you were close to her; then you moved away from her. Care to explain why?"

"What, no 'were you OK, Ben? What was the hospital like? Was it serious?'"

Fee dismissed it all with a wave. "You're here. It's not important."

"That I died?"

"You died?" Her face lit up with concern.

"No. But it's nice to know you care." I smiled.

She threw her napkin at me. "Don't do that again. You know that if you lie to me, I will have to mention it in my report."

"Don't worry, I know what's at stake. That I can assure you of with complete confidence."

The coffees arrived.

"We'd better plan for tomorrow," I recommended. "There isn't much time."

"What would you suggest?"

"We meet at seven thirty, perhaps an earlier start."

"Where do you live?" Fee seemed a bit coy. "I mean, how long will it take for you to get here?"

"In the central reclaimed provinces, a place of dreaming called Engoori. Oh, should take me a half an hour, maybe an hour, depending on pod availability—they can be a bit stingy out there sometimes. Of course, I would requisition a TC, but you heard Madam Li. I'm grounded."

"You could stay the night with me. I mean, at my residence." Was Fee blushing? "I have a spare room. If not, the community center has a dormitory."

"I'd be honored. More time to talk. Your home sounds an excellent idea."

"Very well, then."

The waiter arrived, asking who would pay. I raised my hand. It was done. Visual recognition payments were so much more convenient than swiping plastic or typing in "ass1."

The night was dark; some stars were visible. No longer did strong city lights block almost the entire view of the crystalline night sky— soft ground lights lit our path. The air had the slightest of chills. Fee's uniform jacket and my fleece-lined stock jacket more than compensated, though Fee did seem a bit cold at times. She led the way, chatting about the subjects she taught at the Institute and some of her more challenging pupils. She hoped to take up her first community arbitrator's position next year. I instinctively knew she'd make a great peacemaker and guide; any community would be fortunate to have her.

Her modest new dwelling bordered a few others. Their lights were on, but we respected their privacy. We entered at the back. She gave me "the tour"—the tidy, modern kitchen, bathroom, sleeping facilities, dining and living area. It was all very spartan, minimalistic, and clean. We exited to the front through large sliding glass doors onto a broad balcony facing a common park area that several units maintained and shared. Some of the trees were lit from underneath. It was a magical and calming site, like living close to the spirits of a friendly forest. Fee suggested I sit—chairs were on the deck—as she gathered refreshments.

"Beautiful sense to this place," I shared, looking out at the splendor.

"Oh, yes," she replied, handing me a glass of water. "I sometimes spend hours out here. It's become a special place." I could see why.

She soon returned with an assortment of pickled vegetables on a plate with some cheese, a lovely combination. We nibbled away.

"So, to be clear, you found Mari alluring." Fee by now was sitting comfortably.

"I'd noticed she was attractive, yes. But that was it. Don't worry, I was already creating narratives of how we wouldn't—couldn't—be compatible."

"So, what happened?"

"She did, and a series of troubling events."

∗ ∗ ∗

I was in a daze, images floating uncontrollably through my mind. I remembered scenes and feelings of being afraid of my father as a young boy, when he often raised his hand, and how I'd peed my pants. The time I resigned from my job, and my mother telling me I was being foolish—how could I do such an immature thing? My unexpected joy when I was accepted into the Institute, one of their youngest—a career I'd never dreamed of just a few years earlier. Then I remembered soft lips, or was I imagining them?

Vaguely, as if out of focus, I felt a warm kiss and the concerned whispers of a familiar voice. "Please wake up, Ben. Please wake up." I felt a gentle squeeze of my hand. It was like fighting through clouds to see clearly. At times they would get thick, and vague images would surround me. Now I felt drawn to the sensations, to noises and lights. *Very odd*, I thought. I would have to consider this during my next contemplation.

When I opened my eyes, I noticed the head of a woman with blond, curly hair resting by my left hand. Who was she? *Oh, that's right.* I gently squeezed her hand in mine and her head popped up.

"You're awake!"

I smiled.

Her relief was outpouring. "Thank the mother spirit. Are you feeling OK?"

"I think so. Was I out long?"

"Over eight hours. How's your head?"

It felt kind of sore at the back. As I raised my right hand to touch it, I noticed a tube in my arm and something wrapped above my elbow.

A woman in a white uniform appeared from behind a light-blue curtain. "Good to have you back with us, Mr. Dubois. My name is Tasha. I'm one of the nurses here. How are you feeling?"

"OK, I think."

"Good to hear. Would you mind if I took some observations and asked you some questions?"

I agreed.

She pushed a button on a machine on a stand beside me, and the wrapping above my elbow became tight. Then she pointed a device to my forehead. As I looked up to my right, there was a screen with lines and numbers. On another screen, which folded down on an articulated arm, she started typing. "Could you give me your full name and date of birth?"

"Benjamin Michael ... Dubois. December second, two thousand and ..." I strained to recall the numbers I was supposed to memorize. "Nineteen ... seventy ... seven, no, wait ... nine?"

"Correct."

Thank goodness.

"Do you know where you are?"

"Australia."

She smiled. "I was thinking a bit more local."

"A hospital, of some kind. I'm not sure."

"You are in the Sunshine Coast Hospital intensive care."

Intensive care? That sounded serious. She asked me more strange questions and checked I could move all my parts. So far so good. I informed her I had a Medicare card. "Yes, we have those details, thank you."

"I gave them your wallet and phone. It's all taken care of," Mari reassured me.

My phone?

"Any allergies? Taking any medications? Any medical conditions or past operations?"

"No."

Soon the examination was done.

"Just rest. The doctor will be here soon. You're a lucky man, Mr. Dubois. It could have been much worse," she said as she closed the curtain.

I looked to Mari. "Did you get any ice cream?"

She almost cried.

A kind-looking young woman of Indian appearance showed up wearing blue, and a stethoscope around her neck. "Hello, Mr. Dubois. My name is Pita. I'm one of the physicians. How do you feel?"

"Fine."

She checked the computer screen. "Any pain, nausea, pins and needles, shortness of breath?"

"A mild headache."

"As we might expect." She asked similar questions to Tasha, then, "Can I examine you?" It was over in minutes.

"You are very fortunate, Mr. Dubois. It was a serious knock to your head. Hitting the back can seriously damage the front of your brain. Thankfully, scans don't indicate any bleeding or fractures.

You'll have a bit of a bump for a few days. If it's OK with you, we'd like to keep you for another six hours observation, just in case. If something more serious is going on, it will usually show itself by then. Will that be OK with you?"

I looked to Mari. She nodded.

"OK, yes."

"Fine. Someone will be checking on you hourly. Good to meet you both. Good day."

Tasha returned. "I have a very nervous gentleman outside saying he is your friend—a Mr. Alfonsi? He has been here for at least an hour. Would you like me to ask him to come back—?"

"No, please, show him in."

How had he found out? Martino poked his head around the curtain, looked Mari up and down, then stepped into the cubicle.

"How are you, old friend?" Not very convincing. "Looks like you had a serious knock to head. You good?"

"I'm good, Martino. I'm good."

He looked to Mari.

"Hi. I'm Mari." She smiled, offering her hand.

"Martino. We are old friends." He pointed back and forth between us.

"Martin, is it?"

"Martino. Martino to my friends."

"Martino. So, how long have you two known each other?" Mari asked.

We looked to one another and simultaneously blurted out, "A long time."

"Yes, we go back years," I interrupted. "He's been helping me with work."

"Yes, with his work. Hard worker, Ben, hard worker," Martino exaggerated.

I looked to Mari. "Could we just have a minute?"

"Sure."

After she left, Martino whispered, "This … this is not ordinary!" His finger circled the room. "*She* is not ordinary!"

"Yeah, she's nice," I whispered back with a smile.

"This is trouble for Martino. Why you do this to me?"

"How did you know I was here?"

"Hospital call." I didn't understand. "Emergency feature on your phone," Martino explained. "I am who to contact. They call, I'm here. Why you here?" he asked. "You sick?"

"Oh, tripped over, hit my head on some steps. Knocked me out."

"You better?"

"Yes, I think I am, thanks for asking."

"Good, we go." He grabbed my arm to help me from the bed.

"Now? They want to keep me under observation for six more—"

"We go, now!" He started searching around the bed.

"What are you doing?"

"Your clothes, must be here." He looked under the bed.

"Wait, why? What's the hurry?"

"New visitor. You must talk to them. Very urgent. He'll listen to you." Martino stood up, raised his right hand above his head to about two meters. "This big, arrived after you. You understand? You are arbitrator, no?"

Martino pulled off the monitor leads, the pressure cuff, and the tube from my arm. Alarms started sounding. Tasha appeared.

"What are you doing?"

"You wouldn't know where my clothes are, would you?" I asked.

"You're leaving? You know we can't take any responsibility for your safety—"

"Clothes, please?" Martino insisted.

Tasha pointed to a cupboard. Mari entered. "What's going on? You need to be resting."

"Family problem," Martino explained. "Very urgent."

"Someone sick?" Mari asked.

"Very sick," Martino affirmed. "Very sick."

I removed the hospital garment and put on my shorts. Tasha left, and Mari turned her eyes away.

"I'm sorry. Have to leave. Have you seen my phone and wallet?" I said, getting dressed.

Mari took them from her bag, a worried and truly caring look on her face. Tasha returned and asked me to sign a form saying I was leaving against medical advice, and handed me another paper with symptoms she told me I should look out for. "If you have any of these, you need to seek medical attention." Martino took it and folded it into his pocket. I signed the disclaimer, didn't read any of it. Martino almost pushed me out. I stopped and returned to Mari.

Grasping her hands between mine, I gazed into her concerned eyes. "It has been special, thank you. Can we communicate tomorrow?" I asked softly. I didn't think it was fair that this would be how she saw me for the last time. Mari gave me a short kiss on the cheek, nodded, and gave a concerned smile as Martino returned to lead me out.

"Wise man, huh?" he whispered as we left, his disapproval obvious.

The vehicle was much bigger than Mari's, with windows blacked out. I sat in the back, Martino in the front. Tina was behind the wheel. "Hello, Mr. Dubois. Glad you could make it."

"Hello, Tina. Did I have a choice?"

"Let's go," Martino ordered.

"What can you tell me?" I asked.

"Landed two days after you," Tina replied. "Wrong place, wrong time. He was set upon by a group of local kids out on the town, high on drugs or alcohol. It doesn't matter now. He's in a bad way and won't go out."

"What has this to do with me?"

"He's being picked up tonight, in around … seven hours. He won't move, petrified. We're thinking probably not a good look bringing him to his people sedated. We're hoping he'll listen to you."

Martino spoke up. "You're an arbitrator. You arbitrate."

"Wait, they're picking him up? Perhaps they could return me."

"If only." Martino looked to the heavens.

"Sorry, we have special instructions. You are to stay, for now," Tina explained.

My head was thumping, and I was feeling a bit dazed. "You OK?" Tina saw me in the mirror.

"Just a bit sore. I'm OK."

"There's another reason we need you," Tina added.

"Yes?"

"Probably better that you see for yourself."

We pulled up outside a tall, narrow house. The address was the same as on my license. It looked like it was under major repair. Cut timber and dust was everywhere. Many of the walls inside were open and exposed, revealing pipes, cables, and what appeared to be some form of insulation. In the back there was barely a kitchen. Bob rose from a chair beside a flimsy table as we entered. Martino checked with him.

"Not a peep," Bob replied. "Good to see you again, sir." He looked to me.

"You too Bob. Where is he?"

Bob looked to the door beside us. "He's asleep."

I slowly opened the door. Huddled on a double bed in a small, plain room was a large figure, motionless under a blanket.

Tina followed me. "I have a translator. Speak into this," she whispered, as she handed me her phone. I was expecting our smaller translator from our time.

I kneeled beside him slowly so as not to scare him. Then I saw his face. "Holy crap!" I whispered. "What's happened to his face?" His eyes opened. Startled, he quickly crawled to the corner, the blanket over him. "What have they done to you, my friend?" The translator was on. His face was a mess.

The right side of his face was swollen, his right eye completely closed over. His left jaw was big too and irregular. It was probably broken. His blond hair was wet, with some crusted blood clumping above his left forehead and ear.

"It's OK. It's OK," I said softly. "You are safe. You are safe." He was still shaking. "Was he on the same craft with me that exploded?" I softly asked Tina.

"Yes, apparently so."

I wondered, could he have been the one who saved my life?

"Remember me?" I asked. "The ambassador? Did you put me into the emergency pod, before the crash?" The translator was doing its work but he didn't flinch. "Did you save my life before the …" I used my hands to express the explosion. I saw terror in his eyes; then I thought I saw a smile or recognition.

Martino entered the room. "Do what you do. We need to move."

I led the crowd of three behind me out and shut the door.

"What the hell? Why didn't you get him medical attention? He obviously has a fractured jaw, and who knows whatever else."

"And a busted knee," Bob added.

"Great, so he can't walk either? What is wrong with you people?"

"He is alien. No doctors," Martino insisted.

Tina interjected. "We thought his heart on the wrong side of his chest, or a spleen-like organ that looks like it might hatch, might be a problem."

"OK, fair call, but this?"

"We need you to talk him down so we can move him. Can you do it?" Tina asked.

"I'll try."

"No try. Do," Martino insisted as he checked his phone and paced the room, nervous as ever. "Arbitrate," he ordered.

"Actually, I'm very glad it is you," Tina added.

"Why's that?"

"If I was a Noretian and some race did this to one of our own, I'd be pissed. I'm glad you are skilled in this stuff. I'd rather you talk to them than me."

She was right: this could set off repercussions. This was an advanced race, hundreds of years ahead of us. The damage they could do if they wanted to could be substantial.

I gently returned into the room and asked whether I might sit on the floor not too far from him. He agreed. It was time to build rapport, as they teach us at the Institute, build a bond of friendship. I would focus on what we had in common first, about how much I was impressed by his home. This was a guy I probably owed my life. To get him home to his people so they could care for him properly was the least I could do.

It took several hours to gain his confidence and trust—this man had been severely assaulted and traumatized. Translation was a problem. The phone could translate what I was saying OK—though there was a delay, and I wasn't sure how accurate it was—but it had trouble translating what he said. Not surprising, really, considering how much his mouth was swollen. By the end, he let me sit beside him. I comforted him with a gentle hand, a known form of reassurance among many social species. Calmly and slowly we connected as I was hoping we'd do.

Tina soon slowly poked her head through the door. "We have to go."

I explained to Horst—it was as near a translation of his name as I could manage—how we were going to take him to his people so he could return home to his family, so they could give him the care he deserved. I described walking to the car—we would help him—about the drive, the time it would take, and the type of location where we would meet—Tina informed me. There is less fear if we know what is about to happen. He agreed.

Bob helped him to the car. He was the tallest, acting like a set of crutches. By now it was dark, and Tina used the light on her phone to lead the way—not all the house lights worked. We drove north out of the city and along country roads, some covered only in gravel. Martino opened and closed gates. In a clearing with forest nearby, we waited.

They were on time, their glowing, disklike, smooth craft landing silently. As a doorway appeared, I helped Horst from our vehicle. When they saw us struggle, two Noretians promptly came to help carry Horst aboard as I followed. I met their commanding officer. He looked completely shocked and initially very displeased. He spoke English; that was useful. He was very philosophical in the end. He said all creatures who traveled the stars had a "time of pain," as he called it, a time of hostilities out of control. That was why they only traveled to the times when they were more "mature," to consider initiating contact then. He gave his thanks that I was all right and apologized for my experience—the failing of their craft apparently was a one-in-a-million event. He was a tall, wise, compassionate, and understanding gentleman, someone I was glad to have met. In minutes they were ready to leave.

As I stepped clear of their craft, I sensed a feeling of homesickness, of missing the familiar, an opportunity missed on a new world among a lovely people. Don't think asking them to take me home didn't cross my mind. It did. But I thought the better of it: it would only cause more friction between our two races, them complicit in helping a rogue citizen who wasn't following his own race's instructions.

When I returned to the group, I think Martino was pleased to see me. He smiled and tapped me on the back as if to say, "Job well done." We watched as the majestic craft silently rose to a hover, then darted in the blink of an eye to a thousand meters, instantly turned at right angles at an even faster speed for several hundred meters, then disappeared.

On the drive back to my accommodation, everyone seemed in a jovial mood. Even Martino looked relaxed.

Unfortunately, none of us had noticed that the whole transfer had secretly been recorded.

7

I stared into the still darkness beyond the realm of the balcony. All the other units' lights were off, the tree and path lights faded. Not even moonlight embraced this balmy night. Fee indicated no wish to sleep, and I was more than happy to continue—neither of us watched the clock. She kept my glass topped up with water, darting back and forth to fill a bottle we shared between us. Otherwise, the only breaks were the obligatory bathroom stops.

Returning with the blue bottle filled, she sat, leaning forward, her elbows on her knees, her pose one of curiosity. "Fine. Clearly, she cares for you. I take it that made her even more attractive?"

I smiled.

"But you still haven't told me why you pulled back from her. Is there something you're trying to hide?" Her eyes searched my own.

"It doesn't bother you that our transfer with the Noretians was witnessed? Or the implications to early Earth if they found out aliens were living among them, many from different times?"

"They called them UFOs and were none the wiser. Very unfortunate about that Noretian fellow. I feel for him, I do, though it sounds like you did all you could. And yes, I get it, the fellow probably saved your life, but Mari is the real reason you are here now: it's because of her you want to go back. You were clearly attracted to her, even before your little accident, and yet you pulled back. Your thoughts?" Fee wouldn't be distracted.

I think I squirmed a bit in my seat. "I needed to keep my distance, clearly," I admitted.

"And what distance was that, two millimeters from her lips?"

"OK, I let it get out of hand."

"Really? And you couldn't say goodbye to her in the hospital? Sure, you could. So why didn't you?"

"It's like I said: I didn't think it would be fair—"

"Oh, so now you think about her feelings."

"I had every intention of calling her, meeting up, and telling her it was over."

"But you didn't, did you?"

"I was having glimpses."

"Glimpses?"

"From within. Have you ever wondered, if we ever fully immersed ourselves with the heart of another, whether we could still be trained to look as deeply inside ourselves as the Institute trains us to do?"

"Oh, I get it. This had never happened to you before; this depth of feeling was new!"

"Maybe … OK, yes. I mean, think about it a moment: imagine no longer being the observer in the playground, to be completely immersed and emotionally connected like a child."

"So you really were humbled by these feelings? You, an ambassador standing?"

"Tell me, Fee, have you ever met someone you felt so much for that you would consider abandoning the person you had felt for years you had always wanted to be, the person you had worked tirelessly for decades to become?"

"Sacrifice my sense of self for someone else?"

"To save yourself."

Fee stood up and walked around the balcony. "OK, the feelings you were developing for her were strong. I get that, but what about the friendship imperative?"

"What about it?"

"Friendships should always come first. You and I both know it; our relationships are but fragile shells without them. And true and close, lasting friendship is built on trust."

"Your point?"

"The strong feelings from the dream you were building about her were being built on a lie. You were lying to both of you."

"Yes, I knew I was deceiving her; she had no idea who I really was—"

"Then you should have just left. How could you even consider being with her, knowing, whether you left her and returned here or not, it could never work, it was always going to be doomed from the start."

I smiled, knowingly.

Fee's eyes widened with realization. "You didn't tell her, did you?"

I turned, looking vaguely into the distance, sipping water.

Fee covered her mouth with shock. She knew I had broken a critical law of nondisclosure.

* * *

When I woke, my head was still a bit sore. I had a shave with a quaint, big-by-our-standards electric shaving device. I then showered and clothed myself appropriately for the day before attending a small buffet breakfast downstairs.

From the moment I was awake, all I could think of was Mari—I think I'd dreamed of her too. It was early, so I decided to wait, then called her, as promised. There was no immediate answer; then I heard her voice saying I should leave a message.

"Hello. This is Ben …" I didn't know what else to say. As I was thinking, the phone hung up.

An hour later she called back, apologizing. "Ben, great to hear from you. How's your head? Sorry I couldn't get back to you sooner. I was with a client."

"Fine, thanks," I said. "How are you?"

"It's good to hear your voice."

"And yours."

"Look, I'm busy today, running a bit late, was wondering whether we could catch up tonight?"

"Tonight? OK, yes."

We arranged a time and place. Later that morning she called again. She wondered whether I'd mind if we had dinner at Kelly and Mark's place, if I was up to it. Kelly was very insistent. Apparently, Mark flew out tomorrow for work for a few weeks and wanted to catch up, and they wanted to see I was OK.

"Sure," I said. I was trying to be ordinary and polite, not seem suspicious.

"Dress casual," she said. Whatever that meant.

In the end I sorted it out. I asked a very nice gentleman by the name of Marshal at reception, with blond, spiky hair—reminded me of home—who gave me some suggestions. Thankfully, no shopping trip was required: the clothes were already in my wardrobe—thank you, Bob and Tina.

I spent the day walking again, returning to the garden by the river. Images and feelings of Mari and our brief time together continually floated through my head. This was new and very disturbing; my mind was usually better ordered than this. I found its obsessions very disconcerting.

By the afternoon I was well prepared. I felt joy just to meet Mari again. Would I let doubts about the future—such as how much time I could be with her—cloud my feelings for her? Not right now, not again. For now I would let nature be my guide—let the web and intricacies of time take their course. I knew it wasn't being very responsible, but it was what I felt I needed to do.

She arrived on time. When I entered her car, I was completely and unexpectedly taken aback. Amazing! "Your hair is lovely," I think I managed to blurt out. The aroma, divine. Her dress—the top half I could see—was trim and tight, strapless, an enticing royal blue. I "buckled up" more easily this time as Mari pulled away.

"Would you mind?" she asked. "Could you hold the bottle?" It was moving between my feet in a small long bag. It wasn't polite, I was told, to show up without a present. I placed it on my lap. Mari queried whether my relatives were OK. I assured her they were. We didn't have much time to really talk. Before I knew it, we had arrived. Thankfully, this time the drive was uneventful. I didn't feel the need to grip the seats, and I didn't throw up.

The streets we drove through were immaculate and lined with big, tall houses—at least three times the size we have. There were rows and rows of them, all packed together, all facing the same street. I didn't see any parkland. At least there were a few trees and walking paths. It was hard to tell, as it was night. When I asked Mari where the community hall was, where everyone met, she had no idea what I was talking about. The closest thing, she said, was a local church, but people only met there once a week for an hour. Momentary sadness once again gripped me as I thought about the local children—where did they all play together and meet, dance, create, build close friendships, meet great role models? A strange and sterile environment, this suburb.

The house we stopped in front of was as big and impressive as the others around it. Columns framed two large wooden doors with glass inlays. The lawn was well trimmed, and the shrubs and flowers appeared well kept. As we alighted and headed for the door, I struggled not to stare at Mari: her very being seemed exquisite and enticing. Smartly walking to the doors, she pushed the button to the chime. The sound of giant bells reverberated.

"You're looking nice." She smiled.

"Mari! Ben! So glad you could make it."

"Kells, thanks for inviting us. This is for you." Mari took the bottle in the bag I was holding and handed it over.

"You didn't need to." She pulled the dark, long bottle out of the bag. "Mark will be pleased. Good choice—a shiraz. Come on through. He's out the back."

The foyer was like something I'd imagine in an old Russian castle—marble floors, columns, curved staircase, and a chandelier.

"Where are the kids?" Mari asked.

"Sorry, they're asleep," Kelly explained. "Emma tried to stay awake for you but couldn't quite make it. Big day at the Worm."

"The Worm?" I asked

"The Happy Worm, a day care just a few suburbs away. They're very good, hard to get into but a real lifesaver."

I later found out many families placed their children in paid care while they worked, some for five days a week. I wondered whether this was where they played and made friends. It was strange they had to pay for it. Stranger still, the parents and relatives didn't collectively care for them first, make them a priority, as they do in our communities.

Kelly led us past a large living room and a huge kitchen onto a rear outdoor area. To the right was a large swimming pool, fenced and glassed off, with wooden deck surround. To the left, a large table, chairs, granite floor, and Mark standing by a large silver barbeque, wearing a black apron, with a drink in one hand and tongs in the other, smoke billowing into the air.

"Ben, maaate! Good to see ya. How's the head?" He put the glass down and gave my hand a vigorous shake.

"Fine, thanks."

"Hi, Mars." He politely kissed her on the cheek.

"Hi, Mark. They look nice."

"Prime ribeye. How d'ya like 'em? A bit raw?" He smirked. There were sausages on the hotplate, cooking beside already well-cooked onions. He was sounding a bit drunk.

"Well done, thanks," Mari replied. I asked for the same.

"Hon, the sausages are almost done, and I could do with a top up. Oh, and don't forget to get these fine people a drink."

"What would you like?" Kelly asked.

"Water for me," I said.

"You sure? We have Four-ex, Corona, Heineken, Asahi, bourbon, Coke …"

"No. Water is fine, thanks."

"That's right, head injury. Probably for the best. Mars, you?" Mari offered to go with Kelly to get the drinks, and maybe take a peek at the sleeping kids.

"Big house," I commented.

"What, this old shack? Planning on an upgrade in a couple of years. You?"

"Oh, not as impressive as this." Mark finished putting the sausages on a clean plate as he turned to thick, raw steaks on another plate and threw them on the open grill. They sizzled as they hit the grated bars of metal.

"Hear you are off to work tomorrow, overseas?" I asked.

"Part of the job. Two weeks in Asia every couple of months. Pays the bills, with a couple of perks."

"Perks."

"Thailand," he said with a smile. "Stop over with the lads. Ever been?"

"Can't say I have."

"You're missing out," he said as he grinned. "So, what do ya do for fun, Ben?"

"Hiking, sailing …" It was true, I did.

"Sailing? How big's your boat?"

"Just a little skiff, a bit of a challenge in a wind—"

"Have an eighty-footer berthed at Redcliffe, twin V8s, inboard, outboard, all the mods. We should take you guys out. You fish?"

"As a kid, a couple of times—"

"We can fix that."

Kelly and Mari arrived with our drinks. Mark almost grabbed the full glass of dark wine from Kelly's hand. I graciously accepted mine and offered thanks.

"Mars here tells me you're staying in a hotel, but you live in Windsor. Is that right? Something wrong with your place?" Kelly asked, unexpectedly.

"What? No, um, renovations, very messy, very messy. Just a few more weeks."

"Make sure the bastards don't rip you off," Mark commented. "Hold them to the contract."

"Thanks, Mark, I'll keep an eye on them."

The conversation turned to holidays and taking the children on a long trip. Europe was mentioned, and the United States. Mari wondered how the young children, one still a baby, would go, being on a plane for so long—apparently, it took almost twenty hours to get to the United Kingdom from here. Isn't that just ridiculous? We can travel halfway across the galaxy in less time. They didn't think there would be a problem; Mari wasn't convinced.

Dinner was served. It was buffet style—meats, condiments, salads, and the wine we'd brought. I stayed with water, Mari a glass of white, Kelly a glass of red, and Mark kept the bottle nearby. As Kelly and Mari spoke about personal challenges at work, Mark turned to me, ignoring them. "What d'ya think about the market? In for a crash?"

"The market?"

"Stock market. You dabble?" I shook my head. "They reckon we're in for a fucking major collapse. What d'ya reckon?" Kelly stopped talking and looked at Mark. "What?" He looked at her, then dismissively turned away. "Worse than the GFC, fucking disaster just waiting to happen. Will chuck interest rates through the roof! Gold's the answer!"

"Gold?"

"Shit hits the fan, buy up gold, big. Better still, do what I did. Buy it now. They never fuck with gold. Gotta think of the kids."

"The kids, right."

"You bet, the kids. You got kids?"

"No, I don't."

Mark became all teary. "Goddamn best fucking thing. Little Ems, breaks my heart, the shit happening in the world. Gotta protect them, give 'em the best, you know what I'm saying?"

"I think I do."

Mark poured himself another glass. Some missed and went on the table.

"How about I get you some water?" Kelly suggested to Mark as she started to take his glass.

Mark snatched it from her. "Stop fucking controlling me!" he shouted.

Kelly stood up and left, clearly upset. Mari followed her. I looked to Mari to see whether I could help, but she waved me to sit down.

"You stay here. Us mates have to stick together. Let her wail a bit, ungrateful …" Mark insisted with a slur to his speech.

"Nice steak," I remarked, trying to change topic and calm him down.

He grabbed a chunk on his fork. "Good old Aussie beef. Nothing like it." He roughly cut some and started eating, taking mouthfuls of wine as he went. For a time he just ate, and drank, in his own world.

We finished, and Mark insisted he take me to his "office." As we passed the kitchen, he raised his voice. "More fucking mess!"

I suggested we clean it up, but he said to leave it; it was Kelly's job. As I actually did start cleaning, he pulled me away.

His "office"—study—was bigger than most dining rooms I'd seen. It had a large desk in front of a window, bookshelves covering some of the walls, a few paintings, and on the desk—ornate wood covered in green leather—was a computer screen, keyboard, and mobile interface device they called a mouse.

"Check this out," he said as he brought the screen to life, sitting back in a large, high-backed brown leather chair. I stood beside him.

On the screen were pictures of vehicles, some low and sleek. Some with scantily clad women posing on or near them. "You on Facebook?" he asked.

I had no idea what he meant. "No," I replied.

"You're in IT and not on Facebook. What's wrong with you? You gotta get on it. A real crack up. Here, check this out."

On the screen appeared pictures of people, places, and cars. He focused on the cars. Under the entries were "comments" where people apparently "chatted" to each other or left remarks. He showed me his business's site. It was an international robotics company. There were a few pictures of him clearly drunk with his "mates" and some Asian women under their arms. "What d'ya think of them?" he asked.

"Nice-looking guys," I commented.

"No, them." He pointed to the women.

"Very nice," I said. They appeared happy and well dressed.

"They let you do anything over there," he said with a smile. "They love it!"

Was he saying what I thought he was? "You pay for—"

"Fucking everything's cheaper over there, everything."

I was appalled and started to leave.

"Here, check this out!" he insisted as I kept walking. "Fucking aliens!"

I walked back—aliens? On the screen was a video playing of a glowing TC landing in a field. It seemed familiar.

Just then Kelly and Mari walked in. "Mark, you owe these people an apology." Kelly stood opposite his desk.

"What the fuck for? Here, check this out. Aliens!" He waved them over.

Kelly and Mari came around. The picture on the screen was out of focus and in black and white with a tinge of green. It showed the doors of the TC open, and two tall figures stepping out. Then it focused on them carrying a comrade from a wheeled vehicle, and one of the people following them in. The camera then focused on the person standing beside the vehicle. It was Martino!

"It's fake," Kelly said. "Photoshopped."

"Tony reckons it's the real deal. If it's fake, they did a great job."

Mari started looking at me.

"Yes, it's a fake. Look at how they walk," I said. "It doesn't look right."

"I dunno," Mark commented, skeptical. "Anyway, plenty more of them around. Kells is right. Probably a sample of some movie they're making to suck us in. Have you seen the ones with the *Star Wars* ships over San Francisco?"

"Mark, the apology?" Kelly insisted.

"All right, whatever. Sorry." Suddenly the screen started to show naked people having sex. "Oh, shit." Mark fumbled, and the screen went blank.

I started for the door, concerned, and disgusted. Mari suggested we leave. It was a work day tomorrow and she had an early start. We said our goodbyes at the front door; then as it closed, we heard shouting behind it. Mari headed for her vehicle, and I followed.

We sat in the front seats, silently, for a while. Then we both started talking together.

"I just want to say—"

"—I think you have—"

I started. "Mark is a—"

"Pig," Mari interrupted. "I'm sorry. I didn't know it had come to this."

"'Interesting' is probably what I would have said. You have interesting friends," I commented. "You and Kelly are close?"

"Well, we're not best buddies, but yes, we're part of a group of girls who hang out together. Kelly said she was thinking of leaving, but he said he'd changed, he was getting better; he'd agreed to couple's counseling."

"It was worse?" I was genuinely surprised.

"Apparently."

"Your friend is aware her husband is seeing other women?"

"He's what?" Mari seemed genuinely surprised. "She mentioned nothing ..."

"He's quite proud of it, actually. Many times, with Asian women on his travels. He pays with money."

"The bastard!"

"It would seem the essence of a woman is clearly not something he values or seeks to respect. I think your friend is in trouble."

Mari put her hand to her cheek in apparent shock and exasperation, perhaps thinking what to do, like whether she should tell her. In a way I was kind of relieved. In just a few minutes, I had learned that Mari valued fidelity and friendship, especially among other women.

As we drove home, Mari explained how Kelly was a receptionist at work, studying a counseling diploma. They had become friends over time. When she'd arrived and felt alone, Kelly introduced her to the girls group, a positive, supportive mix of women, many working, many devoted to being mothers—a role she said they all respected. But "having it all," as she described it, was proving elusive. Kelly was a case in point; the more she and Mark worked to build a better life for their children, the more they found themselves driven apart. Of course, we know why, but in this time they hadn't figured it out yet.

Back in the city, Mari suggested we go for a walk. It was still a fine night and we hadn't had much time together. It sounded good to me.

"I hope you don't hold this against me," she said. The mall and streets were virtually empty.

"What is that?"

"The whole night. My instincts told me it was a bad idea. I should have listened."

"It wasn't all bad. We're here now," I reassured her.

As we strolled, she asked, "Funny about that video, don't you think?"

"Video?"

"The UFO." My heart missed a beat. "That guy looked awfully familiar, reminded me of someone."

"The bald guy? I noticed it too. Looked the image of Martino."

"That's what I thought," Mari sparked up.

"No shortage of short, bald guys these days. I'll have to show him. He'll get a laugh."

"Uncanny. Had the same style of jacket too."

"You don't think the video was real, do you?" I asked, half-hearted.

"What, that aliens live among us? Don't be silly." That was a relief. "With so many faked photos and stories going around these days though, it's hard to know who or what you can trust."

"I guess that's where instincts come in, searching beyond what we want to see, towards a greater truth," I suggested.

Mari stopped, holding both my hands, her body close. "A truth based on trust and honesty."

I was about to move on when she kissed me, soft at first; then her passion set free. I felt a release I'd never known before.

I was alive!

And in trouble.

8

The glow of day's early light said hello, introducing us to the new day. Fee decided to shower first and prepared some coffee, a home brew. She said she'd left a towel on my bed. Lights in adjoining units started to flicker on, and birdsong began to fill the air. I was only the slightest bit tired.

"Ready!" she shouted. I guessed the bathroom was now mine.

As I walked in, I stopped in shock. Standing at the mirror, in nothing but lingerie-quality bra and panties, her body taught and trim, Fee was applying the finishing touches to her makeup. Her skin was unblemished but for a small triangular-shaped birthmark, no bigger than a walnut, on her left upper back, near her bra shoulder strap. Paying me no heed, she confidently strode past me as if thinking nothing of it.

I showered quickly. Fee offered to steam my clothes, and I passed them to her from behind the almost closed bathroom door. In minutes she passed them back, clean and crease-free. Resplendent in a white casual blouse and navy skirt, she stood by her kitchen bench, eating some toast and sipping on her sweet-smelling brew. She handed me a cup.

"Toast?" Her hand was on a half loaf on the bench.

"No, thanks. Coffee's fine."

"Have some errands to run this morning. Thought I'd get them out of the way early. Do you mind?"

"No problem."

"You are welcome to join me," she suggested.

Not a bad idea. Perhaps more time to talk. "Sure," I replied. It wasn't like I had anywhere else to be.

After another quick bathroom stop, we were on our way. We left by the front entrance this time. We passed others on a path, and Fee said hello to everyone by name. Some introduced themselves. Kids were already playing in the common parkland in the middle of the houses, and families were starting to gather with one another there too, especially several mothers and grandparents.

In a gap between the circle of houses, we followed a wooded path with still-young trees on either side to a large community hall. It was octagonal in shape, and its curved roof reminded me of roofs from ancient China. A large sign beside the path espoused the community values. Prominent among them were respect, care, protection, and support—commonly shared values recognized on signs in many districts. Above the broad and tall open entrance, with large wooden doors opened inward, was a sizable sign with three words united in a triangle: "Community," "Family," and "Self," with a representation of the earth in the center, a similar symbol to the Institute insignia we wore on our uniform lapels, only ours had no words.

Fee strode in. The place was open and inviting. As we entered, I noticed a large stage at the end of the central hall, and to our right was a corridor and many offices. The place looked rather new. We headed down the corridor.

This was the hub for just under two thousand people, their lives intertwined by activities and meetings organized in a central place. Everyone virtually treated this as a second home, a safe and completely welcoming place.

Fee led us down stairs to one of several subfloors. She knocked on a door. The word "Arbitrator" was printed on the door with an emblem of family unity underneath. Next door the sign indicated this was a meeting place of the "Circle of Welcome."

"Hi, Fee. Great to see you." A short woman of Indian appearance, in her fifties, dressed in standard arbitrator uniform, came over with a big smile.

"Chetna, this is Benjamin, from our ambassador division. He is visiting for the day."

Chetna hugged Fee warmly, then gave a similar hug to me. "Please come in. Session doesn't start for another hour."

We followed her to her office, its walls covered in a moving, three-dimensional landscape of lush rainforest. As she touched her desk, calm, soothing light-blue walls replaced it—I preferred the forest.

"Please sit," she insisted. "What can I do for my favorite recruit?" she asked.

We sat in plush office chairs to the side of her desk—Institute instruction had taught us that unless official matters were involved, it was impolite to talk over such formal furniture.

"I'm afraid important matters of a sensitive nature have come up. I will be unable to assist on the welcome today. Can we make it another time? I thought I should inform you in person," Fee explained.

"Nothing too serious, I hope?" Chetna asked.

"Can't say. I'm sorry."

"No problem. There are only five cases this morning, minor disputes and accusations only. Their families will all be in attendance; we should be fine."

This was one of the jobs of a community arbitrator, to settle disputes and alleged crimes. It involved being chair and facilitator in a community hearing process where family, friends, and community members involved would gather to bond and seek understanding and emotional resolution so we were confident that whatever slight, abuse, theft, damage, or disrespect had occurred wouldn't happen again. As arbitrators we often found crimes were more commonly committed against those people the other party wasn't emotionally connected to—a stranger—or because the perpetrator was ignorant of their actions. The aim was to create a circle around the accused in an intimate setting, welcome them, listen to them, share our care, value, and appreciation for them—that was where family and friends often came in—and help them to help us to understand what we could all do to prevent the incident or perceived crime happening again. Often it simply required education, for a person to see and feel the consequences of their actions for those they cared about. Showing care was the key: it was a powerful tool for positive change—we are less likely to hurt those who care for us, and if they care for us, we are more likely to care about them. Often the meetings involved lots of healthy crying.

Fee was supposed to be on a morning sitting of her local community circle. It was her honor and duty to attend, as it was for all community members. It wasn't just a way to resolve disputes, it was a way for members of the community to intimately play an important part in each other's lives—further increasing the care and bond. Unfortunately, today we had other, more pressing matters that still needed to be discussed.

"It's just lovely to have you by. We must have dinner next week. Toby would love you to share a meal with us." Chetna then looked to me. "My other half is a great gourmet chef—if he does say so himself. You would also be most welcome, Benjamin."

"I'm honored by your invitation, Chetna. Thank you, but unfortunately, I must decline. Work is, let us say, uncertain these days."

"Very well, I understand."

Fee and Chetna hugged. "Take care of yourself, young lady. You know you are always welcome. Always."

"I know. Be true."

"And you."

"I will call soon."

As we left, Fee looked slightly sad.

"Special person," I commented.

Fee slowed her pace. "Sponsored my application. Love her like a mother. A wonderful mentor."

We walked past clinic services rooms, counseling, physical and creative therapies, and a meditation group in session. Morning was a busy time: everyone was preparing for their day.

Out the back of the building were two smaller buildings, several hundred meters apart, one designated for men, another for women. Fee approached the round women's building, its center open to the sky, closable if needed. I waited way back. This was the place of the spirit of women. No man ever entered this space, just as no woman ever entered the place of the spirit of men. It was what in ancient cultures was considered a sacred place. Inside there was always a kind, caring woman in the women's place, and a supportive, amiable man in the men's place. There were times men and women just needed to be with their kind, perhaps to listen, perhaps just to show support. Our communities recognized many good reasons to keep men and women separate yet united by mutual respect. These were places where we could enhance an important part of our inner nature.

A group of women appeared at the entrance, led by Fee. They looked at me, smiled, then laughed. Fee explained there was a community women's group meeting that evening, a sacred circle, which she was also unable to attend. She told me there was an initiation ceremony the next day, a coming-of-age practice of welcoming young girls into womanhood and sharing the expected womanly roles and responsibilities of the community. This, too, unfortunately, she wasn't able to attend. I asked her about the joke between the women when they'd looked at me. I was informed it was a secret. I let it be. I trusted it would not intentionally be disrespectful—it wasn't our way. The women all hugged. We left.

As we continued, the center came alive, people of all ages welcoming each other, talking, and letting their children play together. Some had already started working in the large communal garden. Seeing technology in most of these places was rare. There were society-based mutually respected rules—a set of nationally agreed-upon guidelines—that saw devices such as phones and screens and advanced mechanical devices used only very occasionally so community connection could be the focus. The result was deeper bonds and the virtual elimination of loneliness. Sure, there were differences and disputes—they were to be expected—but that was what the arbitrators were for, to help smooth any sharp edges.

As I walked, I took in the sense of the place, felt its warmth, the joy in the children's play, the occasional child crying or having a fight. Fee was soon accosted by some six- and seven-year-old children. They called her Aunty and hugged her before they left. This felt close to the home I'd left when I decided to take up my ambassadorial role not so long ago—the community in central Queensland. For a moment I truly missed it.

Tasks complete, we headed to a small secluded area of grassland surrounded by bushes and trees, and sat on some large rocks carved out as seats under a tall eucalypt. Fee said it was a favorite spot, like an out-of-the-way retreat; she was rarely bothered by anyone here.

"Thank you," I said.

"For what?"

"Reminding me, of this." My hands outstretched toward the expanse.

"Ah, yes, the glue of loving people."

"Yes. Thank you."

"A life you have willfully decided to abandon and take away from all of us."

"It's not quite like that."

"Then how is it?" Fee said firmly. "Threatening the joy of millions to satisfy a fantasy founded on a lie and self-indulgence?"

"That's unfair."

"Is it? What could possibly make you even think of telling her and risking all this?"

* * *

Mari had rescheduled her afternoon appointments and was able to devote time for us to be together the next day. We met at Kangaroo Point, on the opposite side of the river to the city. To get there required walking over the long light-gray Story Bridge, an interesting reversed-arch structure with tall fences next to the walkway. It was a sad testament to the troubles of the society, I thought, that they needed to create imposing physical barriers just so disaffected people couldn't use it to voluntarily plunge to their demise.

The walkway I was after was down some stairs to the right. I followed the path past a building that hired paddle boards. The concrete walkway stayed close to the river for the most part. To my left was a sheer rock face at least ten meters high, and to my right, river water flowed endlessly. In a small area of parkland further along, where Mari described, I found her sitting on large broken dark rocks by the water's edge. She was pleased to see me. As we found some shade, I noticed she seemed distracted.

"Everything all right?"

"It's nothing, just work. Oh, Kelly says hi, by the way. She wants to send her deepest apologies for Mark's appalling behavior—her words, not mine. I said I'd pass the message on."

"Please thank her. I hope she is OK. Did you mention about the other women?"

"The prostitutes? Not yet, but I will, I will."

"Did you want to talk about it?" I asked.

"What, about Kelly?"

"About your work. You seem troubled. A difficult morning?"

"You have no idea."

90

I suggested she tell me as much as she was comfortable with. Mari was cautious at first. Eventually she focused on one case in particular. The client was in her late twenties. I gave Mari my full attention.

"It all sounded so unbelievable." Mari explained that her client had known the guy for over two years; they'd been dating, traveling overseas. He seemed quite well off, said he worked in finance. After a while he'd slowly confided in her his greatest secret. He told her he'd previously worked for the Australian Secret Intelligence Service, had gone undercover, and even worked for the Australian Federal Police and Australian Defence Force. It suddenly made sense to her why he always seemed a bit paranoid, would only really talk in person, in open places, was always looking around when he was on dates. She'd fallen for the guy. She'd even moved a few times interstate when he'd told her they weren't safe. It left her isolated and afraid, always anxious. She was having trouble sleeping at night and couldn't trust anyone to talk to. It really messed her up; not even medications helped.

Then a friend had convinced her to confide in a counselor. The therapist suggested putting his story to the test, as something about it, the counselor had told her, didn't make sense. That wasn't how she knew the Australian agencies worked. So she tested him.

One day, when he came home, she mentioned she'd noticed a car parked all day across the street. She knew it belonged to a neighbor. The next day, he said he'd had the car traced; they'd been found, and they had to pack up and leave. She was devastated. Had he been lying the whole time she'd known him? Was every car he was afraid of, every call, every person who looked at him suspiciously not what he'd said they were? It turned out he hadn't been lying; it was more subtle than that. He suffered from what is known as delusional disorder, not quite paranoid schizophrenia, but disturbing nonetheless. To him it was all real. The conspiracy, his paranoia: he believed it was true. And perhaps he really had worked for the government once.

"It took her ages to get the confidence to even consider seeing another guy," Mari explained, "though she did make some girlfriends, which helped settle her social anxiety. But with so many guys lying these days—on dating sites, out at clubs—she gave up. Now she has trouble believing and trusting any man, ever."

I didn't know what to tell her.

We sat looking out across the river a moment.

"Trust is important in any relationship, don't you think?" Mari asked.

"Yes, of course."

"And I sense you like me. Am I wrong?"

"No."

"Then why, why don't you trust me?"

"What do you mean?"

"Look, I get the secret work business, I do," Mari said earnestly, "but you said it yourself: you told me I should listen to my feelings, my instincts, search deep inside, and my feelings are telling me you are holding something back. I felt it at the beach. I felt it when we first met. I'm feeling it now. You do trust me, Ben, don't you?"

I didn't know what to say.

"Please, please," Mari pleaded, "I know we barely know each other, but I need this. Please."

Mari then kept silent. She held my hand patiently.

What could I say? She was right: I did have a secret, a huge secret with global implications. But I couldn't lie. I knew she could sense it. Besides, I was never very good at it.

Eventually Mari looked me in the eyes, searching. "Ben?" Then she stood up, letting go of my hand. "I thought so." She turned and started to leave.

"You're going?" I asked. She kept walking. "Please don't."

She turned toward me. "Whatever you tell me will only be between us, just us," she said reassuringly.

Did I trust her? Yes, I sensed she would be very trustworthy—she kept the confidence of her patients after all. My mind searched and searched. What would … what *could* I tell her?

"Goodbye, Ben. Please don't ever call or contact me." Mari turned and walked away.

"What?" I watched her leave. For a moment I thought it was for the best, but burning pains grew and grew; my heart was being torn asunder. I couldn't disconnect; I couldn't let the feelings go. I just couldn't.

"Wait!" I ran after her. "Please!" I begged, standing in front of her, noticing a tear on her cheek. "Why? Why can't we at least get to know—"

"Well?" Mari wanted an answer.

Suddenly I saw a once-in-a-universe chance teetering on the edge of a precipice, my whole future determined in an instant. I couldn't move.

Mari stepped around me.

"OK!" I shouted.

She stopped. I felt like fragile, unstable rocks were crumbling under my feet.

I walked in front of her, drawn by an instinct deep within, stronger than any I'd ever known, bigger than me. I looked into her bloodshot eyes. "OK, please don't think I'm being dramatic, but it is absolutely critical you never tell another soul. Promise me."

Mari nodded. "Of course. This is only between us." She held my hands.

"And please, please don't think I'm a crazy person. I know how this is going to sound, especially after what you just told me."

"How what will?"

Mari waited, curious, anticipating the words as I stumbled to find them.

"OK, I'll just come out with it. I'm from another place."

Mari seemed confused. "Like, another country?"

"If only. No …" I hesitated. In my mind this was sounding worse and worse. "I'm from … what you would call the late twenty-second century. Last week I crashed and was stranded here …"

Mari let go of my hand in disappointment, then walked around me and kept going.

"It's true! Think about our first meeting. You sensed I was out of place. It was my first day here. In your vehicle, that was my first time in a …"

She stopped.

She started walking again.

"The video at Kelly and Mark's, it wasn't fake!"

Mari turned toward me.

"Search inside yourself," I said. "Listen to your heart. You know it's true. Why would anyone want to make anything like this up?" I pleaded.

"You can ask that after I just told you—?"

"I'm not delusional. I'm not crazy, I assure you! Well, no more than anyone else."

Mari stood a moment. "Then that means Martino …"

"Yes, he's from the future too. My minder, if you will. Oh, Martino, he's going to kill me for this. Be ordinary, he said. Be good, he said."

"So, the aliens … are real?"

"Yep. A new species we've developed a relationship with. One of their comrades was injured and trapped in this time. We were helping him get back. Nice people, actually."

Mari looked faint. I helped her sit down on the grass, let her take it all in. Soon she stood. I moved toward her. She stepped back.

"No." Mari shook her head.

"I'm sorry, I never expected any of this … us," I said as I moved toward her. "I wasn't supposed to get involved, but …"

She stepped back. "I can't, not again," she said, then turned and ran away.

That was it.

I was dumbstruck.

My heart collapsed.

What had I done?

9

The sculptured rocks we sat on were polished smooth into just the right shape; they were more comfortable than they looked. Before us was a small area of well-trimmed, short grass. As we spoke, a magpie swooped down onto the most distant area of grass, five steps away, and stood motionless for seconds at a time on the ground below. Not having much luck, it came closer. We both stopped and gazed upon our curious and intelligent visitor. It trusted us so implicitly; it came right up to our feet. For a time, it rested on another, smaller rock beside us, then flew away toward the chatter of another magpie not far away. Fee told me they'd become friends over a couple of weeks and now the trust was mutual. She hadn't yet started to feed it.

The morning was warming up and late. We both decided we could do with some water, so we headed toward the nearby village. Then, without warning, suddenly Fee collapsed, briefly crying out in agony, then holding her right ankle. She swore, then apologized. She swore again when she tried to get up. I had to hold her under her right shoulder. Even to hobble was excruciating.

"I think it's broken," she said.

"Would you like me to get help?" I recommended. "Or there is plan B."

"What's plan B?" she grimaced.

I swiftly lifted her off her feet and held her in my arms.

"OK," she agreed. "Plan B. You're sure you—?"

"If I collapse, we go for plan C."

"Plan C?"

"I'll let you know it when I do."

With her right arm around my shoulder, I carried her back to the medical clinic between the community center and the village nearby. Like being in a small hospital, we were assigned a room. Fee knew the medical attendant, Anna. Of course she did. Anna was about the same age as Fee and obviously pregnant. They had much to talk about.

She scanned the leg with a handheld imaging device and clipped on a thin circular plastic ring below her knee—it blocked the nerves to the lower leg and stopped the pain. Then Fee was asked whether she preferred to have it fixed now or to let it heal naturally over two weeks—it was a sprain, not a break, and would heal on its own without any real problems. She decided on the treatment. She said she didn't have time to be confined to a chair or bed, or use dreaded crutches. The risks of the procedure were explained, and Anna soon returned with what appeared to be a white cylindrical lattice frame—the healing device.

First Anna put on gloves, applied a cream to the lower leg and above the knee, then placed the frame around her lower leg and foot. It was tightened to fit. Setting the device with the controller in her hand, she told Fee to just rest back and press the button by her bed if there was a problem. It would be good as new in an hour or two, and she'd be back later to check.

How did it work? It was just another spin-off of temporal travel technology. The cream increased the blood supply to the leg, and the lattice created a small time variance around the limb so it was running at a faster rate of time compared to us and therefore seemed to heal more quickly. It had to happen slowly over an hour, or the blood supply couldn't meet the demands of the leg, which was aging more quickly within the field of the device. In that case, the leg or foot could wither and die. It also had to stimulate the muscles so they didn't waste away with disuse. I knew the basics of how it worked. Not being a med-tech or doctor, I had never been taught the intricacies.

When Anna left, Fee suggested I take a seat beside her. Fee apologized for the inconvenience and thanked me for the "lift" to the medical facility, before requesting, "Tell me about your last relationship. What was it like?"

"Is it relevant?"

Fee looked at me as if to say, "Are you kidding?"

I was reluctant, not proud, and I wasn't keen to share.

Fee persisted. "Help me put this into context."

"I was in my early twenties …"

Fee's eyebrows rose. "Almost two decades ago?"

"There were a few short relationships after, but if you want to know …"

"Sorry, you were saying."

"I was twenty-three," I began to explain uncomfortably. "I'd barely known any women for more than a few months when Jacinta took me under her wing. In her early thirties, attractive, kind, she was loving in ways I'd never experienced—let alone imagined—before. We met through work when I was still at the research lab, before I joined the Institute. For six months we'd be together twice a week and the occasional weekend. Had I listened to my instincts, it would have been two weeks."

"You noticed something wrong?"

"I sensed something wasn't as it should be, as if her heart was somewhere else. I remember one night I booked an evening at Dino's—upmarket and well beyond my pay grade. She was quieter than usual. It had been a long day, she said. Work was troubling her. But she was also smiling at other men, not me. I'd never noticed that before. That night, let's just say the physical intimacy was brief—nothing for me, all for her. Then it struck me: we'd spent most of our time together alone, as if it was a secret. So I asked her about it—the secrecy, her apparent disinterest in me. She became angry and annoyed at first. 'What, now you want to control me?' She made it very clear this wasn't the way a mature relationship was supposed to be. Hey, what did I know? I'd barely had physical relations with two women in my life. Yep, I was hooked. She had my heart like no other woman ever had. Then, on a hunch—following my instinct—I did some research. What I discovered almost ended me."

"She was unfaithful?"

"She had a family in Montreal—three children under nine and what appeared to be a devoted and loving husband."

"What did you do?"

"Confronted her, of course. She blamed me, made me feel it was all my fault. When I cried, she told me to grow up and be a man, I was being pathetic."

"It almost ended you?"

"I felt like a total waste of air and space, completely worthless, like not wanting to be here anymore. I was a piece of dirt to be trodden on and scuffed off a boot."

"That's terrible."

"Yes, it was."

"But that means somewhere in your past, you were made to feel—"

"Not good enough, not worthy of care and attention? Yes, my childhood wasn't great."

"So, when Mari walked away—"

"It was the second time my heart had been thrown off a cliff. And yes, it was even after barely knowing her. Should I have worked through these issues by now? Sure, and many I have. Then I found a few I'd been avoiding."

"Perhaps more than a few?"

"OK, several."

"And your work, your training through the Institute, helped you avoid them?"

"Work is good at that, particularly our line of work. Hard to get hurt if you practice remaining detached."

"I'm sorry," Fee said, with genuine compassion.

"For what?"

"For being so quick to judge, to trivialize feelings that meant so much."

The machine began to beep. A nurse came in to check. Happy with it, she left.

"It must have been particularly painful on many levels, then, when Mari rejected you," Fee empathized, then asked, "What did you do next?"

What could I do?

* * *

I spent five days alone, holed up in the hotel room, ordering what was called "takeout" or sometimes ordering room service from the hotel menu. I tried to call Mari several times on the day she walked away. I even managed to work out how to leave a message. No reply. I did the same twice the next day, then decided to stop. If she wanted to speak or meet, she had my number; it would be disrespectful to persist.

Hours upon hours of meditation, and still images of her flooded my thoughts, and how it might have turned out some other way. If only I'd prepared her better. If only we'd shared other secrets first so she would more completely trust me. I knew I could have done it differently. I was sure of it. In the end, resigned to the pain of the loss, I imagined what I might recommend a client of mine as an arbitrator—what would I suggest they do in a circumstance like this, after a torrid, emotional breakup? There were many recommendations. Perhaps most pressing would be to get out among friends.

Ah, friends. Where were they? Mine weren't even an itch in their grandmothers' ovaries. The potential for friends here? Next to zero. Martino and his team were flat out. Finding people on the street? No one even looked at you. There were ways the locals did it, according to Marshal, the trusty hotel receptionist.

Marshal recommended I "go out and find a good club or pub and get pissed." All his other recommendations involved loud music, recreational drugs, or hooking up for casual sex—he showed me a few meetup apps I could download to my phone. What was wrong with just finding friendly people and simply talking, getting to know one another? Having said that, did I really want to know other people or let them know me? I could imagine how it might go: "Oh, hi. My name's Ben. I'm from the future. How are you? Not really interested? Perhaps you think I'm crazy. I'm not surprised. My only other friend in this time period felt the same. Correct that: the only person more than a friend in this time rejected me. Have a nice day."

No, searching for friends wasn't an option.

What about getting out, to a park or sitting under a tree, as I had done when I was struggling in the past? Nature had a way of healing me. I found myself a park, in New Farm. It had some lovely trees, even some impressive rose beds with blooms of varying color and perfume. It was nice, soothing for a time, but as I watched couples and the occasional family, I felt lonelier still. A forest would have been ideal. Unfortunately, there was no easy access—I wasn't prepared to risk public transport. That left meditating or, dread the thought, watching TV—their audio-visual entertainment and information device.

I looked. No shortage of wars and violence. The building tensions in Asia were as I expected they would be. Movies seemed obsessed with war, violence, unrealistic romance, silly science fiction, or crime and revenge—great for historians like Martino or Tina perhaps, but not for me. Reality TV seemed the most absurd abuse of people I'd ever seen, and all for money, apparently. Had they no self-respect? Apparently not. Then I noticed their politics. It seemed there was an American presidential election this year.

I was horrified. The lies, deceptions, the money, and corruption. What do they say in our time? Wealth, power, and status beget mass misery? And they were letting men vote? What was with that? Oh, that was right: they hadn't realized lasting peace only came when only women voted—countering men's need to often-unnecessarily compete and fight. That wouldn't happen for another couple of decades or so. It wasn't until then that men truly listened to and respected women, and families and communities truly stabilized.

With nothing worth watching, I switched the TV off. Meditating was now my best option. And the hope Martino and the powers that be would finally get me out of this hellhole. I solemnly vowed I'd make sure the next time there was another alien recovery, I'd be on that ship, no matter what.

Then I heard a chime from my phone. It was a text. "Would like to meet." There was an address and time. It was tonight. "If you agree, please reply with a Y. We need to talk. Mari."

Mari had contacted me! For a moment I was elated, then in two minds. Once again I could end it here and now, step back, be the arbitrator I was supposed to be—detached, wise, careful, nonthreatening to the world. Now was my chance. Yet there was that inner calling again, churning my insides. I felt compelled to answer.

I replied, "Y."

I'd never used a taxi before. I was happy the credit card did its job. I arrived in smart casual—I was beginning to understand what the different types of dress codes meant. I was ten minutes early, standing on the path outside the two-story collection of units they called townhouses. My palms were sweating, my heart racing. I took some deep, calming breaths. Composed, I knocked on the door.

"Hi. Come in." Mari was wearing a pair of torn blue-and-white jeans and a mauve jumper. Her hair was tied in a ponytail. There was no kiss or hug; it was kept very formal. She led me to her living room, average size in our time, neat, ornaments and paintings adorned the walls, and nothing looked out of place or too over the top—mostly very conservative, even by our standards. "Please sit."

I sat on the sofa, Mari in an adjoining chair. On the coffee table was a folding computer.

"Tea, coffee, water?"

"No, thanks. You wanted to talk?"

Mari seemed nervous, rubbing her hands, pulling her hair over her shoulder. "OK, you have to understand something about me. Back several years ago, I dated this guy. He was confident, a real charmer; he lured me in via some friends. He told me things, special things that made me want to believe. I completely trusted him. Then it went south in a big way. I mean a big way."

"He deceived you, like the delusional gentleman your client described?"

"Worse, much worse." Mari seemed quite distressed. "He believed in much crazier stuff. I mean *crazy* crazy. You have to understand, it hit me hard back then, really hard. I vowed I'd never let myself be tricked like … Anyway, so when you told me you were from, what, the twenty-third century—"

"The twenty-second, actually."

"Fine, the twenty-second. When you told me, it was like all I could remember was …" She swallowed hard.

"Something you never want to experience again?"

"Exactly."

"You felt threatened?"

"Paranoid, scared, afraid who to trust. Never again. Never."

It made sense. Then the thought occurred to me: what if at some time someone started looking for me and they learned my secret? Then I, too, would be on the run. I, too, would be looking over my shoulder, and anyone with me would no doubt feel scared and paranoid. Could I now do this to Mari? Could I put her in a position she'd clearly struggled in before? Oh my, was I making a huge mistake?

I stood up. "Thank you for sharing that with me, Mari. It means a lot. I think I should leave."

"Excuse me?"

"I promise I will not call you again. It has been wonderful." I made my way to the door. My heart was breaking, but what else could I do? It was for her.

She pushed it shut. "Don't you see? I'm apologizing!"

"You are?"

"Come with me." She led me to the coffee table and flipped open her computer. She played a video. It was the one we saw at Kelly and Mark's.

"I've seen it. It has a guy who looks like Martino—"

"Wait for it …"

The video continued and showed a figure coming out of the craft. As he shook the bald man's hand beside the vehicle, he turned toward the camera. There was a close-up … of me!

"Oh, crap."

"I found this last night. At first I thought, not again, not another dud—I was having the worst luck with guys—but something gnawed away. I had to know."

"You know they can fake it these days, with Picture Shop."

"It's called Photoshop. Anyone who works in IT and owns a computer—in this century—would know that."

"Double crap." I sat on the sofa

"Sure you don't want a drink?" Mari sat next to me and held my hand. For a moment I enjoyed it and held my hand over hers; then I let go and headed for the door again.

"Ben? Stop! Why?"

I turned toward her. "Martino was right; I'm big trouble. I'm so sorry. I shouldn't have told you. I should have seen it earlier … Stick with me, you could be in real danger. I can't put you through—"

"Now you are being selfish."

"I'm what?"

"You don't think I know that? You don't think I didn't sleep a wink all night imagining what it might be like once I realized what you said is actually true? Don't you think I at least deserve the respect of being able to make that choice myself?"

She had a point. "So, you know it could get rough?"

She nodded.

"You know it might get dangerous if I get found out?"

She nodded again.

"I think I could do with a drink."

I was stunned. What had just happened? Mari returned with a glass of water each. Water was fine right now, though I knew if I drank alcohol—and I don't drink—I'd probably have asked for a Scotch—no, a double, no ice.

As she sat down, she extended her hand. "Hi. My name is Mariana Jenkins. My friends call me Mari."

I shook her hand gently. "Oh, hi. My name is Benjamin ... Ecclestone. I prefer just Ben."

"Nice to meet you, just Ben. Are you from around here?"

"Uh, a small place way out west called Engoori."

"Engoori, I don't think I've heard of it."

"Probably because it hasn't been built yet."

"So, you're from the future, then?"

"Yes, from over a century from now, 2183 to be exact."

"Lovely to meet you, Ben from 2183. I can't wait to hear all about it."

The weight of the galaxy had been lifted from my shoulders. I found I could actually smile again. Mari wanted to know how I got here, so I began by sharing with her about being an ambassador, the new post off-world, the terrifying experience of the explosion of the Noretian craft, and my fortunate escape. Somehow now I felt I could completely trust her, no reservations.

"Why Brisbane, and why now?" she asked.

I explained I wasn't sure of the technicalities but suspected it was because we'd left from the transit center at West End, and that once we'd left Earth and the ship malfunctioned, the emergency pods tried to return us to its last place of origin. Since the craft often traveled back in time to move around the universe, it was just a coincidence we ended up in 2020. I could have ended up thousands of years in the past.

"So it's fate," Mari said definitively. "We were destined to meet!"

I smiled: it was looking that way.

"What happened to that fellow in the video, the alien guy?" she asked.

"He wasn't so fortunate: landed late at night, was attacked by some youths, and was seriously injured before he could be retrieved by the HRU."

"That's terrible. The HRU?"

"Scattered throughout history are History Rescue Units, historians trained to live and blend in to their time to rescue those of us who accidently end up there, or help other historians adapt as they study the people and the place."

"Martino."

"Martino and his team, yes. I owe them my life."

"Tell me about the future, Ben. What's it like?" Her eyes sparkled with curiosity.

I was cautious at first. "Friendlier, quieter, and more spread out."

"Spread out?"

"We can now travel virtually anywhere in minutes or seconds and have unlimited energy to do it. Cities are mostly torn down, with many highly populated countries agreeing to live underground in giant, well-lit, lush caverns to let nature reclaim much of the world. The caverns are easy to build when you have the unlimited energy at your fingertips. I live in a reclaimed area of central Australia, green and lush now we have created underground aquifers. Since the formation and spread of the Institute, we have known decades of growing peace."

"The Institute?"

"An organization whose main purpose is to promote wisdom and personal insight. They train arbitrators and send them out across the world. A respected people whose mission is to resolve disputes, unite communities, and help guide us as people towards ever-increasing peace, purpose, fulfillment, and balance, both within ourselves and without."

"What happened to war, and greed, and famine, and—"

"Puberty, world adolescence, as some of our alien visitors remind us. We grew up."

"We what?"

"Grew up. Stopped blaming and asking the supernatural for our salvation—like a child needing a parent to tell it what to do. Instead, we finally took personal responsibility and defined our own path. We stopped fighting within, with each other, and with the land. We reconnected on a personal level with nature. We relearnt how to be human."

"So it all works out? We make it, as a people, I mean?"

"We more than make it. We thrive and embrace living in ways we never imagined in this time. I know it sounds impossible from the way it looks right now, but believe me, the wonderful future I just described is within reach. The future isn't bleak. The Institute of Mind, or the Wisdom Factory, as outsiders call it in our time, grows its roots in these coming years and helps ground people through the chaos. It helps us see a common truth that can bind and guide us. With the help of arbitrators and considerable individual courage, communities, families, relationships, even countries, unite as never before and resolve our differences with mutual respect. I am just one in a line of many before me."

"You are an arbitrator?"

"Yes. Trained by the Institute since my midtwenties, part of a select and trusted group."

"Did you always want to be one, an arbitrator, I mean?"

I laughed. "Heck no. Never considered it. Way too hard to get in. Hundreds of thousands apply; very few ever make it."

"Then how?"

"A personal crisis that nearly killed me. You really want to know?"

Mari nodded. I sipped some water.

"You could say I had a troubled childhood. Oh, I don't blame my parents: they grew up in a part of Europe that still held on to the old ways, where unless you were a high achiever, had an impressive title and income, you were nothing. Even before we moved to Yackandandah—"

"So that part was true?"

"Oh, yes, and the time spent on long walks in nature and sitting under trees. To my old man, I was never good enough. I'd help him with work around the farm—never good enough. I'd get ninety-eight percent on a test—not good enough. I was considered a mummy's boy, which made it worse. My younger brother was the light in his eye. My mother, kindhearted soul, had to tolerate a lot. I never fully understood why she never left him, but then again, she was a loner without many supports. So when I met Jacinta, I was ripe for the taking."

"Jacinta?"

I explained about Jacinta, the gaslighting, the abuse, how my sense of self-worth was shot to pieces. Mari completely understood. She even told me a few of her clients had suffered the same.

"At twenty-three I felt a desperate need to discover myself and work out what this emotional craziness of life was all about. I read a bit, old religious texts and philosophies mostly. Then I finally spoke with our newly appointed local arbitrator, Lee—he was new to the community where I lived. With Lee's regular conversations and guidance, I began to find myself."

"He counseled you."

"Never had I met a kinder, more compassionate and self-aware soul. He became my role model, the mentor I needed when I needed one most. He suggested I follow my heart. He knew my passion wasn't in computers and technology, the area in which I was trained and worked, and suggested I apply for the Institute as a trainee. He said he would sponsor me."

"You were accepted."

"Not the first year. It took several attempts: the interviewing was long and hard. It didn't help that I still had such low self-confidence.

You know how sometimes we can listen to someone and suddenly we are changed forever? It helps redefine us? There was this one speech."

"What speech?"

"It was on my first day, the introduction to new students. Vitali Orlov, from the Institute branch in Russia, was a small man in stature, but his English was perfect, not even a trace of an accent.

"'Congratulations, friends, and new colleagues,' he said. 'Welcome to our family. I stand here humbled. Before me sit people who have suffered the emotional torments of life and endured, who have stood up when many have stumbled, persisted when many have given up, and had the courage to face the most difficult challenge of all—to face yourself. I know many of you sitting here will be having doubts, thinking you don't deserve to be here, you are not worthy, not sufficient to be sitting here when so many others better than you are not. Let me be very clear: you are worthy, every one of you.

"'You are worthy when you smile to a stranger passing you by, when you help those in need of your care, when you offer an ear and empathy, when you stop to truly listen. You are worthy when you make friends with your colleagues and are friendly and respectful to the people, creatures, and life you meet. I know this is who you are. I know and recognize your special worth. Should you hold any doubts, look to your actions and prove it to yourself.

"'In the coming years, you will be taught secrets few ever learn, face parts of yourself few will ever know, and we will teach you to find a part of yourself that extends beyond it all. Inside each of you is the guidance the world desperately needs. We will help you discover it, connect with it, and make it a part of yourself. Within you is the peace and hope of generations, found inside your heart and beyond. If you learn nothing else but to connect with this greater part of yourself, to the universe from within, we will have served you well.

"'Let me reassure you, we will not abandon you: our task is not to see you fail. We here know and appreciate how precious you are. I hope you find us worthy to be your example and your mentors. If you are struggling at any time, please never feel too ashamed to seek our help. It is through the struggles we overcome that we learn the most. We all know them well.

"'Finally, I hope I may have the privilege of meeting all of you, not as a teacher or a guide, not as a member of the Council, but as an equal, as we all like to regard each other. I hope you find me worthy of your friendship.

"'May inner truth endure.

"'Thank you.'

"From that moment, I knew this was where and who I was supposed to be."

Mari sat motionless, tears welling in her eyes.

10

Fee put her foot to the floor, gently at first. The ankle swelling had gone, and with all devices removed, she said she felt no pain. It seemed to move OK. Even bearing weight, it seemed all right. Fee was very grateful. Anna wished us well and told her to take it easy for a few days just to let things "settle."

Fee wanted to do some shopping, so we headed for the village. All the stores were open. She knew everyone in each store, and they knew her and what she liked. We stopped for a while to talk.

Our supplies in a hessian sack I carried over my shoulder, we made our way back to her place. She offered to cook.

"Roast OK with you?" Fee asked as she spread the ingredients on her small kitchen bench.

"Fine with me. Can I help?"

As I chopped up the vegetables and Fee braised the meat, we shared a hot tea. Soon we placed the meat in one enclosed pot, and the vegetables in another. Then we set her small dining table together, a plain affair, just big enough to seat four. A vase and flower were her finishing touch, and a candle. As we waited, she defrosted a previously prepared sauce. The timer pinged. It was ready in seconds. Fee transferred the half-kilo beef roast to a plate, let it stand for a few minutes, then carved it with consummate skill, its lean, evenly pink insides juicing nicely. The veggies were roasted to perfection and lightly seasoned. One of the benefits of being able to manipulate time was that, if you wanted to, you could slow cook a roast that would normally take five hours in seconds. We sipped on aromatic-infused dark grape juice.

As I savored the lean beef melting in my mouth, Fee asked casually, "I'm curious. What did you think of Mari's self-worth?"

"Why do you ask?"

"For one thing, her choice in men." She took a mouthful from her fork, sipped her juice, and sat back. "Abandoned by her parents, she falls in with, what, someone much worse than a delusional nutcase."

"Your point?"

"Her choices suggest her self-worth is quite low. If it wasn't, would she have let herself be so easily misled?"

"Like me when I met Jacinta?"

"Yes."

"But I've grown since then. What's to say she also hasn't taken the time to know herself and—"

"That is true. I guess what I'm asking is, did you ever consider your status as an arbitrator when you decided to start seeing her?"

"My status? No, it wasn't foremost—"

"So you were OK with her adoring you and putting you on some pedestal?"

"Now wait, I never—"

"Yet here you are, telling her of your special training, raising yourself above her in a world where qualifications and titles mean more to them than—"

"What are you saying?"

"I'm saying, yes, you were attracted to her, obviously. But you know friendship dictates a sense of equality. How is you telling her about your role as an arbitrator, and from the future no less, conducive to a lasting friendship? What were you thinking?"

"That I needed to give this a real chance."

"No matter the huge differences between you? At any price?"

"Yes … no. She was … she *is* different."

"Different, how?"

Fee kept eating, her head shaking in disbelief as I continued to try to fill her in.

* * *

I was finishing a small buffet breakfast when I received the call. We were supposed to meet again this evening, after Mari finished work, but unexpectedly she had to call in sick. She mentioned something about having the flu. It sounded terrible—aches and pains all over, headaches, fever, nausea, shakes, and feeling generally miserable. I offered to come over to help care for her. She declined. She said she didn't want me to get sick, that it was nothing a few paracetamol and ibuprofen wouldn't fix, and rest. I insisted on doing more.

At a local pharmacy, they recommended some cough relief and to continue with the paracetamol and ibuprofen. For anything else, she'd need to see a doctor. Then I spoke to Marshal, my database of local knowledge and custom. He recommended hot chicken soup. He even recommended where I might find it at a Chinese restaurant not far from here. He said he was pretty sure it had no MSG, whatever that was. My mission was set.

Bag of chicken soup and other Chinese delights in hand, I knocked on Mari's door. I heard some thumping coming to the door, and she answered in her bathrobe, her arms wrapped around her to try to keep warm. Her hair was untied—it looked really nice—and her face was without makeup, a more appealing, natural look.

"What are you doing …? What's that?"

"Chicken and corn soup, and a few other treats."

She ushered me in.

"How did you know? I love that soup!"

"Must be fate." I smiled. She opened one of the containers on her kitchen bench and had a taste, then put it in the microwave, a heating device. Learning from her, I suggested she go back to bed and I would bring it out. She showed me where she kept bowls and a lap table. Carefully I brought her the steaming, thick chicken broth and placed it on her lap in bed.

"You aren't having any?"

"Later. Sick people come first."

"Thank you for this. It's really good." She sipped slowly, trying not to burn herself.

"My pleasure." I pulled up a seat beside her double bed.

"I mean, really, thank you."

"I hope it helps."

The bowl empty, I cleaned everything away and came back to see Mari snuggling under the floral quilt and off-white sheets in her robe and cotton pajamas.

She must still feel cold, I thought. "Anything else I can get you?" I asked.

"No, I'm fine thanks." She snuggled some more. "Tell me a story."

"What kind of story?"

"Tell me about your first day at your institute. It must have been exciting."

"More like overwhelming."

"Great, tell me about that."

* * *

I was in awe. I'd seen pictures, even dreamed about this place. It was a Tuesday, I recall. I walked—well, ran mostly, as I was late—to the gates of the Melbourne division, my training campus in the Dandenong mountains just north of the villages of Melbourne. I was struggling to catch my breath, but just as I reached the large sandstone blocks of the entrance, my eyes were captivated by a huge three-dimensional sculpture in the foreground. It was beautiful, over five meters high, an upside-down triangle in glistening silver surrounding a rotating gold-covered globe—the symbol I hoped to wear proudly on my uniform lapel someday, if I worked hard.

There were no guards. If any unauthorized persons stepped past the gate, they would be trapped in a stasis field—frozen in time—and transported to their family and municipality for trial. To break such a law was to bring great shame and sadness to relatives and their community. The field hadn't been activated in over twenty years. As I tentatively stepped past the gate, I recall cringing: somehow I thought the field would trap me, like a fly on fly-paper. I believed there had been a mistake; I felt unworthy. As others rushed past, I started to run again too: the hall's doors would close in three minutes, and once closed, they wouldn't be opened again for two hours. It was here that I would meet one of my favorite and closest friends.

"Uh, you might like to move."

"Excuse me?"

"You're in people's way."

"I'm just taking in that magnificent ceiling," I replied, as I stared above me from the entrance. The high roof arches spanned on high like giant spiders' webs interlocked effortlessly. I'd never seen anything like it. He was a slender but tall guy, a bit older than me, it seemed, clean-shaved, a rather obvious nose. He quickly glanced up and around. "Nice. But you had better find your seat: it's about to start."

"Right."

I followed him and sat beside him.

"Name's Ben, by the way," I said, putting out my hand as we sat down in adjoining chairs, the only two left in the row.

"That's nice," he said, looking at my hand, then looking to the stage and the hundred or so people around us.

"And your name?"

"Shh. It's starting," he whispered.

"Funny name," I whispered back. "I remember someone called Sasha once. Sounds similar. Ever met him? Where you from?"

Everyone stood up as the dignitaries arrived on stage, dressed in gold-and-navy arbitrator uniforms—simple arbitrator uniforms were only a bright navy, undergraduates a lighter blue; I could see some sitting in rows opposite us. The large gold triangles on either side of the delegates' jackets looked amazing. The guy beside me kept silent, his face solemn as he peered to the front.

"I'm from Yackandandah," I continued. "Do you know where that is?"

He turned and looked sternly into my eyes. "Do you always talk so much?"

"Only when I'm nervous."

He looked to the front again. The delegates sat; then so did we. I was a bit slow: I was still taking it all in.

The guy pulled me down. "What are you doing?"

"I'm going to be an arbitrator," I said, proudly.

"You're going to get us in trouble."

Others sitting around started to shush us.

"See," he whispered.

"This is brilliant," I said as I rubbed my hands together. "Don't you think?"

"Why are you still talking?"

The others started to shush us again.

"Promise I'll be quiet when you tell me your name."

"What? Fine, it's Sanjay."

I smiled. "You look like a Sanjay."

Sanjay then pointed to administrator staff standing by the wall, looking in our direction. "See, now look what you've done."

The first speaker took the microphone. My leg started to jiggle up and down—it did that sometimes when I was hyped up.

Sanjay put his hand on it and pressed it down. "Do you mind?" It stopped a moment, then restarted again.

The speaker began, but I hardly heard a word.

"Hasn't anyone taught you breathing exercises to calm down?" Sanjay asked.

"Yes. Should I try them?"

"Do cows eat grass?"

An administrator came over. "Please, gentlemen, out of respect for the others. Thank you." He left.

"Now see what you've done!"

"Which breathing exercise should I try?" I asked.

"Any one!" Sanjay whispered loudly, frustration obvious in his voice.

"What about square breathing?"

"For goodness' sake. Yes, yes, try that one."

So I did. By the time I opened my eyes and looked up again, Vitali Orlov was introduced to the stage. He was so inspiring I was transfixed. Don't think I moved for his whole speech. It was a bit longer than what I quoted. I don't think I did it justice.

After the awesome oratory, the director of the center, Louis Hernan, set out the Three Precepts that all members of the Institute agreed to, and that would form both the foundation and guidance for us for the rest of our lives. It was a big moment. I won't bore you with them.

* * *

Mari interrupted, "No, please. They sound important."

"OK. The Three Precepts. One, we are knowable. Two, we are all things and all things are us. Three, friendship is fundamental.

"Let me keep it brief and try to explain them as some of my tutors did. The first precept, they said, empowers us to recognize that we can know and improve ourselves, that we don't have to live miserable lives. We can know what drives and satisfies us, and work towards making those things real."

"Like Buddhism, then?" Mari added. "We find salvation from within."

"A bit like that, but here there are no great teachers, gurus, or saints such as bodhisattvas. There is no eight-fold path that we hope will lead us to see the truth. No, this is more practical, and personal. The aim is to teach you to learn to listen to and trust a deeper part of yourself so you can then find and live your own path."

"You make individuals their own teacher?"

"Exactly."

"I like it. The second precept?"

"It helps us recognize we are more than what we seem, both on a practical and physical level—we use its principles to help us travel through time and connect inside us, to find guidance within. It is a unifying idea that gives meaning and predictability to all things."

"It answers the questions of life, the universe, and everything?"

"What? Yes … no … in a way. That isn't how we see it. Let's just say it links physics and metaphysics—the real, the mind, and the spiritual."

"You've found a way to do that?"

"Not me. It was developed around this time. We just use it."

"How?"

"It is all founded on the idea that everything that exists is a representation of fields of change, fields like we recognize, magnetic and electric fields, only these fields are set at particular maximum rates that interact with each other. Some call them time fields, though the term is misleading. Time, distance, solidity, the things we know as matter, even gravity and electrical forces, are an illusion created by simple interactions of these fields. As fields with measurable and predictable effects, they bind and give apparent observable order to all things everywhere. They blend with each other with no ultimate beginning or end, only the illusion of it."

"So we are literally part of everything?"

"Yes, and everything is part of us."

"Oh my. So the ancient tribes were right."

"What? Yes. They interacted with their world and saw it made them who they are."

"We are the land and the land is us. That is what they've said."

"And they were more accurate than they imagined. The main difference is we have simply taken this idea to a whole new level, practically and personally. By recognizing these fields exist, and their physical properties, it gives us the ability to travel across time and the universes—the fields are not that difficult to manipulate once you know they are there, and they offer us virtually limitless energy. On a personal level, it is even more useful.

"To recognize these fields tells us the universe and beyond focuses all of itself—past and future—to make us now, and we are part of everything that focuses to make everything else. Personally, this teaches us that by learning to delve deep inside ourselves, we connect with a part of us beyond our self. We can connect and learn to read the language and stories of the universe from within. The universe is ready and waiting to open up inside us."

"The universe becomes the source of the wisdom?"

"I'm impressed. It takes years for some of us to make that connection. Yes, we connect with what is beyond us to help us realize our place and what it is to be us, our restrictions, our point of view that makes us notice and enjoy who we are and what we do."

"Like the land teaching us to be human."

"Have you learnt this before?"

"No. It just makes sense, the way you describe it, I mean. I'm impressed. And the last of the three?"

"Ah, the third precept is to remind us of the values of respect, care, and protection of all people and things—three of ten fundamentals of friendship we are all instructed in, even as children. Friendship is a fundamental part of us. We are taught it should always be raised and valued."

"Friendship keeps us in balance?"

"Some have argued that, among the initiates. You are sure no one has taught you any of this before?"

"Certain. And these three precepts are taught to every initiate?"

"Yes, on our first day."

"So what you are telling me is you learn, from day one, not to listen to authority, to listen to your heart, to take responsibility for how you feel and what you do, to connect with peace and wisdom from within, and make lots of friends, all as you travel the universe."

"Universes. Essentially, yes."

"Universes. There are more than one?"

"Too many to visit and interact with; a waste of our time to explore them all."

"And I guess we don't want to be wandering around the universes as ego-driven, insecure, scared children with unlimited energy at our fingertips."

"No, that would not be ideal."

"I think I can see why your time is so peaceful. I do have a question though."

"Yes?"

"How on earth did you ever become friends with Sanjay? He seems such a … what should I say?"

"Papaya head?"

"Well, OK, not what I would have said. Papaya?"

"After the tropical fruit. You know, the one that smells off-putting at first—like bad, sweaty socks—but is actually good for you. It was shortened to Mr. P—spoken affectionately, of course. We met again at community functions. I think he took me under his wing out of pity after I was almost expelled for crashing a temporal drone into the director's office."

"You were almost expelled?" Mari asked as she snuggled up in her quilt even tighter.

I smiled, adding, "It was a fun first year."

Mari then excused herself and ran to the toilet, then ran back and snuggled up again.

"You OK?"

"Sure. Tell me about the other planets. What are they like?" Mari asked, her face paler than before.

"I'm afraid I'm not big on travel. I did visit the Noretian home world once. It's big, at least a third bigger than Earth. Their continents are vast; their mountains, many taller than the Himalayas. Their oceans are broad and deep. In many ways, you'd swear you were on Earth, only the gravity is a bit stronger. I weigh seventy-three kilograms here. On their world I would be over eighty, and I'd be considered rather short. There are thousands upon thousands of similar worlds, all across many times, many with primitive life we can visit, even bulky creatures like dinosaurs."

"You've seen dinosaurs?" Mari's eyes lit up.

"Sure. Was almost eaten by one."

"Really?!"

"It was pretty stupid really. I was helping collect specimens when a few small T. rexes ambushed the group."

"T. rexes, as in Tyrannosaurs?"

"They're pack hunters. Our surveillance drones malfunctioned, and we should have gone back—they were on us before we knew it. One grabbed me around the waist. If it wasn't for the reinforced EV suit, I'd be a heck of a lot shorter. Was given quite the shake."

"It bit you?"

"Almost in two. Even the two-meter juveniles, fast hunters, have quite a bite."

"Wait, EV suits?"

"Yeah. Fully enclosed environmental suits—we're careful not to share too much DNA across times. Besides, the higher oxygen content from back then gives you head spins."

"You travel back in time and look at real dinosaurs?"

"I don't. This was an exception, but many of our paleontologists love it, and comparing how the evolution is different on other worlds. A few claim panspermia was a product of traveling through time."

"Panspermia? Isn't that where life on one planet seeds another?"

"Yes, and if you travel through time and from planet to planet, you can leave traces of what is familiar in your time elsewhere. It seems many advanced cultures have spread their seeds with a view to creating more neighbors they can relate to. Current theory in our time postulates it is the reason so many alien races appear similar to us, like the Noretians, and so many planets have dinosaurs. We are just beginning to trace the full history of our origins now among thousands upon thousands of worlds."

"There are thousands of habitable worlds, with people?"

"Many more than that. Scientists in this time on Earth are still thinking linearly: they are searching for signs of life throughout the galaxy, looking for radio waves, for short periods of time when others may have developed the same. The time-field technology leaves no such trace. There is a network of worlds of times dating across billions of years, and many of us connect with each other. We don't just look in the equivalent of our era. We travel to promising planets, then go forwards or backwards in time, and soon we find many advanced cultures. Whether we engage in relations or not, once they have developed time-field technology, we leave it to them—once we know they are settled into their more advanced state. We all have very strict rules about not interfering in each other's temporal path."

"I don't understand. Why wouldn't you want to visit all these amazing worlds? I couldn't wait!"

"Why visit so many worlds when you can find the greatest satisfaction and fulfillment on your own? The way I see it, and so do many of my colleagues, is we are made to be part of the nature of this earth. In it we find our greatest satisfaction—connecting with it. Work to build this connection, let ourselves experience its wonder most fully, and what reason have we for somewhere else?"

"You don't get out much, do you?"

"Not really."

"Thought so. So, there are no wars?"

"Between planets? Definitely not. It's the ultimate MAD."

Mari seemed confused.

"Mutually assured destruction. We travel long distances across many temporal zones using time technology. That means if we wanted to, we could conquer any planet before they developed the same technology. But it only takes one other race with a similar technology to notice us doing it, and they can go back to our planet earlier into our time and prevent it ever happening—wipe us out before we even leave Earth. We can all prevent each other existing and cause ripples across time that can change the universe in the past so drastically that most of the universe itself might never exist. Much simpler to respect each other's development and live in respectful peace."

"Sounds amazing!"

"It's not perfect, but it's something this planet has to look forward to, if everything continues as it should."

"If we continue to develop those ideas you spoke about, from your Institute?"

"If they can continue to grow and gain traction, yes. In my time I have devoted my life to understanding the evolution of minds and how we can harness them to create the most wonderful experiences possible. It was one of the main reasons I was traveling to the Noretian planet, to study their mind evolution and compare it to our own. You could say it was my life—an all-consuming vocation. Now I see things very differently. I have found an important part of the whole picture I completely neglected to fully appreciate—or see."

"And that is?"

"You."

11

We had finished our meals and were having very necessary coffee: it was more than a day since either of us had had any sleep. I helped Fee clean up. We did the dishes. Then Fee, on impulse, decided we should take a trip to get some cool air to help us freshen up. She put on some winter clothes, and we headed for the nearest pod hub.

It was 10:30 a.m. in Zurich, Switzerland, when we arrived. It took us less than thirty minutes total time—including walking to the hub—to get there. Yes, I was freezing, until I bought some cold-weather clothes. We found a lovely chocolate eatery and café; the fire inside was cozy. We sat at a table by the door, and the cold air would intermittently wake us every time a customer came in or out.

"This is your idea of going for a hot chocolate?"

"The shops are closed in the village, so why not buy from some of the best in the world? You have tried it, haven't you?"

"Not much, not really."

"Great, my treat." Then she spoke German to the staff. I was impressed.

As I gazed through the window to the cobbled street, I realized it would be another full day of sunshine ahead of us, and more caffeine. Who needs sleep?

"A regular?"

"Not quite." Fee then leaned forward. "What would it be like if you had children?" she suddenly asked, earnestly.

"Why? You volunteering?"

Fee squirmed coyly. "No, with Mari, in her time."

"Difficult, a challenge. What makes you think I'd want to?"

"It's not just what *you* want though, is it? It's clear she wants them. Isn't that going to be a problem?"

"Not necessarily."

Fee sat back in disbelief just as our order arrived. She was right: the mug of hot chocolate and the morsels were divine.

"Do you expect to bring her here, then, to this time?"

"That would be a Ministry decision."

"But you would ask them?"

"I might."

"And if you had a family here, not necessarily with her, what might that be like?"

"Without Mari, why would I want to? I see where you're going with this: a child's welfare, my child's welfare and wellbeing, would be paramount."

"And she has how many supports?"

"Not as many as I would like …"

"So, no village, not even a sense of assured peace. Their world is about to turn upside down in her time, and you want your children growing up struggling in it?"

"I agree I wasn't thinking this through; I was caught in the feeling. I get it. But she was bringing me emotional clarity to a level I never imagined. No one in this time has done that. No woman has even come close."

"Have you really looked? I mean, taken the time to really get involved with someone compatible? Sometimes the person we are searching for is closer than we think."

"And sometimes they're over a century away. I'm surprised you haven't commented on me revealing Institute doctrine."

"Well, there is that."

"Look, I can't tell you exactly what it was about her that made me continue to see her. All I can say is I sensed something much more, and it didn't make sense."

"What was that?"

"I felt she wasn't who I thought she was."

* * *

I was awoken from pleasant dreams by a gentle kiss to the forehead. I had slept on Mari's couch. It was early in the morning, and Mari was complaining she was getting worse: now she had back pains and the fever was higher. She told me she'd made an appointment online with her local doctor for this morning—apparently, there had been a cancellation and she was able to be slotted in. We shared some green tea; then she had a shower and dressed. She checked her phone, and we were heading for the door when she just threw me her keys. "You're driving. I'm sick."

"But I don't—"

"Just kidding." She grabbed them from me, then locked the door behind us. "The look on your face!" she said with a big grin. "OK, future guy, let's ride." She seemed particularly cheerful. I was suspecting it was her morning dose of pain medications.

It wasn't me that noticed we were being followed. Mari noticed them first.

The car behind us was white and, to me, didn't look that different from any other. Mari took some quick and random course changes through some unexpected streets—I knew this wasn't the shortest way to the medical facility. When we returned to the main road, there they were again, several cars back in the distance. Mari said she'd learned to pick a tail a mile away, thanks to her crazy boyfriend.

"Friends of yours?" she asked.

"I don't think so." That wouldn't make sense. Martino and his crew wouldn't need to follow me: they always knew where I was, as they had access to my phone.

We turned into a car park under the gold embossed sign "Family Medical Clinic." The car continued past. "They'll have to wait. You coming?" Mari asked calmly. "Don't worry. If they had enough on you, why sneak around?"

Mari seemed to take this amazingly well. I was more on the nervous side, constantly looking around.

"You might want to stop that," Mari said as we entered the elevator.

"Stop what?"

"Acting like someone's out to get you. You'll make people nervous."

Good point. "OK." Time for some controlled breathing, a mindful focus. By the time the elevator reached the fourth floor and we were in front of the reception desk, I was much calmer. I tried not to scan the large and busy waiting room too much.

We took our seats. The place smelled of antiseptic. There were people with coughs, runny noses, crying children; some toddlers were not far away in a corner playing with toys.

There was a big TV opposite, high on the wall. It looked like a map of Australia with clouds and numbers. Then a middle-aged man suddenly appeared. He was dressed in a smart jacket, shirt, and tie. "Breaking news," he said. "One Chinese national is dead and two others have been arrested today on espionage charges. Experts believe it is in relation to the major cybersecurity attack fifteen days ago that crippled financial markets in Australia and the United States for over forty-eight hours. Federal Police and the government are yet to make a comment. More on this story as it comes to hand."

Mari leaned over and whispered, "Lucky for you, you don't look Chinese."

A five-year-old boy pushed a toy car my way, waiting for a response, his mother breastfeeding a baby and talking to the lady beside her. I kicked the small toy back. Then he rolled it to me again, and I rolled it back. He smiled, so, needing the distraction, I sat on the ground to play with him, as I'd often done in our community.

"What are you doing?" Mari whispered.

"Playing with a new friend."

"I can see that. You better get up."

"Why?"

"It's not what strange men do with children. People get worried."

"About giving children too much attention?"

"No, that you'll violate them," she whispered.

"What?!" I said loudly. Everyone now was looking. I sat back next to Mari, smiled at the young boy, then refused to engage with him. His mother soon pulled him away. "People here would do such a thing?" I whispered.

"Yes. It's horrible, I know, but these days parents can't be too careful."

Smiling, I then glanced around the waiting room. Most people were soon engaged with their phones. Some were reading, while others were looking at the TV. A new story appeared about a military buildup in the South China Sea and concerns of a conflict between the United States and China. I knew eventually that would not end well. Then Mari was called in. She was back in fifteen minutes. I met her at the reception desk.

"Everything OK?" I asked.

"Yeah. You?"

"Oh, fine. Saw an interesting fellow on TV while you were in with the doctor, saying all illegal aliens should be locked up and deported, even if it meant some were shot."

Mari paid her bill; then we headed to a nearby medical dispensary.

"How are they going to deport you?" she whispered as she was walking. "Call in E.T.?"

"E.T.?"

"The extraterrestrial?"

"What extraterrestrial? There aren't supposed to be—"

"It is from a movie, *E.T.* Never mind."

In the dispensary, Mari handed over a piece of paper. They asked some questions, and she showed them her Medicare card and was told it would be a few minutes. "No problem. Thank you," she said.

"Medicine?" I asked.

"It's not the flu. It's a urine infection that's gone to my kidneys. Doctor said if I had left it any longer, I would need to be in hospital. Hopefully, the antibiotics will fix it. Oh, and I get two days off work."

We wandered the aisles of products as we waited, appearing to be interested in some of them. They still used vitamins? Curious.

"Don't worry," Mari said confidently. "The news often shows some crackpot with crazy views: it gives them higher ratings. You can't take them seriously."

Mari stopped at the female personal hygiene section. Once I realized what it was, I decided to keep walking. Soon her name was called, and we headed for the car.

Driving home, Mari kept checking her mirror.

"Still with us?" I asked.

"Nope. Must be getting paranoid." She sighed.

To hear we weren't being followed was quite a relief. I didn't know what I'd do if I was picked up by authorities—I hadn't been briefed.

When we arrived at her home, Mari pulled all the curtains. She took her medicine, then went to her bedroom to change into casual clothes. "Make yourself at home," she yelled from behind the partly closed door. I had no idea what that meant.

"Ah, much better," she said as she reappeared in a loose white T-shirt and gray—what looked like cotton—pants. "Sit, sit," she insisted as she flopped back on her sofa and covered herself with the quilt from her bed. "You look like you have ants in your pants."

"People put ants in other people's pants?"

"You know, if you are going to hang around in this century, you really will have to work on our colloquial expressions. No ants."

"Ah, yes, about that."

"Your HRU, is it? They should have prepared you better."

"I think they would have if they thought I was staying."

Mari's face looked shocked. "You're leaving?"

"Not right away."

"But you're coming back."

I didn't reply.

"Ben, tell me you're coming back."

I didn't know what to say.

"Fine," Mari said definitively. "I'll go with you."

"You can't. It doesn't work like that. The Ministry wouldn't allow—"

"You're serious … and you are just telling me this now?"

"I was going to—"

Mari raised her hand for me to stop, then began to stare hopelessly at the wall opposite. Every time I started to speak, she'd raise her hand. After a few moments, she spoke to herself. "Fuck! I've done it again. I sure know how to pick 'em."

"It's not like I want to go. Trust me, it's the last thing in the world I want. Five days ago, and you couldn't get me out of here fast enough. But then …"

"What? You decided to have some fling? I don't believe this." She sat back from me. "Just love 'em and leave 'em, hey? Like some swashbuckling Captain Kirk?"

"Who's Captain Kirk? Look, you know that isn't true, that's not me. I would never … Search inside yourself and you know—"

"Search inside, you say. Explore your feelings, you say. Fuck!"

For several seconds she started to pace the room, then sat down and gazed into my eyes.

"You know, you are a bastard," she said calmly. I was taken aback. "You know why?" I started to speak, and she quickly raised her hand again for me to stop. "You know why? Because you are one of the point zero zero two percent, an emotionally aware guy who knows a feeling isn't just some word on a packet of chips. Hell, you even get on well with kids. Do you know how rare that is here? Like gum boots on a bee. Ever met a bee wearing gum boots? Me neither. Now I'm tossing up a couple of options: I don't know whether to kiss you … or throw you out the fucking door! You see my dilemma?"

I could tell she was keeping an inner rage in check. "I think so."

"I'm not sure you do," she continued calmly. "But let me assume you do, and I wouldn't put it past you. What do you think I should do now, knowing it would literally tear me apart to know I'd never see you again? Yeah, tell me, Ben. You are supposed to be the wise one, the great arbitrator. Well, Mr. Perfect Arbitrator from your perfect world I'll never see, advise me. What should I do?"

I sat motionless and in shock.

Tears were streaming down Mari's cheeks. I tried to wipe them, but she pushed my hand away.

"What would I advise? What might I say? I'd say, let him share with you how you mean more to him than you can imagine. I'd ask you give him a chance and let him stay, to say fuck the future and their rules; this is where I belong, and God help anyone who tries to take me away."

I slowly kissed Mari on the lips. She hesitated a moment but didn't turn away.

12

Much of central Zurich remained intact. They had closed off most streets and planted more vegetation; a village-style atmosphere was prominent. That meant all the old buildings were much as they had been for centuries. Fee enjoyed strolling the historic village-scape, but my nose wasn't so forgiving. It was cold and sore, as were my ears. It certainly kept us awake. We made our way across the ancient, dark granite of the nineteenth-century four-span Münsterbrücke Bridge, stopping halfway to look out across the slightly green Limmat river, our breath freezing in the cold.

"I remember my first tutorial on relationships at the Institute, given by Mr. Zec," Fee said as we stared outward down the river. "Well, we called him Mr. Zec. His real name was Jarrad Zeca, a crumbly old bloke from Malaysia, of Asian appearance, bald, hunched over, a few warts on his face, and teeth that could do with a good clean, or replacement. And his breath! Could melt nostril hairs at a hundred meters. He was in his late eighties. Poor old soul unfortunately lost his wife just over three years previously—dementia, we were told. I'll never forget it. There we were, about a dozen of us sitting on chairs in a circle—as we usually did in tutorials—when the old guy takes a ripe apple and orange, and starts throwing them in the air and catching them.

"'What are these?' he asked. Nobody answered. I think we were just mesmerized by how this old guy could throw up two pieces of fruit simultaneously in the air and still catch them—nothing wrong with his coordination. 'It's not hard. What are they?' he asked again.

"'An apple and an orange,' someone finally piped up.

"'Everyone agree? Don't answer all at once. I won't bite.' Everyone agreed. 'Good.' Then he threw the apple and orange randomly at people around the circle. Amazingly, they caught them. 'Now take a bite. Go on, I have more.' The two young women bit them and then pulled back in disgust.

"'Lesson number one: no luscious fruit is necessarily as it seems. If you check these more closely, you will see they are made of a synthetic compound—they are fake. You want to know who someone truly is, then you have to take a bite, look more closely, behind what you think you see or want to be there.

"'Throw me the apple,' he said. He caught it. 'OK, who here hates apples, can't stand them?' Jean-Paul, a dark-skinned gentleman in his early thirties, raised a finger. 'What's your name, son?' Mr. Zec asked.

"'Jean-Paul.'

"'You know, Jean-Paul, me neither.' He then threw the apple over his shoulder. It bounced off the wall, left a mark too. 'But you all like apples, all you weirdos, right?' No one moved. 'Admit it, you like them, don't you?' Some nodded. 'OK, all you weird apple lovers, do you think you can make us, Jean-Paul and me, love your horrible apples?' No one said a word. 'Well, Jean-Paul, can anyone here make you love apples, want to munch them day and night till you sing songs about them. La, la, la!' He couldn't hold a note if he tried.

"'No, sir,' Jean-Paul replied.

"'The name's Jarrad,' the old man said. 'There are no sirs here.'

"'No, Mr. Jarrad.'

"'Just Jarrad. Good, now you here all know Jarrad and Jean-Paul don't like apples. Hate them. Yuck! Now does that mean there's something wrong with us?'

"'Not at all,' I said. 'It's just your personal preference.'"

"'Exactly!' came his reply. 'Lesson number two: not all of us can be close friends; not all of us are compatible to be together in relationships. Yes, we might like the look and feel of each other—we call that lust, if you need to put a name to the feelings—but that doesn't mean we will ever be compatible enough to properly meet each other's friendship needs. Some of us just can't be close friends, and that is OK—some of us just don't like apples.'"

"'Lesson number three: if you are an apple, don't try to be an orange. Just because someone you are attracted to likes oranges more than apples, to become the orange just to please them is to deny the most precious part of human existence—you being you. Never give the essence of you up for anyone. End of tutorial one. Contemplate on what I have said; there will be questions next week. Then we talk about vegetables. Have a nice morning.'"

"What are you trying to remind me? That I haven't taken a proper bite yet?" I asked, as I rubbed my cold hands together, then blew into them.

"Well?"

"Oh, I remember old Zeccy too, as we called him. Really loved his celery, as I recall. I know he also told us we aren't in love until we've seen the compost—the worst in each other—and that can take years before it ferments."

"Precisely."

"Was I in the lust phase with Mari? Sure. But remember, old Zeccy never delved as deep as other initiates. He preferred to live life with a family, and never represented a community as their arbitrator. He wasn't very aware of the deeper feelings and instincts we could tap into to guide us."

"Are you sure you aren't just telling yourself what you need to hear? 'Fuck the future and their rules'? 'God help anyone who tries to take me away'? Can you hear yourself? What, you were together for less than a week? Where's the marinade? Where's the compost? This is lust consuming you!"

"Yes, and normally, I'd agree with you, but as it turned out, my instincts weren't that wrong about her after all. I was in for a pleasant surprise."

* * *

Awakened by an insistent knocking on my hotel door, and with barely a loose robe on, I sluggishly answered. Tina pushed past me and strode in. "We have a situation. There has been a video released of the Noretian extraction, and it's all over the web."

"Is that all? I've seen it," I said, as I headed back for bed.

"You've seen it and didn't think it necessary to report it?"

"Just say it's photo altered or something."

Tina followed me into my bedroom.

"Martino's been reassigned to New Zealand, and we need you to lie low for a while."

I snuggled back into bed. "No problem."

"Good, we need you to stay here for a week." Tina started to leave.

"A week!" I sat up, now fully awake. "I have a meeting today with—"

"Not anymore you don't. Martino has given me full authority."

"To lock me up?"

"If necessary, though I'd rather not."

"Why the panic? I've seen crazier videos on this web than—"

"Contacts tell us local authorities have been alerted. We need time to place in other similar videos to make it look like it's some short film, a fake. It will take time for them to get traction. Until then we need you here. OK?"

"OK, I guess."

"You guess? Need I remind you you're an arbitrator, a responsible member of an esteemed order, with an amazing reputation and—"

"And as an arbitrator, I know flattery and emotional blackmail when I see it. No need for … a week?"

"Perhaps less. I have to go. I'll let you get some sleep."

"Yeah, great, thanks."

Tina left.

How could I sleep now? After our last meeting, Mari and I had decided to make the most of our time together, no matter what. We had plans for the day and I didn't want to disappoint. OK, maybe the authorities were following me yesterday, but like Mari said, if they really had anything on me, I'd be in custody by now. It was 5:02 a.m. I mulled over options, then came up with a stroke of brilliance. Around 8 a.m., I called her.

"Can you bring me some dark glasses and a hat? I'll explain when you get here." I gave Mari my room number. I knew facial recognition in this time wasn't that advanced—it wasn't yet reading more global biometrics. Besides, we wouldn't be in the city, where most monitoring cameras were placed. I thought we could risk it. If we developed another tail, then maybe we'd call it off.

Mari arrived at quarter past nine. I mentioned I needed to keep a low profile for a week thanks to the video but didn't want it to get in the way of us spending time together. She was more than up for it.

Two hats were pulled from her bag, one a stockman's, broad brimmed, another a thin-brimmed, more stylish number, like the type worn in the 1960s. I chose the latter. The shaded glasses were dark and squarish.

"How do I look?"

"Like James Bond."

"Who's he? A politician?"

"Not quite."

I dressed smart casual in a long-sleeved shirt and trousers. I expected that if I kept my sunglasses on indoors and out, we'd be fine.

"Where to?" I asked as I sat in her vehicle.

"It's a surprise."

"As long as it's away from any cities."

"It is."

We drove north. I suggested Mari play some music, and she was very pleased. Her choices this time weren't quite as loud and not quite for singing, but I was beginning to enjoy them, more of the age-old classics—they were still the best. Instead of turning toward the Sunshine Coast, we headed inland and up a winding road. Before I felt too sick, we were in a small village called Montville. It was late morning, almost lunchtime. We started with a stroll.

It was a quaint village with lots of stores. Some sold crafts and paintings, others Australian memorabilia. One sold crocodile-leather belts, vests, and hats. I liked the fine woodwork best. Some were carved from cedar, and others from eucalypts. The wood itself smelled divine. Soon we decided on some lunch. Mari suggested a café with a deck that looked over the coast and out to sea. The view was amazing. On the way, a very smart-looking red vehicle parked near us as we walked by.

"What kind of vehicle is that?" I asked Mari.

Mari whispered, "If you want to fit in, you can't call it a vehicle. We call them cars. That? It's very expensive. It's called a Ferrari."

I liked the look of the Ferrari. It seemed a nice vehicle—I mean, *car*. "How expensive?" I asked.

"About the cost of good-sized house."

"Very exclusive, then?"

"Very. Only the very rich drive them."

As we walked past, two people alighted from the impressive machine, a gentleman dressed even more casually than me, and his partner, with shoulder-length, straight blond hair, dressed in an elegant long white dress, black high heels, and some sparkling jewelry. They quickly strode ahead of us, and everyone else, and seated themselves in the same establishment. I noticed he ordered—she didn't—then both quickly took out their phones—they didn't talk. The place wasn't very busy. Mari said it was because it was a weekday—it was apparently much busier on weekends.

As we waited for our order, we both stared out to the sea. We took off our sunglasses to talk, to better see each other's eyes.

"I'm glad we make it," Mari said. "I mean, the future you were telling me about. Your time sounds amazing."

"After the wars, we settled down fine."

"Wars? You never mentioned wars. You said you lived in peace."

"Not in my time, in the near future, not far from now."

"There will be wars?"

"Afraid so. They'll be cleaning up the radiation for years, until the invention of time-field technology."

"Nuclear wars?" Mari looked shocked. "How many die?"

"Too many," I lamented. "We were this close to wiping ourselves off the planet." My thumb and index finger were less than a centimeter apart.

"What? How?"

"Because of that," I said, pointing to the wealthy couple. And as if on cue, we saw them arguing and shouting. Before we knew it, the woman in white was striding away angrily; the guy waved her off as if she was nothing.

"Because of disagreements? Getting angry?" Mari asked.

"If only. No. For the same reason you are looking at a lonely man and an abused and disrespected woman."

"Hold on," Mari said, skepticism consuming her face. "You know nothing about them. That's a pretty bold call."

"You think so?"

"You're judging a book by its cover, don't you think?"

"Am I?" I replied. "Let me ask you, how deep do you think their level of friendship is? How close?"

"How would I know? I haven't met them."

"OK, let's try the Ten Fundamentals of Friendship we teach our children—the ones we spoke about the other day—and see what it really looks like."

"You mean from the precepts?"

"Yes. Number three, let's apply it. Do you see evidence that the man over there completely respects the woman, treats her as a respected equal, worthy of his attention? You saw how he just dismissed her, like she was some ungrateful servant. He even ordered for her, didn't even give her a choice. Are they the signs of mutual respect, a fundamental of any close friendship?"

"But they could just be having a disagreement. She could have asked him to order for her. There can be any number of reasons they are acting that way towards each other."

"Really? Is that what you see? Is that what you sense as you notice them?"

"Well, no, I guess not."

"And did they show they truly valued each other's company, that they were each other's priority? Did you notice their phones?"

"Yeah, I noticed. Look, I agree it is rude to keep a phone on a table when someone else is with you—"

"But is it just rude? What does it say about how valued the other person is to us if we put this communication device where they can see it, knowing we will answer it any time? Worse, if we actually interrupt to answer it? Do you feel important when others do this to you? Feeling valued is another of the fundamentals of friendship."

"All right, they don't seem to be valuing each other."

"And at what point did they actually stop and listen to each other during their argument? Did you notice any real, active listening, helping each other to feel heard, to truly understand each other's point of view? Feeling heard is another of the Ten Fundamentals of Friendship."

"OK, according to your definition, they aren't acting like the closest of friends, but that doesn't mean he's lonely and she's abused. Check that—he was abusing her, wasn't he? Well, it certainly doesn't mean he's lonely. What with his money, he probably has plenty of friends—rich people often do."

"You believe that?"

"Sure, why not?

"But are they really friends?"

"What do you mean?"

"I mean if you didn't have money, would they give you the shirt off their back, still want to be around and help you? Honestly?"

"Probably not."

"If you can think of any exceptions, I'd love to hear about them." Mari didn't answer. "And that," I continued, "is what almost made this planet a radioactive cinder."

"What, money?"

"No—money is just an exchange—no, the decimation of friendship. When there is a strong desire for wealth, such as wanting more and more money, we can never know true friendship. The one kills off the other. His car tells me he strongly desires money; that makes him a tragically lonely man."

"Now hold on. He could have worked hard for the car. Just because he drives around in an expensive car doesn't mean he's obsessed with money. He could just like working hard and enjoying the fruits of his labor."

"Yes, he could. But then why not share it? Don't people who prioritize friendship share, among their friends? Look, I get it. Even in our time, we work for things we hold dear, but we need to recognize that can be just an excuse to cover something far more sinister."

"And that is?"

"A trio of human desires that can decimate us. It has taken us over five thousand years to learn perhaps the hardest lesson of all, that there are three desires that wreak havoc with us, impoverish, and divide us. We can trace them back, and we have. Once we tilled soil and farmed animals, once we relied upon a piece of dirt to provide for our security, rather than our fellow men and women, we let desires for wealth, status, and power consume us. But this demonic trio drives us away from friendships. Instead of friends, it creates competitors, allies, or compatriots at best, willing to use us or willing to be used. We let friendship die, and with it, basic human respect. All for what? So we can be the ultimate king? Have you seen how lonely your Brisbane Mall is? Welcome to the cancer of the world. There it is, and I'm afraid they have absolutely no idea they are afflicted."

Just as I glanced over to the guy, he looked our way, raised his nose, then hollered for a waiter.

"Sorry," I said. "I interrupted you before. Not very respectful. I apologize. What did you want to say?"

"No, it's OK." Mari stopped for a moment and stared into the distance.

"A hug for your thoughts."

Mari seemed lost in another time. "Oh, I was just thinking of Kelly and Mark's obsession with having to have everything the best. The house, the car, the clothes: nothing is ever enough."

"Obvious, isn't it, once you know what to look for?"

"Then what you are saying is their friendship was doomed from the start."

"A close friendship? It didn't have to be, but if even one of them was focusing on the wealth and status, it was never going to do well, unfortunately."

Mari started looking very sad.

"What is it?" I asked as I touched her hand.

"The poor kids. Little Emma."

I squeezed Mari's hand affectionately.

Soon after, our meal arrived. We tasted each other's and shared some lighter moments. At the end, as we left, just outside the entrance, the wealthy couple we had noticed before were arguing again, louder this time. I stepped forward. Mari tried to pull me back: the guy was bigger than me, muscles bulging from his chest.

"You OK, miss?" I asked. "Do you need some help?" We stand up for every woman in our time: their safety and wellbeing are paramount. They deserved no less here.

The guy stood right up close to me. I held my ground, getting ready for him to try something violent. "Fuck off and mind your own business, little man," he said. Then he pulled the woman by the arm. "Come on, let's go!"

The woman balked and stepped back.

"Fine, then!" the man shouted. "Ungrateful bitch!" Then he stormed off.

The woman started crying.

"Are you sure we can't help you?" I asked, a small crowd starting to gather around us.

The woman wept while trying not to smudge her eyeliner. Then, looking up, she started searching. Seeing the man going back to his car, she suddenly looked angry. "Leave me alone, you creep!" she shouted, then raced to get into the car with her partner, if that's what he was.

"Lovely friendship, don't you think?" I asked Mari, just as I noticed a young guy recording the whole incident on his phone. He came over as I fumbled to put my sunglasses on. Then he unexpectedly gave me a hug.

"Awesome. Awesome," he said, then was off up the street.

Oh, great, more images of me likely to go up on the horrid net. Tina would not be pleased. At least Mari and I had learned we could disagree with each other in a healthy way; it was a wonderful surprise and endeared me to her even more. As you know, being able to disagree and argue with each other well is a very good indicator of long-term relationship success. I knew we could improve on this even further in the future: we both practiced the basics of good—friendship-satisfying—communication.

13

Sick of the cold freezing my ears off, and eyelids feeling like lead, I convinced Fee we should get some sleep. We hired adjoining rooms at a nearby establishment. The proprietor—Elena—gave us suspicious looks: who hired out rooms only for half a day? Fee convinced her it was above board. She revealed her Institute insignia, and suddenly we were all best of friends. Elena would ensure we were not disturbed.

I think I'd had two hours of sleep, enough to feel refreshed, when Fee knocked on my door. She said she'd had less than half an hour and only knocked once she'd heard noises indicating I was up. I welcomed her, and we ordered some room service. The room was cozy; the coffee would be appreciated by both of us.

Fee soon sat on the bed and began to rub it slowly and gently. "Was there ever a time you wondered whether you made the right choice, about joining?" she asked, her shoulders slumped, her voice subdued.

"Have I ever regretted applying to the Institute?"

"Yes, any regrets?" Fee seemed melancholic and contemplative.

"At times."

"Tell me about those … Do you mind?"

"Sure." It took me a while to focus. Perhaps the sleep wasn't as refreshing as I'd thought. I wiped my tired eyes. "There was a time I was sure I would resign."

I sat in the chair beside the bed as Fee continued to run her hands across the bed sheets. She didn't look me in the eye as she normally did, but I knew she was listening.

"I was arbitrating in a dispute between village groups in western Brisbane," I explained. "The Gap village wanted to build a TC landing hub. Many of its residents worked overseas, and some off-world; they wanted it for the convenience. The Ashgrove village wanted nothing to do with it: they didn't want the visual pollution of always seeing TCs day and night. The negotiations weren't going well; hostilities were building. Then one of the Ashgrove councillors, Tim, suddenly died in suspicious circumstances."

Fee looked up in shock and concern.

"The worst part," I continued, "Tim was a good, personal friend, a good mate. We'd sometimes spend days together, helping restore old houses neighbors couldn't afford to fix, running the local youth group, going for long bushwalks. Tim had an amazing affinity for country: his great-grandfather apparently had indigenous roots. Oh, Serina, his wife, didn't blame me, and his kids, well, how do you explain it to children under six? But I knew I could have done a better job; I knew I could have held more meetings, resolved more of their differences, taken more time. Never had I felt so helpless and incompetent. I failed a great friend and a dear, young family."

"How horrible. What did you do?"

"Everything I tell my clients not to do. I isolated myself. Oh, there was an investigation. I was exonerated, but for weeks I could barely sleep. None of our training seemed to help: the mental detachment, the internal focus, trying to reframe the events, make sense of it all in a more realistic way. Soon I couldn't take it anymore. I took a leave of absence. I had to get away."

"Where did you go?"

"A calming place I've visited many a time, New Zealand. I don't know whether you've ever been, but the mountains and rugged terrain have a primal, honest, centering feel about them. I went for long walks; it helped ground me. Then, as I started to reflect on the day, other failings came to mind: some about thefts, some about property damage, one about a cranky old lonely guy I'd given up on. Day by day I was wishing I'd never committed to such a difficult and responsible job. I was ready to resign. Tim's death, the last straw."

"What stopped you?"

"An old lady showed up, out of the blue, and we had a chat."

"Madam Li."

"She had just been appointed a member of the Five; it wasn't like she didn't have anything better to do. She reminded me of the one thing I had forgotten and needed to be reminded of the most."

"What's that?"

"I am human. She reminded me my gift as a human was to make mistakes, and that is OK. It is necessary to find our path, learn what works. The other human gift she reminded me of was that I have the ability to see what others do not, something she said I should take confidence from. We had long conversations on and off over the following weeks."

Fee smiled a moment. "That's Madam Li. So, you returned?"

"Not at first. I needed to see it for myself, to contemplate and realize it. I knew there would always be ups and downs. I take it you are having doubts?"

Fee stared past me silently for a moment. "Have you ever wondered what your life would have been like to know none of it? No teachings, no insights, nothing?" she asked.

"Be completely ignorant of the insights."

"Yes!"

"Just live your life day-to-day and be taken by the tides and currents of destiny."

"Precisely. Not to worry about what you felt or why, not to think about your role in other people's future."

"Not to feel responsible."

"Without being aware of the source of so much pain," Fee said as she stared, forlorn, at the floor.

"I recall a young mentor in my first year, Caleb. A man in his midfifties, he seemed very aloof some days, very down the next. He told us the journey of self-awareness comes with a 'kick in the guts.' It's like a one-way train, he said. Once you are on it, you can get off at any station, but you can't go back. The more you see, the more pains it brings up. But it is the pain that brings the insight, for without it we wouldn't seek to understand and change. It is the pain that also brings great joy when we have found the hope it wants us to see. Then we travel to the next station. OK, so, what if you don't want to be on the train anymore? What if you wished you'd never come on board?"

"Or you'd stayed only at one station, embraced it completely, savored all it had to give, and never got back on the train?" Fee looked into my eyes.

I sat beside her on the bed. "I hear and see you. You are not alone. I believe you offer more than you know."

We sat silently for a moment.

"It's hard, isn't it?" I commented softly.

Fee nodded. I gave her a hug. She rested her head on my shoulder.

"You know, I remember I once asked Madam Li a similar question. You know what she told me?" I said, softly. "Yes, ignorance can be bliss, but only in a blissful world. As she rightly pointed out, if we live in a world of pain, it will constantly seek us out; it will eventually find us. She said some of us have been given a privilege, to learn to see through the pain and make less of it in the world for those who follow after us—the generations to come. We take up this challenge so more and more of those who are ignorant will know true bliss even though we may not. She told me that it is our path, our experience, a most honorable and precious journey for the betterment of us all."

"It doesn't feel precious." Fee didn't look convinced, perhaps even sadder.

"My normal recommendation for a friend, or as a counselor," I said softly and compassionately as I hugged her warmly, "would be to take a month or more of leave, take your time to consider your heart and contemplate your options. Unfortunately, we don't have that time. Do you think you are well enough to continue? I can always call Madam Li and ask her to—"

"Oh, no, it's OK," she said, trying to pep herself up. "Like you say, being up and down is part of who we are."

"Is it all right, then, if I continue?" I asked.

"Explaining why you are so determined to go back? Please."

Fee found solace snuggling up with her cheek against my arm.

As horrible as the personal doubts were for her, for me they offered comfort: it seemed now she could better understand how I was feeling, the changes invoked by getting to know Mari. Perhaps now she could see that sometimes we need to let go of our past and, like a child, be fully immersed in a more emotionally engaging life. Madam Li was right: Fee was indeed an exceptional young lady, insightful, and with an emotional understanding of others well beyond her years—but was that enough? There were some important elements I still needed to share to make my case. Mari was about to shock me to the bone.

* * *

When we reached the outskirts of Brisbane, Mari took a detour. She said it was for supplies. I expected a stop at a large grocery store, or a supermarket—they were popular in this time, even though they are virtually nonexistent in ours. Instead, we attended a "healing center." Mari suggested I come in. The building was a converted house on stilts, typical of others on the street, only on this front veranda, up the seven or eight front steps, were wind chimes, dream catchers, and images of pyramids, dolphins, and crystals.

The moment we opened the door, we were smothered in soft,

melodic tunes and mixed aromatic scents such as sandalwood and lavender. The main room at the front was filled with assorted items: small bottles, various-sized candles, and incense, to name a few. Along the walls were spiritual and self-help books—I could tell by the signs above the collections. Dangling from the ceiling and covering some of the windows were even more dream catchers—circular frames with loosely interwoven strings and beads in the center, with more string, beads, and some feathers dangling down. Poor imitations, I thought, having seen real ones in their original setting among some old North American tribes I had visited years back. Some catchers were quite large. As I quickly browsed the collections, Mari waited at the exit of the room to the corridor that led out back. A shadow of a woman appeared down the hallway.

"Mari, dear soul, what a delight." A woman in her sixties—gray hair in a braid, wearing a loose white blouse and an ankle-length floral skirt, with bare feet beneath the hem—hugged Mari generously. Mari ushered me over. "Who's this?"

I bowed my head slightly. "My name is Ben. Pleased to meet you."

"Hi, Ben. My name is Dinah. An honor." She bowed in return. An unusual lady, her skin and features suggested Pacific Islander origins, yet her eyes were almost green. Instinctively I noticed they reflected great wisdom. "Please, please, come in. Tea?"

Dinah led us out back. All manner of colorful traditional art adorned the corridor and the kitchen walls. A modest place, and contrasting to the older exterior, it had a distinctly homely feel. We sat at a round table. My tea was green with a touch of lemon. Mari and Dinah shared a chai.

"We missed you last circle. Is everything OK?" Dinah asked as she poured the cups.

"Something unexpected came up." Mari smiled. Dinah looked to Mari then to me.

"I see. How wonderful. Ben, I notice you are not from around here."

"No. I grew up in Victoria—"

"Not what I meant, but go on."

That was odd. I continued. "A place called Yackandandah, country town—"

"Lovely place."

"You know it?"

"Quite the community, lovely village feel."

"Yes, very sociable."

"And you are not sure whether this is where you should be?"

"What makes you …?" I looked to Mari. "Have you told her …?"

Mari shook her head.

Dinah interrupted. "So, what brings you here?"

"To Brisbane?"

Dinah smiled. "To now."

"Uh, an accident, a coincidence."

"Interesting. You believe in coincidences?"

I took a calming breath and let myself sense her, not judge, just sense. Then it started to become clear. "Life on the tapestry of destiny. All parts manifest in now?"

Dinah smiled broadly. "Hello, Ben. An honor to meet you," Dinah said again, extending her hand. I shook it in reply.

Mari sat back, sipping her tea. "What just happened?"

"Remember in circle," Dinah explained, "we connected with the mother spirit, the essence of women eternal through tribal mother's past? This old soul has seen beyond."

"As has she." I looked to Dinah.

"To have looked deeper is to more easily recognize others who have done the same. It is a delight we could meet: such meetings in these years are rare indeed," Dinah explained.

"These years?" Mari asked.

"Perhaps they will be more common in the future." Dinah looked to me. It seemed she had refined senses beyond even Madam Li. I was completely amazed: I never expected to find such rare insights and wisdom here.

"So, Ben, is there anything I can personally help you with?" Dinah asked.

I was curious. "What can you tell me of the age of friendship?"

Dinah smiled. "An age yet to come to pass. I have some texts reflecting current levels of insight, if that helps."

"That would be helpful, yes." If I was to stay in this time, I thought it best I know where current insights stood, to see whether later I might be able to "nudge" them along. Dinah led me out front, then returned to talk with Mari. I let them enjoy their personal, private time.

I sat in a chair provided. Several minutes passed, and another customer walked in. Dinah appeared and offered assistance. They said they were just browsing. She returned out back and suggested the customer ring the bell at the counter if they needed her assistance. I didn't look up. I didn't even pay attention to her voice: I was too intent with the books on my lap. When Dinah had left, the customer approached me.

"This doesn't look like a hotel room," she whispered. Tina ushered me outside. "What the hell do you think you're doing?" she asked, clearly annoyed.

"Well, I was reading a nice book—"

"What is this?" She showed me on the phone a picture the young fellow had taken at Montville, then a few short videos of my confrontation with the guy from the red car.

"It's a hat, so no one would recognize me—"

"How plainly do I need to tell you? This is dangerous. You can be picked up at any time. If they do a detailed trace of your past, we may not be able to reach you. That will send the Ministry into a frenzy!"

"Nice to know you care."

"I'm serious!"

"OK, Mari and I decided we'd—"

"There should be no Mari."

"No, wait. There will be and is a Mari. If your ministry doesn't like it, that is too bad. If you don't like it …"

"What?"

"You can mention it to me and I'll give it due consideration."

"Martino said you'd be trouble. I didn't believe him."

"How is the bald cooker?"

"Cooling off. Look, there's chatter about you in local law and intelligence. They take you in, and let's just say their methods are crude but effective. It won't be a nice chat. Who knows who they'll bring in. Getting you out … I don't have the facilities or manpower to lock you up. Can you at least keep out of sight just long enough …?"

I rested my hand on her shoulder as I strode past her and back inside. "You've made your point. I'll be careful, promise." I was actually starting to feel nervous again about the whole matter, like when I thought we were being followed on the way to the medical clinic. Now I find out the people who could catch me might physically harm me? Tina could have told me earlier.

Tina stood there a moment, then turned to leave. "Oh, one question," I said. Tina looked back. "Who's James Bond?" Tina turned and left, clenching her fists.

By the time I returned inside, Mari was saying goodbye to Dinah. We purchased the books and made for her car.

"Seems you made quite the impression," Mari said as she fastened her restraint.

"Lovely old and sensitive soul. It was a true honor to meet her," I said as I looked around.

"She facilitates our women's support group."

"You are all truly blessed." It was a lovely revelation just to know women here had such support groups, similar to the sacred circles of our time, places where women felt supported, valued, and safe, validated as women.

As we drove to Mari's place, I mentioned to her about Tina showing up. Mari initially wondered how Tina and her team had found me. I reminded her of my phone's inbuilt GPS.

It was midafternoon by the time we arrived at her residence. We were both checking the mirrors more than usual. Once inside we relaxed, shared some cold water, and sat closely beside each other on her sofa. Then Mari faced me.

"Can you teach me?" Mari asked.

"Teach you?"

"How to see deeper. Dinah mentioned it. An old soul, she called you, someone who has seen deeper inside themselves. Can you teach me to see it?"

"It's not something you just access like opening an app on your phone. It takes training and hours of—"

"I get that, but I'd like to know and see it for myself."

"You mean, experience it."

"Can you teach me?"

"Now? This minute?"

"Sure. Why not?"

I must admit, I was very reluctant: our training to achieve that state of awareness takes years. Perhaps I might have been able to teach her some of the basics, to begin her on her journey. Then something extraordinary happened.

"All right, I want you to sit in the chair. Are you comfortable?"

Mari nodded.

"Now, I think I recall Dinah mentioning you had learnt to connect with your woman essence, the spirit of woman inside?"

"Yes, through guided meditations."

"Then you know how to meditate?"

"Some, yes."

"OK, how would you prepare yourself during a meditation?"

"We'd sit comfortably, take slow and rhythmical breaths, imagine an ocean. The surface is rough and windy. The deeper we go, the calmer and more peaceful it gets."

"A great start. Then we are going to begin to learn the language of feelings."

"Feelings have a language?"

"When you no longer use words, everything has a language, if you know how to listen and understand how it speaks. First, we have to learn the language so we can hear what it has to teach."

Mari shut her eyes and began her slow, deep breaths. I suggested she feel the presence of the deep, quiet ocean, immerse herself in it, be one with it. Surprisingly for a beginner, she had very little problem with this.

"Now you are centered, with eyes closed, I would like you to recall an emotional discomfort from your past, a disappointment, or time of sorrow. Nothing traumatic—not yet. Can you recall it?"

"Yes, I remember when—"

"Don't tell me. Just notice it. Now I want you to imagine that emotional discomfort is like a large bubble, bigger than you, and you are standing in front of it. Can you notice it?"

Mari nodded.

"Very good. Now I want you to keep that memory and that feeling present. Hold it in the bubble; don't let it go. If you need to, recall what made you feel this way, bring it back, try to recall exactly what it felt like in great detail. Do you have it?"

Mari nodded again.

"Excellent. Now I want you to step forward into that feeling, into the bubble, and let the feeling flow through you. You are not going to want to: it is uncomfortable. We can expect to resist, but step into it anyway. It cannot harm you, I promise. Just be inside it and still. Hold it. Don't let it disappear. Are you there?"

Mari nodded slowly. I noticed her heart rate rising by the pulsations of her neck.

"Now I want you to ask it a question: ask it what it wants. What does it want of you for it to go away? Hold it. Don't let it escape. Keep putting the question to it: what does it want you to do? What action, what change, what way of seeing it differently would answer it, resolve it. Keep holding the discomfort."

I kept quiet a few minutes as I let Mari's mind search and hold, explore the feeling's truth. Suddenly she smiled, and her heart rate slowed. She took a deep breath.

"You can open your eyes. What did you notice?"

Mari couldn't help smiling. "It was a pain of my childhood, after my mother scolded me for not cleaning the kitchen properly."

"What did the discomfort want of you?"

"To do a better job, to impress my mother, to be good for her."

"And when you imagined that, how did you feel?"

"Much better: I knew what I needed to do."

"It seems the discomfort required you to gain your mother's approval."

"Yes, it did, didn't it?"

"I'm impressed," I replied. "Most people need many attempts to feel the connection between the discomfort and the action. I suspect you have done something similar before."

"Actually, I have. We learn something similar in our counseling. A therapist taught us a similar approach. I just hadn't connected the dots—the feeling to the action."

"That explains it. So now you have experienced that particular emotional discomfort has a history, a series of events that create it. In essence it spoke to you to tell you what it was, how it came about, and what it needed from you. You just learnt the early beginnings of the language of feelings."

"So, you are saying all feelings have a history and action they want of us?"

"It has a connection to actions, history, or a future you imagine might be. To read our feelings is to read a story about ourselves and the world. The problem being the more we try to find the words to describe it, the less of the story we see."

"That's amazing!"

"It is a useful tool to overcome past pains and expected pains of our future. It also works with fears. They, too, want something from us, even if that's to know it isn't a realistic fear, or there is nothing we can do to make a difference. Once we read the feeling's story, know it, see it more completely, more realistically, know what it wants of us, and have a plan to deal with it, then it no longer defines our life and destiny."

"They taught you this at the Institute?"

"Yes, but my mentor back in Yackandandah, Lee, had taught me long before that. He said I was already doing it, that it just required some more confidence to know that once we step inside the bubble, to not hold back, to let it give its best shot. Then we can know it, explore it, and be liberated from it. The mistake most people make is they want to deal with their pains or discomforts on their terms, hold back, and never experience it ever again. This doesn't allow its story to be rewritten inside us on the emotional level necessary to truly change it, and change us in the process."

"And you have been doing this for …?"

"Many years. Resolve the biggest emotional pains and fears, and then you get to see and read much deeper."

"Can we try it?" Mari asked, very eager.

"Look deeper? I don't think you are ready."

"Please, please, please?"

"If there are any pains or fears that deeply trouble you from your past, you do know they will show up? It could leave you with terrible nightmares and flashbacks … I don't recommend—"

"I can't tell you why, but I know I need to do this. You have experience in such things; I trust you. If anything shows up, we can deal with them together, right?"

"That may take a long time."

"Dinah has already taught us to connect with the woman spirit. How is this any different?"

"They were guided meditations to connect with a part of you often neglected. This is something else."

"Would you prefer I try it alone?"

"You know, I really dislike blackmail."

"Think of it as a choice. I am offering you a choice to help. If you don't, I will not think any less of you or hold you responsible."

"But you will try it anyway."

"Yes."

"Very well, but I'm doing this with deep reservations."

"OK. So where do we begin?"

I guided Mari through the preparation as before: the breathing, the meditation, the deep ocean, and finding peace. "Now I would like you to imagine a great spirit. It is not human; it is not beast. It encompasses all things. Imagine its influence determining all there is, its essence in what is, what has been, and what is yet to be. Now feel it, as we did that feeling before. Feel its presence, its details, its changes. Feel all it is. Just feel it. Don't try to interpret it. Don't try to know it. Just feel it and let it feel a part of you. Take your time. Just feel."

I observed Mari silently for about a minute. Her breath was slow and regular, her pulse not rising.

"Now, as we did before, I want you to ask a question of it. Search for the essence of what you want to know, the truth you seek. Be open to what it wants to show you. Hold that question before it, within you, in all things. Search deeper inside it, deeper still."

Mari remained composed. For minutes I think she persisted. It was as if time was standing still. Soon she started whispering. I could barely make it out.

"I will endeavor to be in balance with all things," she whispered. "To strive to greatest fulfillment. To find and know purpose. To understand and realize the human view. To connect within to the all beyond. I will endeavor to be in balance with—"

I threw myself back. "That's impossible!"

Mari's eyes opened. "Oh my God! That was amazing!" She appeared delighted.

I kept staring at her: I couldn't help it.

"You OK?" she asked.

"Where did you learn that?" I asked, still shocked.

"From you, of course," she replied.

"No, the Five Commitments. Where did you learn them?"

"What are you talking about? What commitments?" Mari asked.

"You just recited them. No uninitiate is supposed to know them. No one outside the order is supposed to …"

"You must have taught me."

I shook my head.

"OK, now you are scaring me," Mari said.

"Maybe it was Dinah," I whispered to myself. "That would explain … perhaps she isn't who she appears."

"What are you talking about?"

"How long have you known Dinah?" I asked.

"Oh, for many years. She was a close friend of my mother. Why?"

"OK, maybe not, then." I looked Mari in the eyes. "What do you remember of what just happened?"

"Just now, with the meditation?"

"Yes. Do you remember any images, any feelings?"

"I remember images of the world, of the sea, calm and tranquil. I remember everything as if it was a cloud I could float through …" She hesitated. "Everything was me and I was … everything." As she spoke, I noticed her face turn to that of solemn wisdom, the likes of which I had only seen in the great masters from the Institute.

"That shouldn't be possible," I said, still in total disbelief.

"I also felt a connection," Mari said with a smile, then gave me a warm, long hug. "Thank you," she whispered in my ear. "Now I finally know, you are part of me." She gently kissed me on the cheek.

I pulled back in total disbelief. Who was this woman?

Suddenly there was a knock at the door.

Mari answered.

"Federal Police." A man and woman in suits showed their badges and introduced themselves. Oh no, Tina was right; I should have listened. I stepped forward expecting them to take me. They checked me up and down, then focused on Mari. "Are you Mariana Jenkins?"

"Yes."

"We would like you to come with us. We have some questions—"

"Are you arresting her?" I asked.

"Sir, that is none of your concern."

"Can I grab my things?" The female officer escorted her inside to collect her purse, phone, and keys. Her face looked at mine; there was a calm resolve about the whole thing. "Can you lock up when you leave?" Mari asked. "I'll contact you as soon as I can." Then her lips mouthed, "I love you." As she was escorted away.

14

We were still in my rented room by lunchtime, still in our same clothes, still fighting sleep deprivation, only this time Fee was all fired up.

"That's impossible. No one could connect that deeply on a single sitting. You are sure it was genuine insight? She wasn't just telling you what she thought might impress you? And how could she possibly know about the personal commitments, the oath?"

"I sensed there was something more about her, remember?"

"Yes, but this? Had someone mentored her, someone we don't know about from our time perhaps?"

"Could be."

"What do you know about that Dinah woman?"

"A genuinely insightful soul, amazingly so."

"Perhaps too insightful. Maybe she isn't from that time at all."

"Then she would have had to have been there a long while: she knew Mari's mother."

"So Mari says. You believe her?" Fee started pacing the room. "Of course you do." She kept pacing, speaking as she went, to me and to herself. "Surely if someone tutored her from our time, the Ministry would have informed us. Madam Li would have informed us."

"Madam Li, sure. The Ministry, who knows what games they're playing."

"Then she was arrested?" Fee asked, stopping, looking me in the eye.

"Taken in for questioning." I nodded.

"OK, detained, whilst other authorities are keeping an eye out for you. What were your thoughts?"

"All I needed was for it to rain leprechauns, and my day would be complete!"

Fee's phone chimed. She took it from her pocket and extended it to a useful size. "Speaking … I see. Could you please keep us informed of any change? Thank you." She ended the call. "It's Madam Li. She's been admitted to the Mao Clinic in Minnesota in the Independent States. It's her heart."

"Is it serious?" I asked.

"Apparently, it's not good. She wants to meet us there. The Council is convening an urgent session; all available arbitrators have been recalled to Melbourne."

"The Council? They must be making contingencies."

"For a replacement? She's not even—"

"For a temporary replacement, until full elections can take place. Can't have the possibility of deadlock on issues involving many worlds."

"What do we do about your matter? She might be too sick to …"

"We can't assume that. We have to continue as it has been. This only brings matters forward. We can talk as we go, if that's OK with you."

Oh, please, don't die now, Madam Li, I thought over and over. With her passing, I knew any hope of returning to see Mari would virtually disappear. I was beginning to feel Fee was coming around to my side. Madam Li just had to hear her and make a recommendation to the Council before she died. She just had to.

"Fine," Fee agreed.

We gathered ourselves, bundled up for outside, said our goodbyes to Elena, and made our way to the nearest pod hub, at least twenty-five minutes' walk away.

"To be clear, your connection to Mari had become closer than with anyone else?" Fee asked. We walked quickly to try to keep warm.

"And getting closer. Yes, it is true, it began as lust—we barely knew each other—but a lust with a promise the likes of which I had never known or seen. Together we could—"

"But she was keeping something else from you: people don't get arrested—sorry, *detained*—for no reason."

"You are right."

* * *

The next morning, I got a knock on my hotel door. It was Mari; she was safe! We hugged like no tomorrow. She seemed pretty calm.

"I was waiting for the call," I said.

"I didn't want to wake you. They kept me till very late."

"Nothing bad, I hope?"

"Had to do with a patient of mine. Apparently, he's been on terrorist watch and did some stupid things. He's been arrested. I was just assisting with inquiries. Couldn't offer too much."

"You were there almost overnight."

"Had to wait for his lawyer."

"So, that's it?"

"Why, you thinking I'd been arrested? What, going to come and rescue me?"

"I might."

"How sweet. And thank you," she then said.

"For what?"

"Locking the place up … for that … experience."

"Oh, yeah, about that. Your first such connection, you said."

"Amazing, it's like being engulfed in joy. An endless flowing ocean permeating your very being. It's like all the answers are just …"

"Waiting to reveal themselves."

"Yes! And to bring us closer." Mari hugged me affectionately. I wasn't so affectionate. "What's wrong?"

"What can you tell me about Dinah?"

"Her again? Why?"

"Does she do any hypnosis, regression work?"

"Not that I know of. What's this all about?"

"The reason the teachings of the Institute in my time are considered secret is so that people aren't overwhelmed or traumatized. But also so they can't be misused or misunderstood. In the wrong hands, they can—"

"I thought you said people were into friendship in your time."

"Not everyone. Pockets of old and dangerous thoughts remain and cause all manner of troubles around the world. What has built up over centuries doesn't just disappear overnight. Factions still hold on to past hates, prejudices, and greed, especially in isolated areas. What I'm saying is the process of real change takes time, time to let go, time to allow new patterns to settle and create lasting and definitive change, time to allow us to properly connect in a pure and honest way."

"Then you don't believe I did what I said I did?" Mari stepped back.

"No, no. I believe you. I just don't understand how you connected so quickly. For you to do what you did … well … it's extraordinary."

"And you think Dinah played a part?"

"I am wondering. Have you ever experienced missing time or—?"

My phone came to life. Mari indicated I answer.

"OK, I'll be here." Then I hung up. "Tina's on her way; she sounds stressed."

There was a knock on the door. That was quick.

"Tina, lovely morning. You've met Mari. What can we do—?"

"Pack up your things. We need to get you out," she said, her eyes covered by sunglasses, her hair inside a baseball cap.

"Out?"

"The police have cracked your mask. They have traced your credit card to the hotel and are on their way. Pack what you can. We need to move, now!"

Mari stood back as I quickly packed some clothes into a small travel bag. "Can I help?" Mari asked.

"It's OK. She knows," I said.

"I know she knows, or she'd be outside. Not happy, by the way, not happy. Hurry up."

We left the room and headed for the stairs to a shopping level. Mingling with shoppers, we left via the side of the building. Bob was waiting for us in their car. Tina sat in the front, Mari and I in the back. Bob locked the doors.

"Hi, Bob."

"Hello, Mr. D. Nice day."

"Hi. I'm Mari."

"Hi, Mari. Nice to meet you. I'm Bob. Any friend of—"

"Just drive." Tina seemed upset.

"To the safe house?" I asked.

"You have a safe house?" Mari queried.

"Not anymore we don't. Can't risk it," Tina replied.

"Then where?" I wasn't sure what other options there were, knowing the HRU's resources were limited.

"Not sure yet. You had to get noticed. You just had to—"

"Maybe I can help," Mari interrupted. "Sounds like you need somewhere isolated. I have a friend who lives past Charleville, lives pretty much alone. I'm sure she—"

"Charleville? Way out west? I don't think … well." Tina seemed to consider it for a moment.

"You have a better option?" I asked. "I say we go with way out west, lie low for a while."

"It's better than trying to keep hidden up and down the coast. Too many cameras to disable, too easy to trace," Bob added. "Besides, if they see us all together, then …"

"Then all our cloak-and-dagger will have been for nothing. OK." Tina was even more unhappy, then stern. "You." She pointed to Mari. "Make a withdrawal for cash; then don't use your cards. You." She pointed to me. "Phone." She put her hand out. I passed her my phone, and she took out a small card from it, then smashed the screen until it didn't work—her heel shoes were very effective, even in the car. "When you get to Charleville, you buy a prepaid phone and text me you are safe." She told us the number. Tina chose a semirandom address in the southern suburb of Kenmore. "We'll drop you off here, and you can get a taxi or Uber home to retrieve your car," she said to Mari. "He'll be waiting at the bus stop. It doesn't seem they've made the connection to you yet, but if they look at the hotel security camera footage, that might change. We'll take care of that. In the meantime, you might like to ditch your phone too, just in case. Any questions?"

Mari was dropped off. Later I was too.

"Any idea how long this will take?" I asked as we pulled up.

"How long's a piece of string?" Tina replied. "Text me; keep safe. We'll contact you when it's been sorted. Oh, and grow a beard."

"Really?"

Tina gave me a scowling look. They drove around the corner to watch me from a distance.

About forty minutes later, Mari picked me up. She had her own bag on the back seat. Tina and Bob drove off the moment Mari arrived. I suspect they were checking whether Mari had anyone following her. As we pulled away, Mari put on some music by an artist called Madonna. "Holiday. We took a holiday …" Then turned it off. She gave my hand a comforting squeeze. It was barely nine o'clock, according to the clock in the car.

Nobody told me driving could go on for so long: almost ten hours, even without allowing for regular stops. To pass the time, we decided to chat but also to relax. Mari took the mindset of "let's make the most of it and keep the mood light." There was no more talk about her experience. We laughed at a few jokes, about funny things that had happened in our lives, or what made us feel stupid. There were plenty of the latter, both privately and professionally. By the time we arrived, it was late evening, and we decided to stay at one of Charleville's caravan parks, a cabin with en suite.

I have this rule, and Mari said she had a similar one too: no sex until we've known the other person for at least a few months. Courting was important; getting to truly connect and know the other person came first. Mari slept on the bed, and I was on blankets on the floor. I can't tell you how much I wanted to break that rule. I was so close.

Next morning, we visited a local clothes store. I bought some regular farm gear—shirt, pants, belt, boots, stock jacket, and hat— using Mari's currency so I wouldn't stand out. Once outside we scuffed them up a bit. Then at the local gas station, we filled the car, bought plenty of water, a local map, and for me, a prepaid phone— Mari had already bought hers before she'd picked me up. The young man behind the counter wondered whether we were on holiday.

"Actually, we're here to visit an old friend. Perhaps you know them, the McCullough property?" Mari replied.

"Crazy Betty? Up towards Gowrie Station?"

"That'd be it."

"Well, be sure to duck."

"What do you mean?" I asked.

"You'll find out. Give the old chook my best. Say Ian at the Servo reckons her fuel pump is shot."

"I'll be sure to tell her," I said.

Ian gave us instructions for how to get there. He was very helpful and friendly. His hair was a bit scruffy, and he could have done with putting on some weight. Some of the locals filled their vehicles too, smiled, said hello, as country folk do—it was certainly friendlier than Brisbane.

As Mari drove, I texted Tina about our safe arrival. It took us another forty minutes, taking a few dirt roads, before I opened gates, then shut them, as the signs on them recommended. The land was sparse, the dirt red; there was grass in some paddocks more than others. A few houses were scattered far in the distance.

We alighted from the car and approached the nearby farmhouse, fenced in with a feeble garden. A lady appeared and walked briskly toward us—with a gun!

"Whoever you are, I don't want any."

I waved. "Hi. My name's Ben—"

"I don't give a rat's ass who you are. Turn around and shut the damn gate!" The woman was rough and covered in red dust. She wore old leather boots, work trousers, and an old khaki work shirt, torn above the rolled-up sleeves on both shoulders. Her hair was in a loose ponytail. She cocked the rifle. It was a weapon I remembered from war footage. "I won't tell ya again." She pointed the weapon toward me. She was less than five meters away.

"Aunty Betty?" Mari asked.

"Who's askin'?"

"Where's Aunty June?"

"Minnie Mouse?"

"As true as the day is a bastard," Mari replied.

She lowered her weapon, clicked something on it, then walked over with arms outstretched. "Show me yourself. You should have called. I could have blasted fancy-pants's head off."

Mari and the partially gray-haired lady, slightly bowed legs and a bit of a limp, hugged fondly. Then Mari waved me over. "Ben, I'd like you to meet Aunt Betty. Like I said, she was a good friend of my mother." We'd spoken about who she was in the car. June and Betty lived together. "Where is Aunt June?"

"Passed on." Betty didn't seem very upset about it.

"Sorry to hear it," Mari lamented.

"Nah," Betty replied. "She was always looking forward to going back home."

"What's with the assault rifle? Expecting an army?" Mari asked.

"Damn fracking companies, wanting to sell me some kinda lease so they can screw up the water. Not on my watch, and it's pretty handy taking out feral pigs."

"Ian at the Servo told me to tell you hi, and that your fuel pump is shot," I added, trying to build rapport. It sounded like they were friends.

"That sparrow fart? Tell him his tiny balls could do with a lube!" I had no idea what that meant. It sounded like farmer's talk, and not very complimentary.

"Come in, come in. Mind the mess," Betty said as she guided us. "Oh, you can park your truck over here, in the shed by Bess."

Mari parked the car as instructed, next to an old tractor. The house was square with a veranda all around. Outside its surrounding fence were rusting machinery parts and big old tires. There were some large and old gum trees out back, what appeared to be a machinery shed, and some stockyards—some for sheep, others for cattle. Two old windmills were off to the right, one spinning, the other missing blades. A water tank stood nearby, tall on metal supports. The sky was clear, the air dry and dusty. I hadn't smelled anything similar since the droughts of my early childhood.

As we stepped inside, to my left was what would have been a bedroom. Inside were all manner of televisions and electrical goods, some covered by old fabric, possibly old curtains. The place smelled of … cow shit, unmistakable. The corridor leading down the center of the house was lined by well-worn hardwood. It looked like it hadn't had a broom to it in a while. Out back was a small kitchen, and what a mess. Clutter all over the table, chairs, and benches, even some machinery parts. Betty threw some of it on the floor, and some into another room.

As we entered the kitchen, Betty asked, "What brings you to Aunt Betty's?" Before we could answer, she grabbed open the door of a dented and rusting old refrigerator. "Wanna drink?" She pulled out three small beers before kicking it shut, a couple of times; the door needed an extra kick to stay shut. Twisting the tops off, Betty threw them into her cluttered sink and handed the beers out.

"Water's fine," I said.

"Water's for cattle. What, you got hooves?" Mari and Betty clicked bottles. "Cheers."

I sucked on the beer, reluctantly—never did like the taste.

Mari explained we needed a place to lie low for a while. Betty offered the old stockman's and shearer's quarters out back. Mari graciously accepted.

"This about you, or him?" She gave me a cursory look.

"Ben and I need to stay away to let certain things play out."

"Little things or big things?"

Mari didn't answer.

"Oh, shit. Fair enough. So, you two hitched? I'm thinking no rings, but … am I right?" Betty winked.

Mari smiled; I remained silent.

"Damn, girl, you sure … about this?" She looked at me like I was a waste of space.

"Thanks," I replied.

"Does he know?" Betty asked, as if trying to protect an important secret.

"Know what?" I asked.

Mari was quickly dismissive. "It's a family matter. We'll talk about it later."

"OK, it's like that, then. Here, let me show you the place. It's been a while."

"Too long."

Betty and Mari walked beside each other, sharing memories as I walked behind. She showed us our accommodation. It was very basic, mostly just corrugated tin with some sort of wall cladding, with a few holes. There was a small kitchen, and the refrigerator surprisingly worked, when we turned it on. The mattresses were old; Betty said she'd supply the blankets and sheets. Soon we moved on to the chicken pen.

It was a three-by-six-meter wired-in area with a walk-in shed toward the back. The brown ten or fifteen healthy-looking adult chickens seemed ready to be let out. As they gathered, Betty whispered firmly, "Keep perfectly still."

I didn't see it at first. It was a meter-or-so-long brown snake. It started to come toward us. Mari was closest. "King brown," Betty said quietly. "Kill you in ten minutes. Just don't move." For a moment we were all still. Then the snake headed for Mari. Suddenly old training kicked in. I noticed a pitchfork beside us in the small garden beside the cage. I gently lifted it.

"Don't move, dumb nuts. You'll piss it off," Betty whispered.

"Ben, don't," Mari protested.

Slowly picking the snake up with the fork, I carried it away past one of the trees. "There you go, old mate. No more scaring the ladies," I said as I watched it take off into the nearby dried-up grass.

Mari and Betty just stared at me, stunned.

"Old trick a stocky neighbor taught me. We had a snake problem growing up." They were still staring at me. "What?"

"You'll get no more shit from me," Betty said as she let the chickens loose and led us back to the house. Mari whispered, "Why did you …?"

"Sometimes they leave you alone, and sometimes they don't. If it wasn't so close to you, I would have left it."

"Holy shit," Mari whispered under her breath.

Betty cooked us some steak and veg. The beef was her own, cut up by the local butcher, she said. After dinner I admired the clear, starry, moonless sky, Mari cuddling up beside me.

"This is something I could get used to," I said.

"Same," Mari replied.

Just as we spoke, we both noticed three sets of lights heading down the road in the distance. Betty came out. "I think we have company. Your friends?"

Mari grabbed my hand firmly.

Betty walked back inside, then came out, with her war gun.

"What are you doing?" Mari asked.

"These aren't the neighbors coming for a chinwag. You want, I can buy you some time. If you head off now, you have three places you can go to hide out." She pointed their directions and told us about how far.

"Who knows what they'll find out if they get me," I said to Mari. "You can stay here. You'll be safe."

"I'm not leaving you," she replied.

"You gonna make a move, now's the time," Betty said. "The locals will take care of ya. Just tell 'em you're mates with ol' Betty."

"You sure you're up for it?" I said as I looked Mari in the eye.

Mari looked to Betty. "What about you?"

"Just an old, scared lady with a gun, protecting her property. Don't worry about me."

Mari grabbed me by the hand. We ran.

As I looked back, I could see the car lights start to head down Betty's road. They stopped at each gate.

"C'mon," Mari urged me.

We ran. We stumbled: it was hard to see.

I heard shots.

I stopped and turned to notice flashing colored lights.

I heard some shouting.

Then beams of light searched the area. They started to come in our direction. We took off.

For hundreds of meters, we ran and ran, the lights behind us bouncing up and down, searching. Mari stumbled in front of me; I caught her as she fell. We didn't stop. I kept slightly behind her, to protect her.

We ran, faster and faster.

I tripped.

I fell.

Mari kept running.

Suddenly I was pulled from behind.

There was blackness.

Mari was gone!

A wave of mild nausea come over me. The dark turned to light. I was being led onto … the bridge of a TC!

I couldn't believe it. On the screens before me, I saw Mari stop, turn, confused, searching for me.

"No! No!" I protested. "You must take me back. We can't leave her!" I searched for the exit, but it was too late. We were already in the air and watching the scene from above. It broke my heart into shattered dust as we slowly pulled away, watching as Mari was taken into custody. What would they do to her? I wondered. Then the greatest heartbreak of all: wondering whether I'd ever see her again.

15

We arrived at the Mao Clinic within thirty minutes. Apparently, there were some delays due to maintenance on some of the pod tubes. Unfortunately, we didn't have a chance to discuss matters further: there were others in the pod—we took the first one we could get. Outside was hot; we carried our winter jackets in our arms.

As we entered the modern, smooth-shaped three-story building covered partly in growing plants, I took Fee aside. "Can we have a few more minutes? We need to talk." This could be my last chance before Fee spoke with Madam Li. Fee graciously agreed.

We found what seemed like a quiet, empty patient waiting area. I sat beside her, facing her, trying to gauge her expression.

"So you see," I said, "this is no ordinary connection I have with Mari, no ordinary opportunity."

"Yes, and I could see you were prepared to die for her."

"Of course."

"Then just one question: how do you see your life if you go back?"

"I'd have to keep a low profile, obviously—"

"Can you?" Fee asked earnestly. "I mean, you've given me ample examples where you failed to keep yourself hidden at all and disobeyed explicit HRU directions. The travel to Montville, the confrontations with a gentleman in full view of the public, a picture taken of you, then transmitted worldwide, being admitted to hospital after an un-necessary visit to a beach. You even managed to get noticed during an HRU-sanctioned recovery!"

"That was hardly my fault—"

"But that is the point: you do not retain a low profile, no matter what you do. You stand out like a beacon."

"I'm sure Mari and I—"

"Ah, yes, Mari. I don't suppose it escaped your attention that she likes to enjoy life, not be stuck hidden in some hole absent of all worldly light. Can you really give a firm assurance, to the Ministry if required, the two of you won't, in some significant way, disrupt the past?"

"It is as Mari said," I tried to explain, "we can stay on the fringes, on a farm. We don't need to be around many people; we can help a local community grow and further unite. We can write books under pseudonyms, help the world through the transition."

"Are you hearing yourself? How is that not interfering? How is that keeping a low profile? You have just told me you want to change the world."

"Not change the world. One person doesn't do that. We all—"

"Another question, then."

"OK." I was cautious.

"What would life be like if you didn't go back?"

"That isn't an—"

"An option? Sure it is. You know it is but are reluctant to want to see it. Tell me, what is so bad about this time that you couldn't find deep satisfaction and live a fulfilling life, find someone who loves, connects with, and cares for you as much as …"

I shook my head. "Now I'm in real trouble."

"Why is that?"

"I felt you understood." I leaned forward. "You said it yourself: who we are, going through the training we have, makes it difficult.

It is the burden we suffer in our profession. Detachment is the price, but when we get one opportunity … What if we could get off the train, be the child again?"

Fee gently touched my hand. "I get it. I really do."

Both our phones chimed. We checked them simultaneously. Madam Li was calling for us. So far, she was still alive.

As we arrived outside Madam Li's room, I noticed Taylor leaving, still dressed as I remembered him in the debriefing room. He smiled, nodded. We did the same. A nurse appeared. "She is ready for you now."

"Both of us?" I asked.

"Yes, this way," the young lady replied, then left.

I tentatively entered. Madam Li had a few devices attached to her chest and arms. She coughed, then smiled as we entered.

"Ah, Fiorella and Benjamin, what a pleasant surprise."

"You called for us," I said.

"I did? Of course I did." She seemed confused. Now I was worried. Were we too late? Was her mental state too far gone for the Council to even listen to her? Then she suddenly sat up, as if all fresh. "Just kidding. Have to keep you young ones on your toes," she said with a naughty smile.

"You look well," Fee said.

"My heart's being fixed as we speak. Wonders of modern medicine. Fortunate you didn't see me yesterday. I take it you have had a little talk?" she asked with a smirk.

"We have," I replied. Fee nodded.

"Excellent, excellent. Seeing as this new heart-and-lung procedure only has a forty percent chance of working, I thought we'd speed things along."

"I don't understand," Fee interrupted. "Can't they replace—?"

"Changing the motor won't make me a new model. We all have to go sometime, dear. It either works or it doesn't." I knew Madam

Li was one of many who believed in not pushing the limits of the human body too far. Long ago I had come to respect her decision. "Shall we begin?" she asked.

We nodded.

"Good. Then, Benjamin, if you'd step outside, I'd like to talk with Fiorella alone."

I bowed slightly and left, my eyes meeting Fee's, her face blank and hard to read. As the door behind me shut, I had this distinct impression it was shutting me out of more than just a room.

I think I wore out the corridor. I paced, I sat down, I paced, I drank water from a nearby dispenser, I paced, I sat down. Minutes ticked by, then an hour, two hours, two hours and thirty minutes, two hours and forty minutes. I tried meditating many times, with mixed success—any relief wouldn't last very long. The nurse walked in; then the nurse walked out, smiling to me as she left. As an arbitrator I should have been more easily able to detach. I couldn't make sense of why I was finding it so difficult.

Finally, as I sat quietly, I recalled images of the last week. Of the coincidence of meeting Mari for the first time—if only I hadn't forgotten my wallet, we may never have met. Of her smiling and bouncing her head to the music in her car, before I threw up. Her head resting on my hand and the genuine relief on her caring face as I finally woke up from unconsciousness. Her laugh, her smile, the feel of her close to me in the water. How happy she was playing with children. How wise and knowing she appeared sitting in her home, meditating deeper connection—a wisdom well beyond her years under the surface. Our only disagreement. Her despairing face as I just disappeared into the darkness—our last moment together snatched away unexpectedly and unjustly. Did I still want to be with this woman who in such a short time had captured my heart as no other ever could? Would I still do whatever it took to get back to her, to give us an opportunity to grow together? The words of my great friend Sanjay came to mind: *Does a cow eat grass?*

The nurse went in again. Moments later Fee slowly came out. She stopped, looked at me; tears were streaming down her face. Then she ran, crying, past me down the corridor.

I wanted to run after her, and almost did, but I stopped when the nurse called me in.

"Madam Li will see you now."

Fee? What had been said?

The nurse left as I entered.

Madam Li motioned me to sit in the chair beside her. "You have been a source of great trouble, haven't you, young Benjamin?" she said as I sat.

"Fee … is she OK?" I asked.

"You tell me." Madam Li then asked, "Well, Ambassador Benjamin, wise and trusted friend, tell me, what have you decided?"

"Decided?"

"Your choice."

"I have a choice?"

"We all have choices, some with consequences tainted with bitterness, but choices nonetheless."

"I think you know my choice."

"It hasn't changed, then?"

"Should it have?"

"That is a shame."

"A shame to complete a life, to know—"

"That you miss it. That you have become so obsessed you fail to let your deeper senses guide you. It never fails to astound me how even our most insightfully trained men often miss the obvious, even when it stares them in the face."

I had no idea what Madam Li was talking about.

"You will recall," Madam Li continued, "I wanted you to convince Fiorella on whether we should permit you to go back. Would you like to know her decision?"

"Of course."

"She said no, you shouldn't be allowed to return."

"What? Wait, that can't be right. There has to be a mistake."

"No mistake."

I couldn't believe it. It was as if I'd taken a blow to the stomach. Time slowed. The lights on the machines flashed slower; the blink of Madam Li's eyes took over a minute, her voice barely audible.

"Ben. Benjamin!" Madam Li raised her voice. I couldn't look at her. This was it. I had failed. "Don't you want to know why?" Madam Li asked. I was barely hearing her.

"Would it make any difference?"

"To my decision, no. Fiorella told me in confidence, but she knew it was not a confidence I could keep."

"Fine, why?" I was ready to leave.

"Because she wants you for herself. The poor child—"

"She what?"

"I told you, never fails to astound me, right in front of them. It is like a cloud covers—"

"Oh no."

"Only now do you see. She said there could never be another."

"But it has only been days."

"Yes, she mentioned that. And I believe with this woman in the past you now wish to go back to, it was also only days, perhaps two weeks."

"Yes, but—"

"But you still have a choice. What shall it be, I wonder?"

I rubbed my face in disbelief. Could I have been so blind? I searched my memories of time with Fee, and it was all starting to make sense. At the beginning, open, inquisitive, and caring—what I'd expect of an arbitrator. Then sharing, opening her life—the time in her home, among her friends, some of the people most important to her in her community, when she could have just called them. And the children, I missed it—her warm desire and affinity with children. Then she'd changed. That was why she was more disagreeable, so critical about the level of my relationship with Mari and almost solely focused on it rather than any way I might make it all work. That was why—oh no—why she was so sad. It was once she realized that no matter what she said or did, I only wanted to be with Mari. And my comforting her so openly … only made her more emotionally connected—to me. "What have I done?"

"You tell me, young Benjamin."

I was still dumbstruck, thoughts of the time with Fee still running through my mind.

"So, what will it be, Mr. Ecclestone? Stay, or go back?"

"I don't understand. You just said Fee recommended I not be permitted to return."

"Yes, but that is not my recommendation—not yet."

"Then why did you have me convince her?" Then it struck me. "Oh no. Oh no, you didn't."

"Help you see your options more clearly?"

"You wanted me to stay. You wanted me to fall for Fiorella. That way it would be my decision. Fee was your way of luring me to stay!"

"You said you couldn't find a deep connection with another woman, not like the lady in the other century. And yet, here we are. I know you feel deeply for dear Fiorella and could have a most fulfilling and wonderful life together, and as you now know, she feels deeply for you."

"Then the threats of temporal crimes?"

"Very real. The Ministry of Time is still considering charges. If they had their way, you would be eating coconuts and talking to fish and turtles by now. Then I read a report passed on by operatives of the Ministry of History, and another option became apparent. They were very accommodating."

"So, there is a choice!"

"Remain here and have a deep and fulfilling life, with wonderful people to care for you, your wife, and your children; be part of a growing community that loves you. Replace me on the Council …"

"What? That's crazy."

"Young Benjamin, young Ben. I'm over one hundred and forty-seven years old. My time is well past. I have put your name before the Council, and I expect they will accept you as one of their own. Your world, our world, is calling you, its future in your hands."

"Wait, I need time to consider …"

"The meeting of the Council is later today to discuss your nomination. Unfortunately, there isn't much time." Then Madam Li began to laugh; that started her coughing. I passed her some water.

"What is it?" I asked.

"Here we are, mastering time travel, and now I'm telling you we don't have time. That's humorous, don't you think? You don't have time?" She smiled.

I didn't find it funny. Then it occurred to me: why did Fee leave the room crying? "I'm curious, what did you tell Fee that left her so upset?"

"That I, and the Council, would be allowing you the option to go back."

"But I haven't made up my mind."

"According to young Fiorella, you already have. Which is it to be?"

16

I tried to find and talk to Fee, but she was nowhere to be found—not at her home, among her friends, the Melbourne Institute informed me she wasn't there; not even Chetna, her confidante and trusted mentor, knew where she was.

"Is there something wrong?" Chetna asked. "Should I alert the—"

"No, it's fine. Nothing too pressing. If she does show up, would you mind asking her to call me?"

"No problem, Ben," she replied. "I'll let you know when I hear from her."

I swear, I'd looked everywhere—or had I? Where was that place again? As I came around the bushes to the stone seats, I was expecting to find her sitting, staring into the distance, perhaps feeding her feathered friend. I acquired a phone from a local outlet and tried to call, but Fee's was turned off and untraceable. I left message after message. With the afternoon sun beaming down, I made for a pod hub and directed it to take me home.

There wasn't much to do. My place was as I left it, cleaned up, some items in storage. I had been expecting to be away for at least six months, perhaps longer. It was always expected to be a temporary posting.

There was a knock at the door.

"Enter."

"Now there's a face I wasn't expecting to see," the familiar baritone voice commented.

"Hi, Simon. Come, come." Simon Garringe was a local tribal elder of the Mithaka people, the local traditional custodians of the land. He was also a good friend and neighbor.

"I heard what happened. You well?" he asked. I stood up and gave him a quick hug.

"Not a scratch," I said as I sat back on the sofa. Simon sat in the adjoining chair.

"You going back?" he asked, as he clasped his dark hands on his lap.

"What's that? Back to Noretia? No. That position is filled."

"So you'll be wanting your home back. Wonderful." He smiled. "I like our late-night chats."

My mind was elsewhere. "What, no, sorry, old friend, I still have to leave."

"You'll be back soon?"

"No, I'm afraid not. Just came to pick up a few things and have one last look at the old place. Can you let my brother know all the old family things are at Martin's storage, in town? I'll leave permission to take whatever he wants."

"This is it, then?" he lamented.

"Please let the community circle and elders know they can put the place up for permanent residency. Make sure it's a lovely family, with a couple of young kids. This place deserves it. Promise me."

"You will be missed," Simon said.

We stood up and I hugged him again before he left.

"Stay well and true," he said.

"You too. And say goodbye to your lovely wife, Elma, and your two brussels sprouts. May they have wonderful dreaming."

"And you."

I checked the time on my credit card–sized phone. 14:46. Time to go.

* * *

It was a large, grotesque, circular clock; I'd never liked it, too dark and otherwise for me. Give me a good old digital any day. Yet I had to walk through the archway underneath it before I could reach the tall metal doors that would slide open to greet me. The Ministry of Time building always gave me the shivers. Part gothic, part art deco, part Greco-Roman, columns here, sculptures there, gargoyles somewhere else, it was hardly a place that brought feelings of tranquility and peace. It was situated in West End, near the TC landing facility so they could have easy access to their own travel craft.

With mixed feelings, I made my way through the sparse and almost empty large, open, and high-ceilinged foyer to the one-person reception desk to ask to see the Ministry official assigned to my case. The young gentleman behind the small wooden structure was nice— he wouldn't have looked out of place at the Brisbane hotel I stayed in over a century ago. He suggested I take a seat; the Officer would be with me shortly.

I sat in the only seating I could find, way opposite reception and near the entrance. It was more of a metal bench really than a proper seat. People came and went, some wearing business clothes, some wearing more casual attire. Some looked as if their clothes had been torn apart and barely stitched back together again.

A few minutes later, a young guy, probably mid to late twenties, a third of his hair shaved off, the rest at varying lengths, sat beside me.

"Hi. I'm Sloth." He held out his hand. I shook it.

"Hi. I'm Ben."

He was dressed in tatters, probably worse than the rest. Soon he was chewing gum. He sat there for several minutes, every now and then looking over at me.

"Can I help you?" I asked.

"No, but I think I can help you." He smiled.

"So, you are …"

"You got it." He winked.

"You're a minister?"

"Well, I prefer specialist, but yeah. I've been tracking you," he said. "Way too interesting: spots, eddies, wow, you've got the lot."

"Sorry?"

"Perhaps we should go to my office. I think I'm losing feeling in my butt cheek." He stood up straight. He was very tall and thin, and slapped his bottom a few times.

"Should I follow you?" I asked. He was standing still beside me.

"What? Yes, probably, yes. We haven't done this before, have we?" Sloth led me to the elevators and down to level B6. The corridor was plain and so were the many bland doors.

"This way," he said, giving his buttock another slap as we headed down the end. There were no numbers; all the doors looked the same. Sloth opened one and invited me in. Inside it was a tiny office with desk and computer. There were papers and books scattered around, some on the floor, and two chairs that appeared to be for visitors. I started to take a seat.

"No, this way." He walked to the opposite blank wall and just stood there. I joined him. "Give it a minute." A double sliding door soon appeared. "There we go," he said. "It's a bit slow this morning—recognition system glitch."

"It's afternoon," I reminded him.

"Is it? There you go. This way." When the doors finally opened, I was speechless. It was huge, the size of a football field. "Welcome to my office," he said.

The place was covered with desks, screens, time-field coils, and bits of TCs. He quickly sat at a bench behind several screens and typed on an old-fashioned keyboard. His long workbench was covered in all manner of tech from different time periods. Another guy of similar age appeared; he was dressed in business clothes.

"Don't worry about Dillon. He's just here to clean up," he said.

"Like a janitor."

"Kinda." Then he shouted, "Hear that? Ben here says you're the janitor."

Dillon didn't pay us any attention as he started working on his own screens and equipment.

Sloth then brought up all manner of images on his screen, some lines interconnecting. Then the image turned three-dimensional, with different-colored dots and swirls.

"Oh, thanks, by the way," Sloth said as he focused on the screens.

"What for?"

"The temporal interfacing on the computers. Much faster." Then he pointed to the screen. "See, there it is." He focused on a spot on a line, then enlarged it. There was a video of my making a breakthrough for my thesis. Then he scanned to another region. "2020 … gotcha!"

I had no idea what he was doing.

"Should have yanked you back, I reckon." Then he shouted again. "What do you reckon, Dillon?" There was a grunt in the distance. "Dillon agrees. Hates having to clean up after us, but orders are orders."

"Orders?"

"Someone ordered you a day pass, or a week pass … never mind. So much for forty-eight hours and clicking your ruby slippers."

"You're saying someone actually gave orders I stay in 2020? Who?"

"Above my pay grade." Sloth stopped and smiled to himself. "You know I always wanted to say that, considering I don't get paid, well, not really." He continued typing.

"You have no idea, then?" I asked.

"Nope." Then Sloth started chewing more vigorously. "Now, you see this?" he said. "This is an eddy." It looked like a swirl on the screen. "We don't like eddies." Then he shouted, "Do we, Dillon?"

"What's an eddy?"

"That's when you screw up time. To heal itself, and keep everything running smooth, time creates an eddy."

"Like in a river?"

"Now you're getting it. We call them a paradox. A causality loop?

I've been running the numbers, and if we place you just here, we might just avoid a couple. Except for one thing."

"What's that?"

"You go blabbering and this happens, or it's happened—I can't quite tell sometimes." His whole screen came alive. "In this case the planet fries. No world gardens. Get it?"

"You're saying I have to keep quiet about the future?"

"Bingo! Give the man a star." Then Sloth gave me a clear coin that ejected from a slot in his desk and handed it to me.

"What's that?"

"Your lucky ticket. It will get you to five days after you last left. The TC will drop you off at this park at night." He pointed it out on the screen on a map. "Take this upstairs; give it to departures on level one. They'll give you your package and you're set. Kapow! Back to crazy land," he said as he swiveled in his chair.

In no time he was back to typing and sliding his fingers over his desk to control the screen, sometimes touching the images in front of him. He kept this up for minutes.

"I can leave now?" I asked.

"Yeah. The door's over there."

"When do I go back?"

"Whenever they have a TC free. That's departures; we don't do departures. See you again, if I haven't seen you already. That's a time joke. Get it? Never mind. Bye."

The second floor was also plain, but with a longer desk than reception, and a few more staff. I gave a middle-aged lady my token. She put it into a slot. It ejected; then she gave it back, and a package that included clothes, credit card, license, Medicare card, and some cash appropriate to the time—over a thousand dollars. The name on the cards: Matt Damon.

"Is this my new identity?" I asked.

"You will have to talk to the HRU division about that. They are on level ten in the Ministry of History building, four blocks—"

"No, it's OK." Fine, Matt Damon it is. The name meant nothing to me.

"Your flight departs in—" she checked the numbers on a holographic screen appearing in front of her "—an hour and fifty-five minutes. Your assigned HRU team will contact you on arrival. Have a nice trip, Mr. Ambassador."

Great! I could give it one more try.

"Hold this for me. I'll be back soon." I grabbed the token but left the package on the desk and rushed to the lift and outside the building.

I tried calling. No answer. I tried her unit again. No answer. I even checked out the café with the apple Danish, the garden by the river. Nowhere to be seen. It was almost time to head back. Then I tried my one last option.

There she was.

I sat beside her on the polished stone of her quiet place. She didn't move. We sat silently for a moment.

"I'm happy for you," Fee said softly, staring ahead. I put my hand out to comfort her, but she pulled her hand away. "Don't you have somewhere else to be?"

"I just came to say—"

"You don't need to say it."

"No, I think I do."

"Then I'll walk." She stood up to leave.

"Please don't. I'll keep it brief. I promise." Fee sat back down, still not looking at me. "Madam Li told you?" I asked.

"She would let you go back, yes."

"And that she had plans for us, it was her way to keep me here."

"Well, that worked."

"What will you do?" I asked out of genuine interest, especially after her bout of melancholy.

"That is no longer your concern." She continued to look ahead.

"Will you be OK?"

"Why? Will you be here?" Fee stood up and started to walk away.

"Wait, I need to say this." Fee kept walking. "Thank you for your honesty. I truly valued our friendship." Then I whispered to myself, "Perhaps more than you will ever know."

Fee stopped and turned to face me, her face sad and solemn.

"I truly wish you every deep life satisfaction possible. Be fulfilled and true, Benjamin Ecclestone. Be true."

I started to speak, to offer her the same, but she put her finger over her lips to indicate that I shouldn't speak. I kept silent.

Then she turned and slowly walked away. I watched her every step until she disappeared behind some bushes, each step a possible beautiful lifetime together that I was letting walk away.

I sat and let out a sigh, then pulled the clear token from my pocket and rubbed it momentarily. It was time to discover my new future, in the past.

17

The air was warm and slightly humid, the sky dark and covered with a blanket of low gray cloud. Beneath my feet, I soon noticed the softness of trimmed grass. Wearing a sports jacket, matching trousers, and business shoes, necessary cards and cash in my pockets, I stepped forward warily, not wanting any nasty surprises. The night was still; to my left, familiar city lights appeared. I walked several paces, turned around, and all I saw was black—the TC that had brought me here was nowhere to be seen and had probably left. Then I heard a familiar female voice behind me.

"Welcome back."

"Thank you, Tina. Good to be back."

Using the light from her phone, she guided me a few hundred meters to their car. She sat in the back with me.

"Hi, Bob."

"Hello, Mr. D. Good to be working with you again."

"Same." There was a new guy next to him, in the front passenger seat. "And you are?"

"This is Troy," Tina said. "New staff, had to fill a shortage." The young to middle-aged man with short, bristled hair turned to look at me and nodded.

"Troy," he said, brusquely.

"Hi, Troy."

Tina handed me a new wallet filled with license, cards as before, and a separate passport. "I already have some cards and cash," I said. "I'm Matt Damon.

Tina chuckled. "No, you're not. Hand it over. Keep the cash."

I handed them to Tina, and she put them in a black bag beside her feet. I checked my new wallet and the cards.

"So, you found a way to keep my old identity?" I asked as Bob drove us to the nearest road. "What about local authorities?"

"They're 'cops' or 'police'—you'll need to get better with the local lingo. We sorted it out, gave you a longer background, made it a change of name through a witness protection service running many layers deep. If they trace it, we have a few people who can offer you a cover. Law shouldn't be a problem, if you keep out of trouble." Tina shook her head. "Of course, we know how good you are at that."

"I was keeping a low—"

"Right, just try to keep a *lower* profile. We don't need the extra hassle."

"Mari, how's Mari? They took her!"

"She was detained for a few days, out on parole. It seems your lady friend has a bit of a record."

"Parole?"

"If she even so much as jaywalks, they'll lock her up."

"A record? What record? As in criminal?"

"She didn't tell you? You'll have to ask her. Not our problem."

"OK, I will. You can drop me off at her location—"

"Hey, hold on, hotshot. We still need to do a debrief, update, and acclimatization—HRU procedure. And we need to start teaching you to drive."

"Drive, like a car?"

"Bit strange holding a license and not driving. Bob here will teach you, five times a week for the next month."

"You'll get the hang of it," Bob said reassuringly as he suddenly accelerated, then swerved on the road violently. "See, it's easy." I gripped the seat in front of me as I was being tossed around. If dread had a look, it was all over my face.

"OK, I think he gets it," Tina said. "Now, about income. We've given you a portfolio."

"A what?"

"A combination of shares and investments, to cover expenses, as part of your profile. Don't blow it or you'll be on your own. We'll give you a file with instructions, including your tax information. We have an accountant we use, Gina; I'll send you her details. She knows not to ask too many questions. Now, accommodation."

"Finished my renovations yet?"

"Very funny. You'll see on your license you have a new address. It's a modest house in the suburb of Chermside—new, fully stocked with furniture and clothing, with new neighbors. Remember, most people keep to themselves. The socializing aspects I'll leave to you. The house is owned by a trust—Gina will explain it."

We drove for at least half an hour. The park was remote and well north of Brisbane. This time they made sure no one watched. It helped that our TCs were less conspicuous than those of the Noretians—our new alien friends weren't used to being secretive among the worlds they chose to visit. Eventually we reached the safe house; it was still a mess.

"Like what you've done with the place," I said as I stepped over more building work. "Any more visitors?" Tina didn't answer. Troy went ahead of us, Bob behind.

For more than a day, I was stuck in the same room where the young, injured Noretian had been kept. I was given several videos to watch of local customs, such as avoiding eye contact with most people, not smiling, and not spitting or blowing your nose on the sidewalk. There was even a short clip on using the local toilets. It was amusing, but I was pretty sure I'd mastered that. Then there were clips on local news items and politics, global and local. It wasn't to compare where we were in history—the history of my future time—it was more just a way of getting a greater idea of the problems the world and local people faced. Besides, it could help with conversation—not that too many locals, apparently, liked to talk about it. Complain, maybe. Properly discuss? Not so much.

The next day, Tina handed me a new phone. "You break it, you get a new one," she said as she handed it to me as she was passing by.

"Can I call her?"

"If you must."

I fumbled with it. "It doesn't work."

"You have to set it up first." Tina smirked.

"I have to what?"

"It needs to know it's you. Create a password, six numbers. Look at the camera and it will remember your face and open automatically when you look at it."

"Primitive biometrics," I mumbled under my breath as I had to rotate my face. Finally I dialed in the number I remembered, but didn't press the green button. No. I'd meet her in person, surprise her. I rang up where she worked and found out when she finished, and confirmed her hours to see whether she was seeing clients the next day. I couldn't believe I was actually nervous.

That evening I ordered a taxi to pick me up. The drive seemed to take forever, though the nice Asian taxi driver told me the traffic was very good for this time of the evening. Eventually we stopped outside her townhouse. The lights were on. My heart skipped a beat. Before I knew it, I'd paid the driver with credit and he was on his way.

I stood motionless, looking at the door; my hands were sweating buckets. I rubbed them on my trousers several times.

After some slow, calming breaths, I started striding toward the door.

Before I knew it, I noticed the garage door opening beside me. I was turning to look inside when suddenly a car pulled up behind. As I turned back, the lights hurt my eyes and startled me.

"Ben? Is that …? Oh my God!" Mari raced over and gave me a

huge hug, then kissed me. "I don't believe it," she said as she looked into my eyes. Her touch, her feel, her smell were glorious. "When? How?"

I wanted to tell her everything there and then. I had just opened my mouth when she put her finger over my lips.

"Hold that thought." She raced back to her car, parked it properly in the garage, opened the rear compartment, and lifted out several bags. "Would you mind?" she asked. I helped her carry the bags inside and put them on the kitchen bench. Her place was just as I remembered it, as uncluttered and sweet smelling.

Once the bags were on the bench, she virtually jumped on me, her hands around my neck, joy expressed all over her face. We kissed as if a built-up passion had accumulated over decades. Then she broke free. "Just a sec!" She rushed back to the kitchen and hurriedly placed items into her freezer, then some into her refrigerator. I helped her as best I could, but we'd hardly packed anything away before we started kissing again.

Then I stopped and looked deep into her smiling eyes and softly caressed her smooth and gentle face. "I missed you," I said. "I've so much to tell you. Ah, but where are my manners? You first."

"Me?" she said, surprised. "No, you. One moment you were behind me, then …"

"They pulled me back, plucked me into a TC. There was nothing I could do. Are you all right? I saw what they did to you."

"Back to your time?" she asked. Then her face changed to one of concern. "How long do we have?"

"How long could you put up with me?" I smirked.

"You're serious?" She smiled.

I nodded. Then Mari looked very businesslike, putting her hand to her chin. "Well, that depends."

"Depends?"

"On whether you pick up your socks." Then she beamed a glorious smile. "I don't believe it," she said. "You did it!"

"As promised. You and me."

Eventually we sat.

"You OK?" I asked again. "They were very rough. I'm so sorry."

"Me? Couple of scratches here and there."

"And no charges?"

"No. Free as a bird. I think they had a few calls from on high once they had evidence that your footprints just stopped. All very nervous and hush-hush. Thank you."

"It wasn't me. Betty OK?" I then asked.

"Betty? She's good. Had to pay a fine for shooting out a couple of headlights. The police were a bit pissed, but she's OK. I'll call her later; she'll be thrilled to know you're safe."

"Thrilled?"

"Well, maybe amused. She was impressed you gave them quite a chase. They were there for days looking for you. Speaking of which, they've let me go, but what about you? They said something about serious fraud."

"HRU came through. You're looking at a person in witness safety …"

"Witness protection?"

"Yeah, that. Tina says it's all taken care of; no more problems with the cops if I keep out of trouble." Then I asked more carefully, "And she also said something about you and a criminal record?"

"Did she?"

"Anything I should know about?"

Mari stood up. "Not really." Mari returned to the kitchen to pack away the rest of the groceries. I went over.

"Not really?"

"Have you eaten? I'm famished," she said as she put some cans in the cupboard.

I stood in front of her; she went around me.

"Trust," I said.

She stopped. "I've put it behind me; it's no matter."

"What, now you don't trust me? You do trust me, don't you?"

"Yes, completely."

"Then?"

"You'll see me differently."

"What could possibly …?"

She turned, stood, and faced away from me. I stood beside her, my arm over her shoulder.

"You know you can tell me anything. Anything."

Mari stepped away from me.

"Anything," I repeated. I stepped forward; she stepped further away.

Mari was silent a moment, then spoke quietly. "I killed my friends."

* * *

This had to be some mistake. I knew this woman, surely. Could my instincts be so wrong? We sat on kitchen chairs opposite each other, my hands holding hers. I asked her to start where she felt comfortable. She was reluctant at first.

"It was about four years ago," she began. "A new friend from a financial organization I was temping with in Sydney, Rebecca, introduced me to some of her group. I was lonely, just up from Melbourne, and I thought, why not? It was fun. We'd catch up on weekends, party—now they could rave."

"Rave?"

"A type of dance—loud, electronic music, thumping beat, almost trancelike. Boy, were there some long nights." She smirked. "I thought he was cool, smart, had a calm energy about him."

"Who?"

"He was a DJ … uh, he played the music. Anyway, my new friends all adored him. Went by the name Tobysun. Seemed nice enough. One night he invited me to join the others at his place. They all met there every Wednesday night, but I'd only just found out even though I'd been hanging with them for over a month. It was to talk about spirituality, philosophy, and how we could make the world a better place, he said."

Mari stopped and looked away, putting her fingers to her mouth as if out of deep concern.

"When you're ready," I said. After a few moments, Mari continued. She seemed visibly upset.

"Everything was going great. For months we'd meet up, have a laugh, some deep discussions, disagreements, some drinking. Thought I'd finally found my tribe, you know?" I nodded. "Then I learnt he was sleeping with all my friends."

"All of them?" I was shocked.

"The women, mostly. One carried his child." Mari shook her head. "I should have seen it; I should have walked there and then."

"But you didn't."

"No. Two weeks later they were all dead, all of them, and it was my fault," she said as she stood up and made for the kitchen window.

I approached slowly from behind and gently placed my hand on her shoulder. She squeezed it and cuddled it against her cheek.

"What happened?" I asked.

Mari let go of my hand and stared into the distance, then continued. "It was a suicide pact. Tobysun—it wasn't even his real name—had us believing, one by one, he was some messenger in exclusive contact with some alien race who lived in the Pleiades star cluster, called the Tylosians, a highly advanced spiritual race who wanted to bring love and peak spiritual attainment to the world. Crazy, huh?"

"You all believed him?"

"Yeah. He was good. Boy, was he good. He had me convinced I was the most advanced and special of them all and that I, I alone, with his help, could help teach the others, and later the world, to all attain the next stage of our spiritual evolution, as beings of light. I was unique, he said, with a special gift to be treasured. I actually slept with the guy," she said as she shuddered.

"It sounds like he was attractive."

"Not really—well, not physically. Then one day, out of the blue, Dinah shows up at work. Hadn't seen her in years. Somehow she knew. She tricked me into going with her and took me to Betty's place. I was fuming. How dare she? She convinced me it was only for a day or so; we'd be right back. It took them, together, over six weeks to deprogram me."

"Deprogram?"

"It's what they call it when they rehabilitate you from a cult. I owe them my life," Mari said with affection. After a brief moment, she continued. "The week I headed back, I got a call from Rebecca's mother; she could barely talk for crying. Rebecca and all the others were gone—all of them!"

'That's terrible."

"What's terrible is even once I knew it was all BS, even when I knew they were in danger, I didn't do a thing about it. Nix. Nothing!"

"What do you mean?"

"I knew the date! I even helped buy the crap they swallowed!"

"They killed themselves with poison? Why?"

"It was the coming cleansing, he called it, where the world would pay for its transgressions, be cleansed, and we who had proven ourselves worthy would be raised into the heavens and be saved, then return and create a paradise. I knew the day. I didn't call anyone, not a soul. I killed them!" Mari held her hands to her face.

"You could have died with them."

Mari looked out of the window again. "That's what Betty said. Good riddance to the bastard, she said, they should have lynched him, poison was too good for him. But they were my friends."

"You still think that?"

"Yes ... no ... I don't know."

"And friends would help kill each other, knowingly harm the ones they loved?"

"But they weren't harming each other, not to them, to us," she said as she glanced over to me.

"And now?"

"Now? I want to cut the guy's balls off and sauté them for breakfast."

"And you still hold yourself responsible?"

"Oh, I know from my own counseling training there is survival guilt in there. I know they all made their own choices. And so did I, and if I'd chosen to put my friends first, they'd still be around today."

"Or, you'd be dead. I'm glad you're not." I hugged Mari from behind.

She unclasped my hands. "You came back for a murderer," she said, distress obvious in her voice as she rushed up to her bedroom and slammed the door.

I slowly followed her, then knocked gently. I knocked again. "May I come in?" I slowly turned the handle and peered inside. Mari was laying on her side in bed, facing away from me. I gradually sat on the other side of the bed.

"You know what I think?" I said. "I think you aren't going to get away that easily. Did you make a mistake? Yes. Were you naive? Yes. Did your actions contribute to the deaths of others you cared for?"

"You're not helping," she muttered.

"Did you believe in the best in people, want to see the love and kindness in us all? Yes. And that is not a crime. Did you screw up? Sure, but that doesn't stop how I feel about you. Would you intentionally want to kill another human being?"

"Of course not," she said, annoyed as she rolled over to face me. "What sort of monster do you think I am?"

"Exactly my point. You're not a monster, but deep down you're still afraid you are. Afraid that if I see this part of you, I'll run away. Well, guess what, kiddo, I'm staying. And if you want to get rid of me, you'll have to find a much better reason than that."

"Then you don't hate me?"

"Hate you? I'd be honored if you were to be the mother of my child."

Mari slowly began to smile. She wiped away the tears, then soon put her arms affectionately around me from behind. Soon she whispered "Only one?" as we snuggled cheek to cheek.

"Let's not get too hasty." I turned to face her. "I am curious, how could this leave you with a criminal record? What could they possibly charge you with?"

Mari sat back. "Some of the parents wanted me to pay for what I'd done and charge me with being an accomplice. I wanted to pay for it too, but my lawyer was able to get the charges reduced to a lesser offense. Now I have a record I'm not proud of."

"Absurd. You will never be a criminal to me." I hugged her. "Cup of tea?" I whispered.

We made our way down to the kitchen.

"I do have one more question."

"Sure, anything," Mari replied.

"So he was the reason you ran away when I told you who I am?"

"Uh-huh. It was the Cult of Light all over again. A charismatic man drawing me in with a secret too fantastic to believe, and making me feel special."

"So, you think I'm charismatic." I stopped and turned back to her on the stairs.

"In a fumbling kind of way." Mari smirked.

"I don't fumble."

Mari looked at me with unbelieving eyes.

"Well, I'm new around here."

"Yes, you are."

"A promise, then?" I asked. Mari looked at me suspiciously. "We will always trust and be truthful to each other."

Mari came over and hugged me. "Of course."

And yet, I was still to learn Mari's greatest secret of all.

18

The next weeks were busy: Mari was working several days of the week, and I was still taking instruction from Tina and her HRU team. I dreaded my driving lessons with a passion.

"Try to look ahead, get the flow of the traffic, anticipate what other drivers will do," Bob instructed. "Loosen up," he said. "Be gentle," he said. "Watch out!"

Five hours a week of this? Was he kidding me? And who ever heard of a "hill start"? Or a "parallel park"? There were no hills when you traveled by pod. No drivers to worry about who might do something rash at any moment and scare the bananas out of you. And we certainly didn't have to park our transport—they weren't ours to begin with. I think I aged ten years in my first week of learning to drive a car. Who invented these abominations? I wondered. I was tempted to contact the Ministry and tell them to go back and stop it before such contraptions were let loose on the world, and on me! But, what with their time eddies, causality loops, and temporal laws a mile long, I suspected they wouldn't be very receptive.

"Same time tomorrow?" Bob would ask as I threw him the keys. I'd simply shake my head and walk away. "Ten thirty it is," he'd say enthusiastically. I would just raise my hand in reply. It had become our little ritual. Did everyone struggle learning to drive as much as I did? I was beginning to admire Mari's driving prowess.

Between lessons on recent history and local and international customs, I availed myself of some bookstores. Eventually I found the author I was after, not well known yet; the book was hard to find. Later I learnt I could find books over the net and order them "online." It would have saved me lots of leg work, but I didn't mind. I liked the walks and the feel of books in my hand, to browse through them physically. Books were like ancient parchment in my time, quite rare, so I savored their smell and feel. Then I came across a poster in a health-food store. That healthy and unhealthy foods existed here surprised me. Why weren't all foods prepared well to ensure good health? I wasn't impressed. The poster on a noticeboard just inside the store was of a small retreat not far from Brisbane. I recognized the location and pictures from the image of the small collection of buildings at once.

I'd finally found them! But would I make contact?

Sloth's words started echoing in my mind, about the need to be quiet or the world would become a burning cinder. Noninterference in the past was the motto of the Ministry, and also the HRU—observe, interact, but keep a low profile, always. I knew neither department would approve of me getting involved with them. I still saw images of Sloth and his dreaded unwanted eddies. But I was curious: what actually happened in the fragile years of the creation of the world's first Institute? What did they talk about? What were their goals and aims? Not much of these fledgling times remained. Most records were destroyed in a fire just over fifteen years from now. I was itching to pay them a visit. And take Mari. I wondered what she'd think.

Evenings and weekends were special times. Mari would either spend them at my house or I'd visit hers, depending on our mood. We cooked, talked, spent days at a time in bed, learning what pleasured each other the most. The physical communication of our friendship was regularly consummated with fun and joy the likes of which neither of us had ever known. It was beautiful.

We started to invite neighbors for dinners. We both agreed

building a community around us was important. It wasn't easygoing: they were so different, and many of them, much like Kelly and Mark, had their sights on achieving greater material and promotional "success." Speaking of Mari's friend Kelly, she soon moved out into her own apartment, not long after she'd confronted Mark about his sexual liaisons. He didn't see the problem. Hey, it was a bloke thing, he said, it didn't mean anything, Kelly should just get over it. They tried couples counseling, but Mark didn't want to be there: he thought this was Kelly's problem, not his. It broke Mari's heart to see her friend struggling. We agreed to babysit young Emma: Kelly needed all the support she could get.

Then we invited Dinah for a Sunday lunch.

"Dinah!" Mari cried with joy. "You made it." Then she gave her a big hug. She hadn't changed a bit, except she was wearing shiny black riding boots, and there were gifts in her hands. She passed them to us immediately, then bowed her head slightly as we invited her in. "It's too much!" Mari protested as she opened hers. It was an expensive-looking wooden box filled with fifteen Australian essential oils. Dinah didn't reply. I received two dream catchers with feathers and beads, each interweaved around a hoop no bigger than a dinner plate.

"Two? You shouldn't have," I said, uncertain what I'd do with them.

"To the man with visions," she said with a smile. "Something to catch them in."

"Uh, thank you."

Dinah slowly peered around as she entered, smelled the walls and doors as she passed, her face cringing as if we'd invited her to a torture chamber, but she relaxed a bit more once we were outside on the covered deck. She smiled at the few potted plants. A slight breeze made the temperature bearable. Mari brought out refreshments; she insisted she do it alone.

"How do you find adapting to the new time?" Dinah asked, calm and curious.

I glanced toward Mari with a questioning look as she prepared to bring the drinks and some cheese and fruit on a large tray.

"Uh, fine," I replied.

Mari yelled out from inside, "It's a new time in our life we are looking forward to." Soon she was passing out the glasses of chilled water with a touch of squeezed lemon, and plenty of ice.

"How's Betty?" Dinah then asked, calmly and slowly.

I looked to Mari again, who had barely sat down.

"She's fine, sends her regards," Mari replied happily. "Cheese?" She passed the plate over.

"We spoke last week." Dinah then sipped from her glass as she looked toward me.

"Oh, great," Mari said, apprehensively. "Hope she's still doing well."

"Says you have a real Houdini on your hands." Dinah's eyes were searching mine.

"Really?" Mari said with concern in her voice.

Then Dinah looked to Mari and back at me. "Planning on disappearing again anytime soon?"

I reached out and squeezed Mari's hand. "No. No repeat performances," I replied.

Dinah smiled.

"How's business?" I asked, trying to lighten the mood.

"You can speak your mind, Ben."

"I can?"

"Feel free to ask what you know you need to."

I peered into Dinah's warm, dark eyes, struggling to see beyond them as I could usually do.

Mari interrupted the building tension. "We're planning on looking for a property outside the city. It'll be a bit of a drive, but I think I can continue with the counseling."

Dinah smiled affectionately at Mari. "So you should, dear. You have the gift." Dinah then looked back to me. I felt like I was being intuitively scanned, as though I was once again in the presence of Madam Li searching deep within. There was more silence.

Mari interrupted again. "Ben plans on writing. We think time in the countryside would do us good—closer to nature, to a connection with country."

"Country, you say?" Dinah asked as she turned to Mari.

"It's a spirituality we both miss," Mari replied.

"A wise and honest source of truth, the country." Dinah soon looked back to me. I nodded approvingly. "I hope you'll let me visit?" she asked.

"Of course we will; you'll be our first guest, I promise." Mari smiled. "Isn't that right, Ben?"

I nodded. "Sure."

Dinah then sat back and stared out into the clear blue sky. "May I make an observation?" she asked.

"You know you don't have to ask. You are family, remember?" Mari replied.

Dinah placed her hand warmly and gently on Mari's arm, then sat back again. "I sense a change in energy between us." She looked to me. "I know you've noticed it."

"I have?" I replied.

"Please, ask."

"OK, sure." I held back a moment; Dinah didn't flinch. I finally came out with it. "Who are you? Who are you really?"

"Ben!" Mari interrupted.

Dinah reassuringly placed her hand back on Mari's arm. "It's OK, dear. It is a fair question. Who am I? Who do you sense I am?"

"This isn't about what I sense though, is it? Care to share?" I asked.

"Hmm. Who am I? I'm a friend, glad to see you are both together and well, and wishing you every happiness in the life you build together."

"Why, thank you, Dinah." Mari smiled. Dinah smiled back affectionately.

"Have you been able to connect with the future for long?" I asked.

Dinah smiled. "I must admit, I'm glad you can," I added. Dinah seemed confused. "Unless you are a very good spy."

Dinah shook her head. "I don't understand."

"Well, how else could you know, right?"

Dinah shook her head again.

"That Mari was in trouble. The cult, no contact for years. You asked what I sense. I sense you don't spy on people: you don't need to. Am I wrong?"

"I would never—" Dinah began to dispute.

"Exactly. I'm truly grateful: your ability to connect with the future saved Mari's life. And to take six whole weeks out of your life to do it, I can't thank you enough."

Mari seemed sad. Dinah leaned over and clasped Mari's hand between hers. "It wasn't your fault."

"It's not that," Mari's said softly. "I miss her."

Dinah stopped a moment, then replied. "I miss her too," she said compassionately. Dinah came around and gave Mari a hug. "She will always love you."

"Miss?"

"You are right, Ben. I did not spy. Mari's mother, Robyn, arranged that," Dinah explained. "There is no mystery, no great foresight or gifts at work, only love and keeping a promise. A promise I should have kept better. I'm so sorry, child. If only I'd been there sooner."

"Robyn made you promise to care for—"

"She sensed her time was near. Those of us close to her accepted the honor of caring for her most precious child. Some were artist friends in the cities. We all agreed to pay for a professional to check once a month but keep their distance, to report Mari was safe, that she was all right."

"You were close?"

"She was a dear and wondrous soul. I could not have been more privileged to be her friend."

We remained silent for perhaps a minute.

Suddenly the cooker in the kitchen chimed.

"I'll get it. You both stay here," I insisted. Mari wouldn't be held back and helped me serve the tofu and chickpea curry she had lovingly prepared, with raita and pappadums. As we plated up, Dinah walked the balcony. We ate on the deck.

The curry was spicy hot, apparently how Dinah liked it. It left me sweating a storm. I think I ate most of the soothing yoghurt and cucumber just to stop my mouth from frying. Mari left halfway through and brought me a small hand towel to wipe my face.

"Gorgeous meal. Thank you." Dinah's face was full of satisfaction.

"Our pleasure," Mari replied.

"Yes, pleasure," I said as I panted with every mouthful.

We all helped clean the table. Dinah put her arm around Mari in the kitchen. "She would be proud."

"Tell me more about Robyn. Hon, do you mind?" I asked as we headed back to the balcony with cool drinks.

Mari smiled, still slightly melancholic. "Not at all. We used to love talking about the old days."

"Old days?" Dinah protested.

Dinah spoke of how Robyn liked to swim naked at public beaches, in the daylight. I had no idea it wasn't legal until I heard how she was arrested for it once, or was that a few times? Then she'd choose a different beach. She was a painter, a dancer, and had a passion for modern history. The oppression of women in the empires of the eighteenth century was her topic of specialty. She was a constant advocate for women's rights, as women; she felt let down by militant feminism. However, she did understand such methods and sentiments might be a necessary evil until the patriarchy gave up its dominating role. Robyn would often lament and worry about the world left for her beautiful daughter; she adored Mari more than anything on earth. It made me wonder how Robyn, and women like her, might react to know their struggle was worth it, to know they did regain enormous power as women in my time. It was a topic I was yet to broach with Mari.

We ate, we smiled, we sat quietly, meditating our connection with the natural world—it was Dinah's idea, not mine. We spoke of our shared respect and love of ancient cultures who once had the wisdom of this connection. It brought us all closer; Dinah was feeling like family, like a wise old aunty you hoped would visit. Soon she was ready to leave.

Walking down the corridor, Dinah and Mari arm in arm, Dinah insisted she have us over next weekend to her place. She reassured me she'd keep the food mild. Complimenting us on a wonderful afternoon, she kissed Mari on the cheek. Then she seemed about to do the same to me. Instead of a kiss, she whispered, "You will know who I really am soon enough. Be true."

Just as I stood back in shock, she left. No one in this time ever used that saying. What did she mean, I would learn soon enough?

"You OK?" Mari asked as she shut the front door.

"Me? Fine."

As we walked back to the kitchen, Mari continued. "I'm glad you two get along. Dinah is very impressed by you, you know."

"Hmm, amazing woman. How did you meet her again?" I asked as we started cleaning up.

19

It was early evening, two and a half years later, and I was driving back with a new friend, Patrick—yes, me, driving—to pick up liquid supplies. The road out of Eumundi—a small country town north of Brisbane—was quiet, the road mostly clear. A crescent moon hung in the distance. The streetlights were small, glowing orbs in the moisture-filled air.

"So, I was wondering," Patrick continued—we'd been talking a while, his crinkling midfifties face a focus of concentration, "whether you wouldn't mind teaching a guided meditation class? I know you'd be great. Not trying to pressure you, mind."

"I would love to."

"Fantastic."

"But, you know what we agreed."

"Look, it's not like we don't appreciate you with the phone calls, the cleaning, the—"

"Thanks, Pat."

"It's just I know there's a massive hidden talent in there yet to awaken, and it would be such a waste—"

A motorbike sped past us, then another. I glanced to Pat.

"WATCH OUT!" he yelled.

A car pulled out immediately in front us. I swerved and braked into the opposite lane. Lights flashed at me from the other lane. They were very close, and directly in front. I hit the accelerator, snapping the car back into our lane just in time to see a huge truck pass on the other side. I pulled over.

Pat sighed in relief. I took a few calming breaths. "Holy witch hazel," I cussed. We gathered ourselves and headed back to a small farm nearby. We were silent. My eyes were scanning everything. My hands tense on the wheel.

There were more than a dozen cars out front, just as when we left. I parked under the shed next to our regular-sized farm trailer. Patrick carried the drinks and ice. Talking and laughing could be heard out back.

Mari met us in the corridor and guided Pat to put the drinks in the fridge in the laundry, the extra ice in the coolers out back, where everyone was gathered.

"What is it?" Mari asked.

"I hate cars. Did I ever tell you that?" I replied. "Infernal machines."

"Only a dozen times. No, wait, a hundred!" She smiled, then noticed I was shaking. "What is it?"

"I can't believe I'm saying this, but Bob's lessons just saved our lives." Mari looked shocked. "Some dingbat," I explained, "just drove out of nowhere and forced me towards an oncoming truck!" I shook my head. "I can't wait till it's all automated. How did you survive so long growing up around these death traps and dingbats?"

Mari hugged me. "Remind me to thank Bob next time I see him."

Suddenly we heard a baby cry. "You want me?" I asked.

"No. You don't have the boobs for it."

"I could warm a bottle ..."

"No problem. You can entertain our guests. Won't be long."

Our farm was a medium-sized house—by local standards—with a large deck and even bigger backyard that we'd cleared when we moved in. We'd invited a group of friends, some from Mari's new counseling center on the Sunshine Coast, and some of mine from the fledgling Institute. They called it the Heart and Mind Retreat. Patrick and his wife, Alicia, were the principle owners, though they were thinking of making it into a cooperative, a decision I firmly agreed with. Yes, Sloth's words were still echoing in my mind, but I was being careful, making sure I kept my input to behind the scenes, mostly a passive participant. Our community was growing. It had a long way to go before it would get close to what I grew up with as a young boy or had known before I left, but these friends were a great start.

As I stepped onto the deck, they all started clapping.

Steve, the partner of Belinda, a colleague of Mari's, came forward and patted me on the back. "We have a new Lewis Hamilton in our midst," he said.

"Who?"

"Pat told us. Such driving skill," Bradley, another friend from the fledgling Institute, explained. "Very impressive."

I just shook it all off and headed for the drinks. "More drinks, anyone?"

Next thing, there were some oohs and aahs. "There's the little man," Belinda said as Mari brought Lincoln, now fully awake, to share time with his community. Most of the women were quick to gather around, and it almost made me cry as I realized these would likely be Lincoln's "aunties." Most of the guys gathered in their own group, some of them more interested in Lincoln than others.

Sarah, one of Mari's new friends, slowly walked from inside with a large chocolate cake and a single candle and started singing, "Happy birthday to you. Happy birthday to you. Happy birthday to Lincoln …"

Everyone joined in and cheered.

"Speech! Speech!" they then insisted.

I shied away. They looked to Mari, who looked back to me as others were holding and playing with Lincoln.

"OK, OK." They gathered around. "I'm at a bit of a loss." I then stood tall. "Firstly, a big thank-you to all of you for coming and sharing this special moment in our lives: the first birthday of our firstborn, Lincoln."

"What? There's more?" someone interjected to a few laughs.

"We'll see." I smiled to Mari.

"We can always do with new members," another piped up. "And our football team is a bit short."

"No, seriously," I continued, "on behalf of Mari, Lincoln, and myself, thank you all for coming; it means more to us than you know. To Sarah, wow, what a cake! Right, that's mine. What's everyone else having?" There were a few chuckles. "To my dearest wife, my closest confidante, my rock who grounds me in the now, I owe you more than my heart can bear. Thank you. May I always remain worthy of being by your side."

"To Mari!" Pat announced.

"To Mari!" all said in unison. I could tell Mari was struggling not to cry.

"To our son, Lincoln Thomas," I continued, "may we all honor you with our loving care and kindness all our living days so you may live the greatest life of human fulfillment possible. Thank you for choosing to be part of our life; we will forever cherish it."

"Hear! Hear!" a voice replied.

"OK, that's it. Short and sweet. Don't forget to eat: we have enough to last a week. Please, indulge and enjoy. Thank you."

"Well said." Pat took my place. "Well said. May I just say a few words?" Everyone remained silent. "Mari, Ben, Lincoln," Pat continued, "it is an honor to have you, both as neighbors, friends, and recent members of our retreat. When we first met, I must admit—"

"THEY'VE DROPPED A BOMB!" someone shouted.

We all turned to see Belinda standing in the patio doorway with her phone by her side, terror reflected in her face. I hadn't noticed she'd slipped inside.

Steve walked over to her: she was barely standing.

"I was just checking the news in the bathroom." Her voice trembled. "China, they've sunk the *Gerald R. Ford*!"

"They've what?" Patrick asked.

"Turn on the TV," Steve suggested.

On the screen, we saw debris in the water, some charred bodies, and damaged US naval ships. Archive footage showed the USS *Gerald R. Ford*, the newest US aircraft carrier, indicating it was commissioned July 22, 2017, and had a complement of over two thousand six hundred crew.

"Just to confirm," the young female presenter said, "there are unsubstantiated reports that a thermonuclear detonation has occurred in the South China Sea. The United States aircraft carrier USS *Gerald R. Ford* is reported to have been sunk, in addition to two other military support ships. Initial estimates put the total lives lost at over two thousand eight hundred, with a similar number injured, though these figures are yet to be confirmed. If correct, that makes this the worst single attack on the United States military since the Japanese surprise attack on Pearl Harbor on December 7th, 1941. A temporary ceasefire is reportedly in effect. The Australian military has been placed on high alert, ready to offer support …"

"Have they gone mad?!" Tony asked, fear obvious in his voice. He'd come with Brie, another of Mari's colleagues.

"It was only a matter of time; they've been pushing for this. Now, here we are," Pat lamented.

"Let's hope it doesn't escalate," Steve added.

"But did you hear? Australia is committing to helping the US!" Wang, another member of the fledgling Institute, spoke loudly. "They're going to drag us into a war with China!"

"We could be just offering them medical and—" Pat replied.

"Are you kidding?" Wang continued. "What American war hasn't Australia joined in? Here we go again, only this time they have nukes!"

I quickly turned the TV off. There were some surprised looks.

"Bye-bye, planet." A voice could be heard from the small crowd.

"I wonder whether we have time to move to New Zealand," another added.

"The children!" a female voice cried out.

"No, no!" I almost shouted. "Let's not do this."

"We need to leave," Steve announced as he held Belinda close.

"Wait, please," I protested as people kept leaving, their heads held low, their shoulders slumped.

"The beginning of the end," Bradley commented as he, too, started to leave.

"Wait, everyone, please! I need to say something! It's important, please!"

People stopped. Many turned toward me; some looked at their phones.

"Look, this is terrible news, terrible, but it is times like this I feel I need to remind you, all of you, we are your friends. What does that mean? It means if this does go to hell in a teacup, please don't ever forget to call us. I'm sure I speak for Mari as well." She nodded. "No matter what. Belinda, if you need someone to listen, please call. This kind of news can leave a lasting bad taste in our psyche. Steve, if you need help changing your mower blades, don't hesitate to pick up the phone. Wang, if you need a few extra groceries for the family, call. Pat, if you need someone to disagree with, you know where I am. Every one of you, please, don't let this trouble make us forget we are friends."

Everyone still looked solemn.

I raised a nearby glass. "To friends!" I toasted.

"To friends!" Pat repeated, loudly. He looked around; most were silent. "To friends!" he shouted louder.

"To friends," most people repeated.

"No matter what!" I added.

"No matter what," the others replied.

Pat and I walked among the group, hugging them. Mari joined in with Lincoln on her hip.

"Thank you for the reminder," Steve said.

"You're right," Wang added. "It is when times are at their toughest that we need to come together. Your offer means a lot."

From person to person, we shared our friendship; we strengthened our community. Within half an hour, the mood had started to lift. Then we called it a night: many wanted to get back to their families. As we dispersed, we made sure we had each other's numbers.

"You know where we live!" I shouted as people made their way to their cars. "No excuses!"

Pat came over, the last to leave. "And don't forget the same applies here. If you need anything. Anything!"

"Mate," I said, "you've got a deal." We hugged the usual one-arm man-hug.

Once everyone had departed, we put our tired young Lincoln to bed, then sat on the couch, cuddled beside each other. We were silent a moment.

Mari then asked, "How bad does it get?"

I pulled her closer. "It will get bad, but not right away. The US will now have to show it means business, call for an evacuation of several Chinese-claimed islands, and use a nuclear weapon on one and destroy the others. China will protest but not retaliate: it isn't ready for a war—not yet. The United States knows, even with China yet to reach full strength, it can't win a war in China's backyard. Soon it will be war again after war—Asia and the Middle East as empires battle it out. But don't worry, we're safe. Besides, we'll be prepared, and we have friends."

Mari hugged me tight. "I hope you're right."

"About history?" I asked.

"A history that can change." Mari didn't sound convinced.

Then Lincoln started crying. Mari headed for his room.

"Shame Dinah couldn't make it," I said.

"I'll visit her tomorrow. Hopefully she's feeling better."

I headed for the study and checked news updates on the laptop connected to a large high-definition screen. Soon I heard quiet. I checked in Lincoln's bedroom to see how Mari was doing. It was empty. Then I found Mari cuddled up with Lincoln on our bed, both asleep above the sheets. What a beautiful sight. Memories of joy together filled my heart, of time in the park, holding Lincoln up in the air as he smiled, playing on the grass, by the water at the beach, cuddling them both; I couldn't help but smile. I gathered a blanket and gently covered them both, then sat in a chair in the room, just watching them, savoring it. Reposed before me lay a part of my soul I'd never expected to be awakened, that I'd never imagined could exist. Gratitude and heartfelt warmth overwhelmed me. It inspired me to get a pen and paper. As I sat before them, I wrote.

To my beloved,

In heart's repose I humble myself before thee, a man once guided by life's impositions, a journeyman once lost. If a heart could melt of warmth divine, this one is pouring within to fill the holes of emptiness and know completeness. This night I am most privileged to gaze upon mother and son entwined. With joy and love raised skyward, I meekly bear witness to the fulfillment of thy divine womanly presence. To cry with pride and gratitude would never be enough. Thy very being, its grace and honesty, unlocks the celestial spirit of bliss, setting the gods in rages of jealously for the gifts thy heart and very being have bestowed upon me. No matter the roughness of road or the height of jagged cliff, know my arms are ever ready for comfort's embrace, my trusted hand to clasp thee from trouble's wrath. In a life all too brief, let time hold no barrier that I may fully honor thee.

Thy dearest friend eternal.

I closed the door quietly behind me when I'd finished. What scribbles I'd made I then rewrote on special stationery Mari kept in the study. Not ready for bed, I decided to clean up. Onto the clean kitchen table, I returned the vase with fresh bush flowers and placed the letter against it, then gathered a blanket and pillow and slept on the couch.

I was awoken by a kiss.

"Thank you," Mari said. "I could have helped, but thank you."

"Sure."

"Toast?" she asked.

"The usual, thanks." I made my way to the shower.

By the time I returned, I found Mari sitting on the couch with the letter I'd written in her hand by her side. I poured some juice. She didn't move. She was just staring forward.

I came over and sat beside her. "You OK?"

No answer.

I touched her hand. She suddenly looked to me as if she didn't recognize me.

"Well, not quite the reaction I was—"

"It's you!" Mari interrupted.

"Yes, it's me."

"No, no. You don't understand," Mari said with shock and desperation. "This, this letter, I've seen it before."

"That would be a good trick. When I saw you were cuddling last night, I—"

"That can't be. Last time I read it …" Mari started to say in total disbelief.

"Hold on, what do you mean, last time?"

"2207."

"But I hadn't finished writing it till at least eleven thirty."

"No, the year 2207. Oh my god, it's all coming back … all of it!"

"What is?"

Mari paced the kitchen, then walked outside onto the deck. I put my arms around her; she pulled back.

"Don't you get it?" Deep concern over her face. "I'm not who you think I am!"

Soon she began to recall the biggest secret of her life, which she didn't even know she had.

20

15:10, May 16, 2207, Brisbane, Cooperative Nation of Australia.

What do I remember of it?

I recall sitting outside the chairperson's office in the Ministry of History, having to stop biting my nails from nervousness. I almost jumped when the door opened. *Ah, finally*, I thought, but alas, a slim woman in her late thirties, wearing Ministry of History insignia, came out and left. Then, I started practicing the relaxation techniques I'd learned—at the Institute!

I know, I can hardly believe it myself, but I also attended the Institute! Only, in my time, it had been decentralized and had far less authority. Every degree or government position now required at least three years at the Institute—they weren't just training arbitrators anymore. Yes, I remember now: my passion was history, like my mother before me. The chair I was about to meet knew her well: they were part of the same tribal community and personal friends. Mother was "on assignment," as we called it. That meant complete immersion. I was hoping I would be given final approval for the same.

How? Why?

Mother and Nana, it was them.

Mother and Grandma went against the grain. The most respected and supported role in our community was to be a mother, grandmother, or aunty. It was considered by most women the greatest pleasure and honor; to finetune the personas of the adults to come was our highest achievement. It was sometimes frowned upon to follow other paths, but not discouraged or disrespected. My maternal role models were far more devoted to being historians.

I couldn't understand it at first. Nana or Mum would be away for a week or two, and when they came back, their faces had new lines or creases, and their hair was grayer or very different in style from before. Later I learned they were spending years living other lives, then debriefing, reacclimatizing, and returning to live with us. I don't think Father was very happy with it. He was an artist, male mentor, and our local community representative. I recall many a heated discussion between them. I thought they were arguing about me. I was too young to know.

But Mum being away meant more time with Nana Fee Bee!

"I'm coming for you, Susan," she would say. "You are driving your car too fast. I'm coming for you."

I loved imagining what cars were like and the anticipation of being pulled over by police. As a five-year-old, the idea of a police force to lock up people was scary but also exciting—to be locked up in our time was almost unheard of.

"My turn to play the policewoman," I'd insist.

Nana was very tolerant. We played at flying in planes, reading real books, trying to make as much money as we could by doing chores to buy new "gadgets"—these things were all completely foreign to me. I even learned to ride a bike, the only one in our tribal community, since everyone preferred to walk or use our—by now much-upgraded—pods and smaller, personalized TCs. Imagining traffic lights was especially fun. I'd turn it red just as Nana would arrive, then give her a ticket. Nana's games and tales of the late twentieth and early twenty-first centuries were the best.

Mum loved the same era too. When she was home, we'd sing to Michael Jackson, Diana Ross, Red Hot Chili Peppers, The Beatles, and my favorite, Queen. All the ancient classics. Modern music was too boring. Mum would say she preferred music of much earlier times, with angst and grit.

So, of course, I was going to become a historian. You can't imagine how eager I was for my first immersion.

What's an immersion?

It's the ultimate history experience—losing all conscious memories of our time, taking on a persona of someone from another era, then returning to share the experience, the insights, the difficulties, and conundrums. This was the full immersion experience. It was time-consuming though. It took years of study and a similar time for the Ministry of Time to painstakingly ensure the right persona was chosen, with detailed-enough life history, so as to not "wreck the ship," as they liked to say. They set up a specialist department devoted to it: the Department of Temporal Personas, or DTP. Their job: to work with the Ministry of History to mold an individual they could send to the past who wouldn't stand out, wouldn't be easily discovered, and wouldn't wreck the future.

I'd done my study; I knew the customs of the era well. The detailed study was my backup in case the memory overlay failed or collapsed. I checked with the DTP; they had a few persona options prepared. I'd made my choice. Now all I needed was final ministerial approval from the chair.

"Susan, come in, come in," Chairperson Peters insisted, her warm smile very comforting. "How's your father?" she asked as she closed the door behind us.

"Oh, he's active as ever. Preparing for the next election, garnering all the local women's opinions before they vote."

"Tell him I wish him well."

"I will," I replied as I remember cautiously sitting down. "And how's Mother?" I asked.

Ms. Peters seemed upbeat. "Doing well as far as we know. No recallable events. Should be back next week."

We sat opposite each other on small double couches in front of Ms. Peter's desk. Between us, a coffee-style table. As she sat forward and touched the desk, a three-dimensional holographic image with data of my request and assignment appeared between us.

"So, this will be your first," she said, her brow furrowing. "Let me see. Good prep work. Your tutors were very impressed. Hmm … I don't know. It's very long for your first."

"I know, but as you see, I have no family of my own, I know the era like I was born there, and I just know, with the right amount of time, I'll find …" I hesitated.

"Find?" Her eyes didn't leave the screen.

"The ability to unlock a deeper part of myself and bring back invaluable insights."

"Ah, I see. Honorable goals. So why these years in particular?"

I didn't want to tell her. She looked up. Then I noticed, on the wall opposite me, a large picture of four women, shoulder to shoulder. One was Ms. Peters, much younger, another, Mum dearest, probably before she'd had me, and now I know who the other two were: it was Dinah and Betty! I'll never forget their faces: Betty looked a bit cross, Dinah serene, and she had jet-black hair. They'd all graduated history together!

"Susan? Ms. Buchanan," Ms. Peters prompted loudly.

"What was Mum like back then?" I pointed to the picture.

Ms. Peters turned to it, then turned back and smiled. "A very determined young lady. These particular years, why them?"

"They seem interesting."

"Perhaps we should send you back further, to a less troubling time. This is a very risky proposition; the DTP has forwarded some serious reservations—"

"What? No!"

Ms. Peters sat back, searching into my eyes.

"It's Nana," I finally admitted. "After she died …"

"She will be sorely missed. The Ministry's condolences."

I nodded my appreciation. "It was her specialty, her time."

"So this immersion is to honor her?"

"Maybe understand her. She was …" I began to reminisce.

"Was …?"

"Let's just say, to understand her is to realize an important part of myself."

"You were close?"

"She was more like my mother than Mum," I recalled with some sadness.

"I see." Ms. Peters seemed to empathize as she looked at her information then to me, then the information, then looked to me, silently for a few moments. "I sense something else," she said as she sat back.

I hesitated, remaining silent.

"May I remind you this is part of risk assessment. Motivations and honesty are paramount. Yes, we can overlay a memory, but not suppress all our subconscious drives. They can still guide your actions and feelings … if there is something unresolved."

Ms. Peters shut down the screen and started to stand up.

"No, wait. OK, it was in Nana's things."

Ms. Peters sat down.

"A letter," I said.

"A message?"

"No, a real letter, on real paper. Dates back to those years—it's been tested." I showed her a copy on my portable miniscreen. I gave her time to read it. She handed my screen back with a knowing smile. "If the era creates this, I want to experience it," I explained.

"You've sourced this letter?" she queried.

"Nana showed it to me after my last partner cheated on me. Not all men are like that, she said, some are like this."

"Do you know who wrote it?"

"No. Even the DNA has been wiped clean. Nana wouldn't say

either; she never brought it out again. I found it in her belongings when she passed. I had temporal forensics do a trace."

"Do you have the reports?"

"No, but I have it with me. Did you want to see it?" I pulled a thin, sealed case from my jacket's inside breast pocket. With a small hiss, it opened to reveal the fragile article. We gently pried it open; it was in amazing condition for its age. The handwriting was rough but with an overall smooth, flowing character.

"You keep this with you? You may wish to reseal it," Ms. Peters recommended.

I gently put it back in its container and my pocket.

Ms. Peters turned on the screen. "You do understand he could be the exception? The history of men's behaviour in such a misogynistic, patriarchal world was far from your Mr. X."

Ms. Peters studied me some more, then pressed a section of her desk. "I see this means a lot to you … Very well. You go in three weeks."

She didn't know the half of it: the letter meant everything to me, for over a year, reconnecting me with Nana, building dreams of warmth and hope. Now it even helped me get my dream assignment. But, I soon found out, the chair had her own agenda. She altered my programmed persona so I'd be cared for by Dinah and Betty, have them be Mari's mother's best friends in the new time, as they had been in this one.

Before I knew it, I was in Melbourne, then Sydney, then here. Everything since my arrival that I've told you is true. I think the letter had such a strong connection it woke me up!

* * *

Mari/Susan paced the room, then stopped. "I'm so sorry," she said as she looked to me desperately from across the room. "I'm not the woman you married."

221

I walked over and held her hands before me. "No, but you are the mother of our son, and I would be honored if you'd give me another chance to be your friend and confidant. If you'll have me."

Mari/Susan seemed unsure. We sat down on the sofa. "So, what do I call you?"

"Mari. Yes, I prefer Mari." She seemed lost in thought.

"Hi, Mari. My name's Benjamin. My friends call me Ben. Welcome to the twenty-first century." We shook hands. "Very pleased to meet you."

Then a thought crossed my mind.

"What is it?" Mari asked.

"Did your mother really die here? Was she even here?"

"Was she just a programmed part of my persona? No. I actually met her; it was Mum, both of us on assignment, only here I barely knew her until … later." I think I saw Mari smile.

"When you reconciled?"

"Remember the plane crash I told you about? They didn't find any bodies."

"And Dinah and Betty, they met her as well?"

"Yes, around the same time I did, though they had memories of her that went further back."

"Wow, your DTP certainly did a job on you guys. Which makes me wonder." Mari looked to me for an answer. "Do you think Dinah and Betty know they are from the future?"

"You know, I have no idea," Mari said, seemingly surprised by the suggestion. "What I do know is for a time Dinah was an arbitrator before they all met."

"I knew it!" That explained her insight. Then it occurred to me: I had married someone from the Institute after all. I wondered what Madam Li would think.

I was still curious. "So, you say your nana inspired you to come here? She sounds a remarkable lady."

"Kind, loving, more than a young girl could wish for. A bit down at times. I remember trying to cheer her up lots as a young girl. She never spoke about it, even when I graduated. Oh, she was so proud of me that day. I was shocked to see her in arbitrator's uniform at the ceremony—she kept that part of her life hidden. They dedicated a prize of accomplishment in her honor: the Fiorella Buchanan Special Achievement Award. I still miss her."

"Did you say 'Fiorella'?"

"Yeah, Nana Fee Bee. She—"

"Describe her. Did she have any distinguishing features?"

"Why?"

"Indulge me."

"A few scars, one on her right thigh, a few on her chest from previous surgery, a birthmark on her upper left back, a—"

"The shape of Tasmania?"

"How did you …?"

"She almost stopped me returning to you!"

I was dumbfounded. Carefully I explained about Madam Li and her plan to keep me in her time. About Fee's affections for me and my different affections for her.

"Eddies!" I said out loud.

"Who?"

"No, eddies in the river of time. That's how Sloth described it. Sloth? Oh, he was a minister of time I met. Well, actually, he preferred to be called a specialist." Mari seemed confused. "Don't you see? If you hadn't read the letter I wrote you last night, two hundred years from now, you wouldn't have come back to this time and we wouldn't have met. If we never met, how could I have written the letter that sent you back to this time so we could meet? It's a classic eddy, a part of time looping around itself. Oh my," I realized, "there's more of them!"

"Time loops?"

"Fiorella, you amazing, loving soul."

Mari looked more confused.

"Only now do I see how you really felt."

"What are you talking about?" Mari seemed lost.

"It was something she said when we parted ways. She told me she truly wished me every deep satisfaction possible. She knew. Once I returned to this time, she worked it out. She knew."

"Knew what?"

"She gave us each other; she gave us now. She really did know how much this meant to me after all," I lamented, then held Mari gently at arm's length. "Without your nana, I would have remained trapped by duty and expectation, never have known the better part of me—us." I gazed into the distance. "She helped me step off the train."

Thanks in large part to Fee, I had a new life, new vocation, a loving family—a new me. I had finally found where I belonged, didn't feel a need to achieve, to make sense of the human condition. For the first time in my life, I felt at home.

I savored the moment in embrace.

Suddenly Mari pulled back, all concerned.

"What is it?"

She ran to her bag, scrambled through it, then threw the contents on the floor. Finding her phone, she touched the screen—then dropped it. "Oh no!" She raced to Lincoln's room, then opened the door slowly. She stepped quietly in and began to gently stroke his head.

"What's going on?" I whispered. Mari didn't answer, tears falling on her cheeks. "Tell me."

"They'll retrieve me in twenty-four days," Mari said.

"Send you back to the twenty-third century?"

She nodded, continuing to stroke Lincoln's head.

"But they can't: you have family here!"

Lincoln started stirring. I grabbed Mari's hand and guided her out of the room. As we entered the hall, she fell to the floor, sitting, her knees up, sobbing into her arms. "What have I done?" she said, her voice muffled.

I knelt before her. "Look at me. Mari. Look at me."

Her red, puffy eyes barely looked at my chest.

"This isn't over. Trust me. You don't think I've traveled across time just to have time keep us apart, do you?"

Holding Mari's hand, I helped her up, but she was reluctant. We opened the door again and stood quietly by Lincoln's bed. I pulled Mari close.

"I promise you, from the bottom of my heart, no one is going to take you from us. Nobody is going to break up this family, do you hear me? Nobody!"

If there was one thing I knew I was good at, it was keeping promises to the ones I loved.

About the Author

In his early twenties, Dr. Winfried Sedhoff faced a life-threatening personal crisis that sent him into self-imposed isolation. A twelve-month solitary quest uncovered solutions to his crisis and a genuine and lasting sense of self. Documenting this journey in his first book, 'A Balance of Self', Dr. Sedhoff went on to write, 'The Fall and Rise of Women', and 'The Friendship Key'. He has practiced as a family physician in Brisbane Australia for over 25 years. With his unique approach to mental health, he offers guidance and training to patients, colleagues, medical trainees, and the general public. Dr. Sedhoff's books are inspired by his vision of a peaceful world that offers fulfilled, balanced and sustainable lives for us all. This is his first published novel.

www.winfriedsedhoff.com

www.ingramcontent.com/pod-product-compliance
Lightning Source LLC
Chambersburg PA
CBHW070452120726
47910CB00003B/1019